A Criminal to Remember

Also by Michael Van Rooy

An Ordinary Decent Criminal
Your Friendly Neighbourhood Criminal

A
Criminal
to Remember

Michael Van Rooy

RaveN
STONE

Turnstone Press
Artspace Building
206-100 Arthur Street
Winnipeg, MB
R3B 1H3 Canada
www.TurnstonePress.com

Turnstone Press gratefully acknowledges the assistance of the Canada
Council for the Arts, the Manitoba Arts Council, the Government of
Canada through the Canada Book Fund, and the Province of Manitoba
through the Book Publishing Tax Credit and the Book Publisher
Marketing Assistance Program.

This novel is a work of fiction. Names, characters, places and
incidents are either the product of the author's imagination or are used
fictitiously, and any resemblance to actual persons living or dead, events
or locales, is entirely coincidental.

Cover design: Jamis Paulson
Interior design: Sharon Caseburg
Printed and bound in Canada by Friesens for Turnstone Press.

Library and Archives Canada Cataloguing in Publication

Van Rooy, Michael, 1968- ꒰ᴏ⊥⎮ /ᴀN ᴈᴏ
    A criminal to remember / Michael Van Rooy.

ISBN 978-0-88801-369-9

    I. Title.

PS8643.A56C75 2010   C813'.6   C2010-902287-4

To Laura, once more.

A Criminal to Remember

#1

I love a fair, a festival, a circus. I was at the Red River Exhibition Fair with my wife Claire and our son Fred and our friends Elena and Alex with their son Jacob. They were a few hundred feet ahead of me, lost in the crowd, as I stopped to tie a shoelace.

While I was on my knee I saw a pack of twenty-somethings, men and women both, about six of them all clustered around the side of the butterfly tent forty feet away. I didn't think anything of them but then I saw a flash-lick of fire in the narrow alley between tents and heard a raucous laugh that grated.

I decided to check it out. I'm very curious; it's a failure of mine, one bred deep in the bone. It's caused a lot of pain, mostly to me, over the years.

I also get bored easily.

Curiosity and boredom are a much underrated combination. I knew from experience that bad things happened when I got bored and worse things happened when I got curious. For that reason I always tried to keep busy; it was one of the few pieces of advice I remembered my father ever giving me.

Between me and the group there was a big tent full of antique farm equipment, so I circled around into it and made my way past hay balers and grain sifters and all sorts of things I couldn't identify. There were a few people in the place, some old men, a puzzled professor type and a guy trying to cop a feel from a recalcitrant but giggling girlfriend, but the tent was mostly empty.

At the back of the tent, behind a steam-driven pile driver, I could hear the group outside clearly through the heavy canvas.

"Here, let me do it."

There was a hissing sound, and then another voice said, "Here, use this. It always works. It's one of those electric igniters."

I pulled out the pocket knife my in-laws had given to me. A little Swiss Army deal that keeps a good edge. The smallest blade made a slit in the canvas and I had a front-row seat.

Two feet away stood six idiots. One was shaking a huge pressurized can of generic hairspray and another was trying to light it with a butane lighter.

The woman with the hairspray said, "I'll show those dumb fuckers to kick me out ..."

The guy beside her finally got his lighter going. "Yeah. Also, Free The Bugs!"

Everyone laughed. They were drunk. Or stoned. Or stupid. Or all of the above. Four men and two women, all egging each other on towards true idiocy. It's amazing how adolescence happens later and later for some people.

I put the knife blade back into the slit and kept cutting, sliding the blade down gently.

The three-foot gout of blue flame twitched at the old,

patched canvas in front of the group and one of them whooped. At a rough guess they were ten seconds away from setting the tent aflame. Which would be a shame. I'd been through the tent earlier. It was called the Butterfly Garden and it held (or so the sign claimed) two million butterflies and moths. I'd taken the number on faith and hadn't tried to count.

Inside it had lived up to its name—a big space full of fluttering, crawling, eating, fucking, birthing and dying bugs. Along with the bugs there were four teenage interpreters and guides and a few dozen visitors. It would be a shame to turn the tent into a torch, not to mention what would happen to all the people and bugs. My son, Fred, had loved them—he'd been captivated into silence and awe by the gentle, lumbering flight of the moths and the tense flickering of butterflies. He could see their entire lives in front of him on one wall—birth, first flight, feeding, fucking, dying. All coloured alternately in gentle pastels and sharp colours that looked blocked out by some talented artistic hand.

Even Claire had liked the bugs, when a moth the size of a coffee saucer landed on her breast, briefly becoming a brooch. It flew away when she laughed but her delight stayed.

It would be a shame to destroy something that had brought my family such joy.

I put the knife in my left hand with the one-inch blade sticking out the bottom of my fist. Just in case.

The woman with the hairspray shook it again as I stepped out.

"Now watch this ..."

Fair fights are fine in the movies.

Really. I like them and I almost always want the good guy to win. But I wasn't in a movie. I cheat. In the real world I was

5

a bad guy—well, a retired bad guy. Which meant I cheated, as a matter of principle.

I balled my right fist up and swung overhand down as hard as I could at the closest guy's right shoulder—near to his neck but away from his spine. The sound of his clavicle breaking was drowned out by his scream and the woman dropped the hairspray as the man crumpled. Lots of pain in a big bone explosively shattered but, fortunately, screams in a fair are not uncommon and no one near by seemed to notice or care.

The others turned to face me as I windmilled my arm back again fast like I was pitching a softball. The guy beside the girl had been leaning up against a support rope with his hand above his head, which made him a good target. He was stepping towards me with his hand still on the rope as I drove my fist up under his armpit fast and felt his shoulder pop out of its socket. It was an easy shot to take because the ball and socket joint is open from below and almost wants to come apart. With a little encouragement.

Anyhow, he started to scream too as he lurched to the side.

By that time one of the other men had managed to find a half-assed martial arts stance. Something he'd gotten from one of those unlimited (or is it ultimate?) fighting shows. Which was cool—whatever made him feel good. Maybe he was trying to impress the women. Men do way too much of that, and it seems to lead to all sorts of idiotic behaviour: wars, mountaineering expeditions, white water rafting, even getting married. I knew all about the urge to impress because I indulged in it myself sometimes.

Although with age it was happening slightly less.

Basically men will go to great lengths to be remembered and to be memorable.

I lunged with my left hand, the one with the knife, and

twisted it gently at the last second to lay the very edge of the blade right across the guy's forehead from temple to temple. It cut a trough maybe an eighth of an inch deep, skipping along irregularities in the bone, but that was more than enough.

For a second nothing happened and then a gush of blood poured down his face, covered his eyes and filled his mouth.

I wondered why they didn't do shit like that in ultimate (maybe it was unlimited) fighting. I might watch it then.

Let's be honest; in a real fight you palm an ashtray into someone's face, you strangle someone with their own hair or you piss on them to distract their attention. Then you hurt them as badly as you can—you do what is necessary to win. Because in a real fight, after you lose, they just keep kicking you until you are way past dead. Then they kick you some more.

The knife wound I gave wasn't serious ... well, it wasn't life threatening, but the guy would have other things to worry about for a while. Head wounds bleed like a bitch. They're very, very scary. I mean, the head is where thoughts are and now blood is pouring out of it. It would keep the idiot busy as he pawed at his face and tried to wipe the blood away and see something.

I ignored him and kept moving. Which is a good idea in a fight, always keep moving, always keep loose and flexible. Always be ready to take or deliver a quick, cheap shot as long as it will be effective.

The two women had fled. But the last guy, the one with the lighter, had turned to face me, leaning back to kick like he was hoofing a soccer ball. Swaying a little from drugs or drink. It was still a pretty good kick, though.

I let him kick, twisting aside and bending at the knees to let

7

it pass. When his foot was at chest height I put my shoulder under it and jumped straight up.

His expression was priceless as his foot went way past his head and then all expression vanished as the back of his head hit the ground from maybe eight feet up. The rest of his body landed seconds later and I took a second to heel-stomp his ribs into about a week of hospital recovery time.

I scooped up his lighter out of curiosity and wiped the knife on the first man's shirt as I passed.

Then I was back in the tent with the farm machinery and walking idly towards the exit.

By the time the rent-a-cops arrived I was hundreds of feet away and meeting up with my wife and son and friends.

Just a normal, average, ordinary kind of guy.

#2

The fairground west of the city was lit up at dusk by a hundred spotlights throwing cones of brilliance into the sky like signals to the divine. And lower down in between the spotlights were ribbons of neon spelling out names and nonsense and pretty lies that I desperately wanted to believe.

Where there were no spotlights and no neon there were shadows, deep and dark and hard edged. And those places I knew very well.

It was the once-a-year, one-week, one-chance-for-fun Red River Exhibition carnival and the place was packed. The noise filled my ears and vibrated my bones. The clank of chains on the Ferris wheel and roller coaster, the clatter of children's feet racing down the asphalt paths and kicking gravel, the cry of frightened babies, the bray of young men, the gasps of young women and the pleas of barkers and shills.

My nose opened to a hundred smells, the salt slick of sweat. The sour of vomit, the sweet of spilled drink syrup. The bravado of hot dogs and the spice of cinnamon. The butter and salt of popcorn and the sickly, slightly burnt smell of sugar turned into pink thread. A whiff of cologne from a man crossing my path, something too sweet, too complex. A young woman passing me in slight rut, flushed pink by excitement or orgasm or both.

I felt the vibration of the machinery rising up through the ground. Echoing everywhere from bone to bone, resonating my sinews.

The look and taste of the place filled me with a kind of eager expectation ...

Elena Ramirez, Winnipeg police sergeant and friend, stood beside me and said loudly, "I LOVE the circus!"

Her son, Jacob or Jake, two years plus a few months, looked up at her from his stroller and blew a raspberry. When she looked back down at him he smiled and raised his hands to be lifted up and out, which Elena refused to do. He was an adorable baby, golden skinned and black haired with sparkling brown eyes, and he was thoroughly and completely wicked.

I checked my son Fred, who was in the second stroller, and he just pivoted his head back and forth to try to take everything in. His hair was blond, very fair and almost luminous in the June evening, and his brown eyes seemed to weigh everything against his curiosity. He fastened on a roller coaster that was painted with blue and yellow diamonds like a boa constrictor and he said, "Let's go! Ya-ya. Ya! Go! Ya!" Loudly and with approval.

I turned partway to Elena and raised my voice to be heard. "I like the circus too, but love it? C'mon. Besides, this isn't really a circus."

Elena shook her head and her short dark hair swayed. "So few real circuses left. I have to be happy with what I've got ... this is about as close to a midway as I can find. And in

May there's the Royal Canadian Circus which comes to town and has some of the elephants and the clowns. That's almost like the big top. And every now and then the Cirque du Soleil comes to town and that's the high wire and acrobats and the rest."

She smiled and showed bright white teeth. "Between the three of them I get a real circus! I just have to wait a little while to get what I want. And I believe that waiting is good for my character."

Beside us a merry-go-round started up. It was populated by centaurs and unicorns and flying horses and even a few seahorses. We watched them whirl around and crowds of people came close and eddied around us, respecting the strollers, perhaps.

I looked at Elena and shook my head. "You are strange. I get accused of being strange but you beat me hands down ..."

Her eyes were alight with mischief. "You are a n'er-do-well, just like my grandma said about certain boys in her home town."

"This is true."

Claire and Elena's husband Alex appeared with white plastic cups of lemonade loaded with too much ice, and corn dogs with mustard. For the next few minutes there was nothing but the sound of eating and drinking. Then both children loudly refused to eat the unfamiliar food.

"Nononononono. NO! Yes. NO!" From Jake and roughly the same from Fred.

Elena stared at her son. "Last year you loved corn dogs and now you hate them."

I got the two brats regular, boring hot dogs with dull, uninteresting ketchup and they both shut up and ate quickly. And messily.

I knew hot dogs were bad for kids. I knew there was a choking danger. I guess that makes me a bad dad. But it was one of those risks Fred was going to have to face eventually in his life and I felt he should face it with some paternal support.

Alex put his arm around his wife while she ate. They made an interesting contrast: he was white and thin with long black hair and she was West Indian, brown and solidly built. I wondered where her gun was but I didn't have the guts to ask for fear she might show me.

Claire knelt in front of Fred and cleaned ketchup from his nose and eyebrow. Then she turned to me, sighed, and cleaned mustard from my cheek with the same napkin.

"I can't take you anywhere." Her voice was melodious and amused.

"Hey!"

The four of us kept walking and pushing our strollers, working our way through the fair. Fred was tired and I wanted to carry him but I was trying to be a tougher kind of parent. Frankly, I was sucking at it, but I kept pushing and tried not to think about it.

We passed plastic slides, chain and canvas swings tied to V6 engines, bumper cars and many other devices designed to zip, shake and agitate.

As we walked Elena kept talking cheerfully. "It all used to be different, back when I was a child … like the prizes. They used to give out bugs on the midway."

Claire wrinkled her nose. "Bugs? Really?"

"They weren't really bugs, they were bright green anole lizards given out in glass bowls. A bug butcher was a salesman, and he would wear the lizard on his lapel, tied with a piece of string to show they were harmless. My granda used to claim he caught bugs for sale to Mr. Barnum when he came down to Sarasota, Florida."

Alex interrupted. "Your granda also used to claim he was a pirate."

His wife gave him a swat. "That was much more believable. He was a dreadful liar and I mean that both ways. But all that's changed. No more bugs. No more trains. And the grifts … oh the grifts. Where have they all gone?"

The word was familiar to me but I asked anyway, "Grifts?"

I had to say something. An ambulance was nosing through the crowds, preceded by two fat rent-a-cops slowly turning beet red. I guessed they were there to pick up my friends back at the bug house.

Alex spoke up. "The frauds, the cons, the schemes. Like the Fiji Mermaid, half a monkey sewed on a fish and presented to the public at five cents a view." He had a childlike look of glee on his face. "I like circuses too. A gentler kind of crime and vice, an innocence."

Elena laughed delightedly. "And the Cardiff Giant, a stone statue shown as a petrified man. Barnum saw it and had a copy made and was sued by the original creator. The judge ruled that there was no crime in copying a hoax."

Claire looked at both of them as though they were insane and then she smiled as she remembered. "Something about an egress?"

Elena nodded eagerly and watched people climb nervously into a centrifuge. "Yes! There once was a circus so spectacular that no one wanted to leave so the owner put up a sign saying 'This Way to the Egress!' People followed it and found themselves outside again. Lots of them went back to the front and paid again." She frowned down at her son and he mimicked her expression exactly. "So many harmless cons not done anymore. The Three-Card Monte card game and shortchanging the flat diddlies on the high counters where they couldn't see it."

Claire said, "Pardon?"

"Cons. Picking the right card. Giving the wrong change at the cash counters to flat diddlies, the customers, which was anyone not in the life."

She flicked hair off the back of her neck. "People expected it. The circus came to town and they'd trade the limelight and spangles for a little harmless graft. Everyone knew the circus wasn't honest but that was okay."

We had gotten past the rides to the booths, and barkers called to us, "Hey Mister, win a pretty prize for a pretty lady!" And "Show who's got the muscles in the family!" And so on.

Claire squeezed my arm. "I believe you promised me a prize."

"I did. But didn't I do that thing you liked last night? Doesn't that cut me some slack?"

She spoke gently. "I don't like that. You do. I simply tolerate it."

I had nothing to say to that patent lie. We ignored the calls of the barkers and watched the games—the baseball tossed into the wicker basket, ringing pop bottles with a plastic hoop and bursting balloons with darts. I watched out of the corner of my eye and saw that the baskets were rigged to make them extra bouncy. And I saw the pop bottles were too close together for the hoop and that each balloon had behind it a diamond of red hardwood. Nice harmless gimmicks designed to separate the mark from the money.

I wondered if the crowd around me knew the games were rigged and I wondered if they cared.

And I wondered if Elena was right about everyone knowing the circus wasn't honest.

Farther down there was a crowd shooting targets with gas-powered submachine guns firing copper-coated BB's.

Claire looked at the guns and then back at me. "Wanna try your luck?"

Elena was smiling. She had a built-in cop instinct that made her always want to bash the cons (in this case me) down. On general principles. Most of the time she controlled it though. Which was fine because I had the same hard-wired need to bash the cops down to a manageable size.

There was a lineup of kids and adults around the guns. I elbowed in and then came back with a report. "Not really. The guns are old and not very accurate. They're also leaking air like you wouldn't believe. I'll keep my eyes open, though. I've got to win you a prize, huh? You're sure?"

"You have to win a prize. At least one. If you want to keep my respect."

"I do. I guess anyway. I mean, if I have to." I looked over at Elena. "Now if it was a real Thompson submachine gun, maybe I'd show this pig something."

Elena snorted and Alex hid a smile. They both knew I'd been a thief and thug and general leg breaker for most of my life. And both knew I'd reformed and was reforming. But Elena was still sure she could take me.

Inside my larcenous little soul I wondered about calling a cop a friend, and then I shut that voice up fast.

#3

I looked at Claire and she smiled and my heart lit up.

It is much, much better on the outside of prison walls. That was a fundamental truth for me. A basic.

Elena, with help from Alex, talked about the circus and we wandered down the rows of game booths and past haunted houses and funhouses.

Behind me I finally heard the sounds of sirens as someone navigated an ambulance through the crowds to carry away my shit-kicked friends. Which meant the cops would be on hand soon but they'd be looking for someone rushing out of the fairgrounds. They wouldn't be looking for someone walking with his son and wife in the company of an off-duty cop.

To celebrate I bought everyone cotton candy and listened to Elena.

"... these days it's not the same. No more burning the territory with bent shows. Which is what happened when someone ran a really crooked circus on a tour. The next circus along would reap the whirlwind of rage and fury." She smiled a little sadly. "Yeah, it's all Sunday school shows these days for the lot lice and gullies. Which were the kids and the marks."

Claire linked her arm through mine. "Elena, you are an amazing font of knowledge. Monty used to work circuses and fairs. Didn't you?"

Elena looked at me, surprised, and I laughed. "Yeah. Back in the old days. It was a good way to travel under the radar back when I was a thief. I remember it fondly."

I didn't, not really. It had been hard work and no glamour, setting up and tearing down badly made stalls and tents mostly. But some of it had been good.

I remembered the face of a local girl in some forgotten Saskatchewan town as she'd climbed into my lap during a thunderstorm. I'd snuck her onto the fairground after hours to see the lions up close. She had had red hair down to the middle of her back and small breasts set far apart on her chest and her smile had been brilliant as she'd come. We were three feet from the cage, up against a pile of rope, and she'd taken off her panties and my pants and hiked her skirt up high as she'd ridden me and watched the lions. When she came the lions purred approval and she came again. It took her by surprise and she made a noise I've never heard again.

The memory flared and vanished and Claire looked at me suspiciously and then smiled to herself when I winked at her.

I remembered the way the children had cheered the clowns and the way the loaded trucks would cut along the highway and throw long shadows at dusk and dawn. I remembered sleeping in a stolen sleeping bag in a partially assembled haunted house, and I remembered eating day-old hot dogs forty feet up while putting together the roller coaster. And I remembered the way storms would come rolling across the horizon, black sullen clouds split with white fury, rolling forward and swallowing whole towns.

Mostly, though, my memories were of hard work and shitty pay, but working the fairs had gotten me out of my home town.

That was enough at the time.

When I'd gotten tired of the fair we were in southern Ontario. I'd waited until a dark and stormy night before I'd tied the manager up and taken the cash box from the red money wagon. Then I'd vanished.

The entirety of my circus experience until now.

Claire and Alex wandered off to check out booths selling antique china, silver cutlery, buttons and other junk at very high prices while Elena went in the other direction to check out a booth selling dirty t-shirts. In between I waited with the two strollers and the boys who urged me to "Go-go-go!"

Claire motioned me over to a china booth and I dragged the boys with me.

"What do you think?"

She was holding up a brilliantly white china plate covered in a pattern of tiny red roses and tight curls of green vines.

"It's beautiful. For us?"

"For my mother. I think it's almost a match to her old set."

The man behind the counter cleared his throat and I looked at him. He was small and dressed entirely in brown, an expensive old herringbone wool suit that looked uncomfortably warm.

"If madam would like to give me the makers mark of her lovely mother's set perhaps I can find an exact match. The one you have chosen there is very rare." He gestured, "This is only a small sampling of my wares."

Claire shook her head very slowly, with regret. "No, I

think. Too expensive right now. But thank you." Her smile was enthusiastic and passionate. The man blushed and she said, "You have beautiful things."

He started to stutter and we left to go look at the Fiji Mermaid or reasonable facsimile of same. Behind us I heard shutters shut and someone angrily say, "Hey."

Eventually we got to the end of the route through the exhibition which had circled around back to the beginning. There we were faced with the choices of doing the route again or of heading off towards agricultural and art exhibits. Claire and Alex leaned towards the route one more time but Elena and I voted for the new horizons. Fred and Jake agreed with us and off we went.

Past the Deep Fried Twinkie stand there was a display of cop cars, Crown Vics mostly. Cop cars and bomb disposal robots and a real, genuine, antique portable prison. Around the cars were some handsome examples of the city's finest and a dunk tank featuring a female cop in a water-skiing wet suit and dress hat daring everyone to knock her off her perch.

Elena saw my face and said, "Community relations."

"And why aren't you up there?" Claire took a found stick from Jake's hand before he could do something bad.

Elena looked offended. "I? I am a sergeant. And mean. I don't have to do that."

"Anymore," Alex cut in laconically.

I stood there a little bemused and a young cop came up and asked if I wanted to ride in the back of a cop car. I stared at him while Elena started to cough and Claire stared politely at the sky. Finally I managed to say, "Thank you, no. Been there. Done that. Frankly, it's lost its lustre."

He looked puzzled but went off to find other victims and

I stared after him. I don't like cops in general, and in specific, I've spent too much time running from them and being shot at by them to feel much affection for them. In my experience cops were either corrupt or blind. The corrupt ones would rip you off and then lie about it in court. The blind ones wouldn't see anything the corrupt ones ever did.

When I'd been stealing they'd been a serious occupational hazard, and even now there were lots of them who didn't want to let me forget my past. Last year a corrupt cop with delusions of godhood had set me up towards prison or the grave and had almost caught my family in the crossfire. Eventually Walsh and I had had it out and I had won, barely.

Then I'd been saved by another cop with a strong sense of fair play, but that wasn't the point.

Elena had done a lot to redeem the whole species for me. But later in the same year I'd been a bystander in a bank robbery that had gone sour and ended up spending time in remand while my lawyer pried me out.

In that case I'd actually stopped the robbery. Out of self-interest, actually, but again, that didn't matter. I'd been innocent and I'd still been bounced through the legal system one more time.

In retrospect, I had enjoyed the actual bank robbery though. Maybe more than I'd expected.

Which left me with an attitude towards cops that was in transition, and watching them play nice was a little surreal.

Not that I held grudges—I wasn't built that way, at least that's what I told myself. They did what they did and I did what I did and, back when we were at cross purposes, bad things happened. No grudges, I kept telling myself that.

Like the midway neon lies, I really wanted to believe them.

Claire was gone when I turned to ask her something and

then she came back holding three old and battered major league baseballs. She handed them to me and I must have looked deeply confused.

"Huh?"

Claire took me by the elbow and led me to a white line painted in the dirt. "Very simple. Stand here. Throw balls at target. Knock cop into water. Raise money to stop child abuse."

The cop on the perch chanted, "C'mon, take your best shot ..."

I looked at my wife, who was about to burst into laughter as she patted me. "It's for a good cause. To prevent child abuse. I mean really, who's in favour of that?"

An angry teenager pushed past me and windmilled three balls that all missed.

Claire leaned in and said, throatily, "Happy birthday."

It was my birthday in a few days; I was trying to forget it.

I used to throw lots of baseballs in prison. I used to be really good. Playing baseball was a good way to burn off stress because you could hit something. And, when I was in Drumheller, my best throw was clocked at seventy-six feet per second, which is not bad and it was bang on target too. In prison baseball was a way to deal with rage.

And outside of prison? I wasn't sure of the role of baseball.

Without thinking I wound up and threw, and it felt like a winner as the ball came off my fingers with everything all loose in my shoulders and back.

The cop had time to say, "We want a pitcher ..." when the ball hit the six-inch steel paddle and dropped her into water.

Behind me there were cheers, and I turned to find Elena and Alex with huge cones of cotton candy and Fred standing up in his stroller. "Good one!"

He sounded very mature and Jake echoed him.

I turned back to the tank and the cop adjusted her hat and got back onto the perch. I waited until she was comfortable and let her call out, "Lucky ..." before I threw again and the cop was back in the water.

Some days are like that.

When I'd thrown my third ball and turned to go, the angry teenager who'd missed handed me three more and said, "Nail da bitch." But he said it with a smile.

And I did. Bang-bang-bang. And when those balls were gone Claire was there with three more and a big smile, and when those were gone Elena brought me more.

It was a John Wayne day, everything went perfect. Just like in the war movies when the bad guy leans around the tree into your site. Just like when the girl turns right into your arms at the perfect moment. Just like when the arrow leaves the string and for a second the shooter and the target are the same thing. Just like when you draw the fourth jack and everyone is betting strong.

Just like when you hit the bank on payday.

Throw.

Those were bad thoughts, so I focussed on the positive; I'd been out of prison more than a year and I wasn't going back.

Throw.

I had a wife and a son and friends, even a job babysitting. All for the first time in my life—I was basically stable and (fairly) honest.

Throw.

Shit, even the cops here were finding this hilarious. Their laughter pulled me partially out of the groove and then I was back in, me and the ball. The ball and me.

Throw.

After about ten dunks the girl in the tank called it quits, laughing, and a fat sergeant in a black Speedo climbed on and clenched an unlit cigar between his teeth as he perched his hat just right on his bald head.

"Ready?"

"You betcha!"

Throw and splash.

I'd never thrown this well before. Claire bought a whole bucket of balls and Elena dragged it over to the line. Elena kissed my cheek and said, "Claire told me it's your birthday in two days, so happy birthday, and many more."

And I just kept throwing.

When I stopped throwing it was because my arm was numb, not because I missed. I don't think I missed once.

As I turned away there were people cheering and they rushed forward to try their luck. I turned and put my face right into the lens of a TV camera and found myself talking into a foam rubber microphone held by an incredibly short blond woman. She was very pretty with a wide smile that made me think of enthusiastic mattress games and no regrets on either side.

"Hi! My name is Candy! And I'm from the station that never sleeps!"

"How utterly wonderful for you." I matched her enthusiasm with difficulty. I was clutching my right arm in my left, cradling it gently; I could feel a good ache. The ache in the muscle and not the bone. The sweet ache that meant tired and not hurt.

"You just knocked cops into a dunk tank for more than an hour. How does that feel?"

"Sore." Rule number one about talking to journalists is don't. Do not talk to them on the record, do not talk to them off the record, and do not talk to them. Do not talk to them.

"Sorry to hear that! Are you burning off some rage?" Long pause and then she added, "Mr. Haaviko?"

That stopped me. "How do you know my name?"

Candy showed bright teeth and brought the microphone back to her face. "Because I do my research. You've certainly been in the news enough!"

Behind her I could see Claire and I knew I had to wrap this up quick. "Ah. No, no rage. Just raising money to stop the abuse of children ..."

"A Good Cause!" She capitalized it enthusiastically. "So, you don't hate the police?"

"No." I tried to back up and she followed, along with her camera guy, a round black man who sweated a lot.

"You've been a felon most of your life?"

"True."

"Yet you claim you don't hate cops?"

"True. You put news reporters in that same tank and I'll be down here just as fast. Probably faster. I mean child abuse, who's in favour of child abuse?" She didn't get the joke.

Candy smiled again. "So what do you think of cops?"

She was not going to leave me alone. I exhaled. "I like cops. Really." I didn't finish the line with "but I couldn't eat a whole one." Instead I added, "There's been four wrongful convictions for murder just here in Winnipeg in your lifetime."

I named four names from Winnipeg's past.

Candy's brow furrowed. "What? Who are they?"

I took a step forward and she took a step back. Around us the cops kept showing their cars and robots and taunting the ball throwers. I went on, "Those are four dead people, people murdered in the past twenty-eight years."

Candy's smile never wavered. "What does that have to do with ..."

I took another step forward. "In each case the cops arrested someone and put him in jail for a few months or years or decades. Then they had to let them go because the person arrested didn't do the crime. Think about that."

Candy didn't have a response and I kept talking. "Because. Those arrests meant that the murderers got to walk free and clear. And do whatever they wanted. To whomever they wanted."

Claire came around and took my arm and I smiled at Candy. "I don't hate cops. They do a very hard job. Frankly, I don't think about them at all. But when I do I admire and respect them."

It was a lie but a good one to leave on.

As we walked back to the parking lot Elena just shook her head. "You pour gasoline on fires too? Tease wolverines? Molest sharks? You are a walking disaster area ..."

Alex took her hand. "True. But at least he's not boring."

Claire was pushing Fred, who had fallen fast asleep. She pulled a blanket over him and stuck her tongue out at Alex. "He's never boring."

On the way out the gate Claire looked back at the bright midway and sighed. "And I never even got a prize ..."

#4

The next morning Claire and I heard the same interview played over and over on three separate radio stations. Each time it was followed by angry callers talking about my behaviour, demeanour, attitude and general lack of respect. We also got nine phone calls from various news agencies trying to get me to comment. Then I got a call from a local right wing radio station that tried to insult me until I got angry but I hung up and finally unplugged the phone.

I stood there for a second and looked around the kitchen. The whole house didn't feel safe to me yet. A full year ago an enemy had booby-trapped the place with grenades, cyanide, shotgun shells, spring razors, spikes and so on. Clearing it had taken me eleven days on my hands and knees.

Eleven days. And I still wasn't sure I had gotten all the traps out. It gnawed at the place I was supposed to have a conscience—I would hate to have Claire or Fred hurt through my carelessness.

I had cleared the place to the best of my ability and I was really good.

But no one's perfect.

Idly I wondered about burning the place down ... just to be sure. Claire interrupted me before I could think it all the way through. "Coffee? Eggs? Breakfast was promised. You still worried about the radio and the phone calls?"

I snorted. "Yep. Kept me up last night screaming."

Claire accepted the eggs I offered and tried to make the best of it. "Well, at least we don't have cable television. There's probably an American Fox news spin on it by now. The right wing demigods probably hate you."

"Well, that's okay. I can handle a little hate. As long as it's not coming from Stephen Colbert."

"He scares you, doesn't he?"

"Very much." I offered a single fried egg to Fred along with strips of toast to dip and he began to devour them. While he did so I spun channels on the radio until I got the civilized tones of the CBC morning show hosts talking about the weather and the chances of forest fires. I looked back at Fred and then at Claire. "Am I supposed to be giving Fred eggs?"

She looked at me and then at Fred. "Let's ask him. Fred, should we be giving you eggs?"

He swallowed and said, "Yes. More—ples."

Claire corrected him. "Please."

Fred looked at her hard and tried again. "Pleass?"

"Better."

I gave him another egg and finally got around to my own. "And what are you doing today?"

"Selling houses. Same thing I do every other day. Also probably renting some. Maybe some buying." Claire had passed her real estate test a few months before and was doing better than fine. She specialized in houses in the North End, the poorer end of town. However, it was the part of the city where bargains could still be found and where the market was still strong. After all, people always needed a roof over their head, no matter what the state of their finances was.

The North End was where Claire and I lived, only we rented. We weren't up to buying a house, not yet. I was taking baby steps—when I was a crook I had lived in hotels and motels, so renting a house struck me as a reasonable step in a good direction. Buying a house could wait, would have to wait—hell, I was still getting used to belonging to a neighbourhood!

I was proud of Claire. Despite a generally tanking global economy she was still selling quite well and with her commissions plus the money I made babysitting we were doing okay, better than most.

Our neighbours the Kilpatricks, for example, were in much worse shape. When the sub-prime economic mess had started the husband had had to come out of retirement and go back to managing restaurants. His wife, who worked at the Manitoba Telephone Service, had had to take extra shifts. When I talked with them about the situation, they were tight-lipped and furious, so I suggested they rob a bank, and they took a very long time before turning the idea down.

Meanwhile, Claire and I just kept lurching along. We were making it from hand to mouth and we never had any savings, which meant we had nothing to lose. I wasn't sure if that was a good thing or not.

On the other end of the spectrum my assorted criminal acquaintances were doing really well. Marie Blue Duck, who smuggled illegal immigrants and poor people into the States, was having an easy time as the plummeting US dollar scrambled the international money market and dropped plane fares, which made it possible for even more of her clients to come over. And Sandra Robillard, who ran her dead husband's CCE (continuing criminal enterprise), was selling grass and tranqs like they were going out of style. That was because sins always became more popular when the world was collapsing, a rule I had memorized before I could talk.

And, of course, Elena was doing fine with lots of overtime as she fought crime in all its assorted forms. Bank robberies by desperate honest men, fraud by desperate dishonest men and familial violence by mothers and fathers under job pressure.

The economy made for interesting times all around.

Our dog, Renfield, came into the room and sat down by his water dish and wagged. When his tail got wet from the water dish he had forgotten he was shocked and confused, so I gave him a little egg on a toast point and he cheered up again. While he was cheering up the radio announcer changed subjects. "And we have with us next a representative of the city who is answering questions about some claims made public yesterday about the police."

Claire winced visibly and I apologized one more time.

The man who came on was angry and energetic. "Thanks for having me on. The claims made last night are completely without foundation and show a profound disrespect for the hard-working men and women of the police service."

"So there's no shred of truth to the statements that were made?"

"None."

I looked at Claire and held my hands together as if in prayer and pointed at the phone. She sighed, plugged it in and handed it over. A minute later I was on the air.

"Hi. My name is Monty Haaviko. I assume your guest is talking about me?"

The host managed to say, "Good morning, Mr. Haaviko ..." and then the other man cut in with, "You have a lot of nerve!"

"Not really." Claire came around and rubbed my neck. "Actually I called to correct something your guest said. It's Mr. Harrow, isn't it?"

"Yes."

"You said I have profound disrespect for the police. That is not true. I simply do not have blinders on. But I do respect them."

"What do you mean?

"Should I respect them for that time when a cop shot an unarmed man and the investigation was questionable, to say the least? Or the recent enquiry when a cop killed a woman and the investigation was botched? Or what about the occasion when a hundred cops faked illnesses after another cop beat up a handcuffed man on camera and was temporarily suspended?"

"This is preposterous ..."

The host cut him off. "Mr. Haaviko, what are you trying to say?"

"I'm clearing up a point. Words that I never used are being put in my mouth. Attitudes are being attributed to me that I do not have. I did not say I dislike cops, I said they make mistakes sometimes. Even when I was stealing I didn't hate cops. They were simply part of the business expense. But, they do make mistakes."

Mr. Harrow came back on, "Well, of course they do, they're only human."

"Exactly. All I'm saying is that cops have made mistakes. That's it. Am I wrong? Not in specifics, but in general?"

There was dead silence and then Mr. Harrow said, "Well, sometimes mistakes are made."

"Okay then, let's leave it at that."

I thanked the host and the guest and hung up and un-plugged the phone and turned the radio off. Ten minutes later Claire was gone out the door and Rachel, the Kilpatricks' granddaughter, and Elena's Jake were in my home, trying to tear the place apart.

The life of a professional babysitter. There's no life like it. As I cleaned up spilled apple juice I thought, somewhat long-ingly, of going back to thieving.

At the park that afternoon Fred, Rachel and Jake played on the swings while I warmed a bench. One of the nicest things about the North End is its vast number of parks. The whole area was laid out in a time with a different civic attitude and the parks survived most types of improvement and develop-ment. Another nice thing is that most of the parks have areas where children can still play on swings and teeter-totters and the occasional jungle gym.

After about twenty minutes a young man with badly pit-ted skin and protruding eyes sat down on the other end of the bench and pulled out a radio/flashlight combo he had to crank to get working. The man was wearing a black hooded sweatshirt, jeans and runners, and the radio, when he got it working, was set to the same right wing talk station that had tried to ambush me that morning.

It must have been a slow news day because they were still talking about me.

"Next caller ..."

"Hi, I just wanted to say that I agree with everything the other guy said. This Mr. Haaviko doesn't understand anything about the situations our city's finest find themselves in day after day down on the front lines ..."

Uh-huh. It was an interesting statement but it didn't really make sense. I did understand. I was an ex-con, I'd seen up close the world cops complained about. And I'd seen it for years, better and more clearly than any cop I'd ever seen.

"Good point. And that caller is absolutely right. Mr. Haaviko, a convicted criminal, has no right to comment on the behaviour of the fine men and women ..."

Right.

I got up, gathered the kids together and started for home. When I got there I found a bundle of dark red, long-stemmed roses wrapped in a recent UK *London Times* newspaper leaning against the screen door. There was a note with the flowers that I opened, written in block letters: "To Claire, In Admiration! So wonderful seeing you at the Fair!"

Nothing else.

I took the flowers inside and put them in a pitcher with water. There were seven flowers and nothing else, none of the greenery or preservative powders that normally come with them. There hadn't been any tissue paper around the flowers either. I got ready to tease Claire when she got home and started to make dinner after plugging the kids into a documentary about particle physics.

Some parents for whom I babysat did not like that I showed their kids documentaries. They wanted me to show them *Sesame Street* and *Dora the Explorer* and other stuff like that. I told them that such programs were against my personal life philosophy and that if the kids wanted to learn about co-operation, a good documentary on lions eating an elephant was as good as anything Hollywood, Tokyo or Seoul could come up with.

One mother told me I was depraved but she kept bringing her daughter back, so I figured I must be doing something right. Either that or she meant depraved in a good way. Or maybe she just couldn't find another babysitter.

#5

Over dinner Claire asked Fred what he learned today. He thought about it and said, "'Article physics are cool!"

She looked at me, "Particle physics? You're teaching our son about particle physics?"

"He's going to have to learn sometime ..."

She forked a piece of lettuce into her mouth. "You don't know anything about particle physics."

"I got the kids a DVD from that rental place across the Assiniboine River; the one about an hour's walk away. The monsters seemed to enjoy it. I'm trying very hard to enhance my mind, I'll have you know. Nice flowers, by the way."

"Thank you. They're not from you?"

"Sorry, no. They had that note. Strange delivery, if you ask me. I just figured it was from one of your many lovers."

Claire looked at the note and put it down. "None of mine. But it's nice to get offers, you know? Weird, the note's cut from a piece of strange paper; it's not a real card at all."

"So who did you meet?"

Claire shrugged. "No one. I talked to lots of people but actually met? No one. Maybe it's a joke."

While we were still eating our doorbell rang and Renfield went nuts, barking ferociously until Claire put him in the guest bedroom. I went to the door and made sure the chains were in place. When I was sure, I pulled the crowbar from the umbrella stand and held it behind my back. Only then did I open the door to the limit of the chain. The door itself was solid core oak, an antique that had cost a mint and a half and which I'd ruined by painting it white and setting into a steel frame. A battering ram might get through it. Normal cop door-breaking shotgun ammunition would be useless.

Claire used to tell people, "It's not that Monty doesn't trust people." She'd pause for a measured two or three heartbeats and then go on, " ... it's just that Monty doesn't trust people."

Standing on our steps were a man and a woman, both wearing dark grey suits and carrying thin leather briefcases. The woman was white and the man was an olive-skinned Aboriginal. They were both fairly forgettable, wearing nondescript, expensive clothes and good quality watches and smelling very slightly of expensive colognes and perfumes. At a guess I put them in their late twenties or early thirties. They didn't look like cops and they were too well dressed to be reporters, so I didn't slam the door but instead asked, "May I help you?"

The man reached into his shirt pocket and produced a business card with a practiced flourish and handed it to me. I took it and read, "Dean Pritchard—Consultant" followed by a cell number, land line, fax number, email address and website. The card was of heavy bond paper with raised lettering, tastefully done with black ink on an old ivory-coloured stock. Reflexively I glanced at their shoes, which were well-shined with heavy stitching, made of a creamy-looking leather that had never been stretched, dyed or sewn. Shoes are an easy way to tell the wealth of a person. Rich people do not buy cheap shoes. I'm not sure they know how to buy them.

When I offered the card back the man refused and I complained, "Your card doesn't actually tell me very much. What do you need?"

"May we come in?"

His voice was smooth and I unlocked the two chains and removed the floor plate lock to let them in. "My wife and I are just finishing dinner. Please come in though. Have a seat in the living room."

I wanted to find out what they wanted and why and quickly. Inviting them in was the fastest way to get answers. Frankly neither of them scared me or I'd insist on meeting them somewhere else. Here, in my home, I had an advantage. And a few assorted tricks that I could always use.

They came in and shook my hand and then Claire came over and they shook her hand as well. When the amenities were over Dean spoke. "We won't take long. We're here to find out if you're interested in a proposal, Mr. Haaviko."

I motioned for everyone to sit down and then I asked, "A proposal?"

"Yes. We saw you on the news and we think you're exactly the kind of person the city needs."

Claire didn't even crack a smile as she said, "The city needs a goat?"

I love my wife but I chose that moment to ignore her. I walked back to the door, spun the crowbar back into the umbrella stand and said, "What are you talking about?"

"You are exactly the person the city's new police advisory commission needs."

"Police advisory commission? I don't think so ... I'm a

convicted ex-felon. We, as a group, generally have very little to do with the police, if we can avoid it. They don't like us. We don't like them. It's kind of a system we have."

The woman, Mrs. Brenda Geraghty, according to her card, nodded. "We know all about you. Convictions for armed robberies, possession of narcotics, possession of prohibited weapons, burglaries, assaults, attempted murders, frauds—it's an extensive list. And arrests for multiple-murder last year, although those charges were dropped."

Dean took over. "Anyhow, that was all in the past. We're interested in having you run for the job right now. It's an elected position and the election takes place in September, so we have to declare soon. Then we can put a support team in place and get your campaign happening."

My head was spinning and Claire was looking profoundly amused. Fred finished his supper, climbed down from his booster chair and came over. I picked him up and put him on my knee before answering, "Uh. Thank you. But I don't think so."

Dean went on, "The position pays quite well. More than babysitting. And it will be very simple to do: not a lot of work at all."

"That's nice." Alarms went off in my head. They knew my criminal record, although the news could have given them that. The babysitting job was less well known. Reporters were loath to mention anything to do with kids, so these two in front of me had done some research.

Brenda reached over, patted Fred and said, "Well, think about it. We can talk about it tomorrow. We'll call you then."

Dean stood. "Just so you know. Off the record, we're offering to cover the costs of the election totally and completely, plus we're willing to help you out with living expenses during the campaign. There's absolutely no risk to you here. We just want you on the board and we think you can win. With our help, of course. Between the two of us Brenda and I have worked on fifteen campaigns. We're the best in the west."

Brenda's nose twitched and she reminded me of someone I'd known somewhere else. They both gathered up their briefcases and allowed themselves to be graciously escorted out of the house. Only then did Claire and I return to dinner.

I was eating the salad when I looked up and saw that Claire's face was bright red with repressed laughter. I put down my fork. "Let it out before you explode."

Her laughter was clear and rich and filled the whole bottom half of the house and made me smile myself. In the living room Fred looked up from his Megablox and then went back to work on his wall.

"Okay, it is funny."

"Funny? It's hilarious! How many ex-cons get propositioned for an elected position? It's beautiful! You gonna take them up on it?"

"No. I'm not really a political type, you know?"

Her eyes twinkled across the cold food. "Oh no. You're a thief and a thug, an arsonist, a killer and a thoroughly bad man."

"Don't forget my twisted sexual desires."

She smiled. "Never. That's why I married you."

Later in the night I untangled my legs from Claire's and rolled over onto my side. "I think that broke some laws."

"Good." She purred. "Got to keep you in practice. Although I think that last one put a kink in my neck."

"Excellent."

"Yep. I think that last one was illegal in Texas."

"Everything is illegal in Texas. Illegal or mandatory."

I pulled her close and whispered five or six things into her ear and she stretched against me. "A thief and a thug. But not a politician at all. That would be a step down."

Eventually we fell asleep.

#6

The next morning I made breakfast and got Claire off to work while accepting the delivery of Jacob and Rachel. Then they watched a DVD of David Attenborough's *The Life of Birds* (also from the movie store) while I did the dishes. Afterwards we headed out to make a tour of the playgrounds and see who was up and about. Along the way I had some nice conversations with a few mothers and grandmothers and many small children of varying ages and genders.

It was boring but a living. That eight-hour day with my son (and friends) paid $50 for the privilege of watching him grow up.

It beat the hell out of stealing for a living. Or gang-banging, dealing dope, pimping whores, cooking meth, growing weed, smuggling, arson, fencing or any of my other previous delightful careers. Although I still missed the buzz and lift of cocaine and PCP and acid. Not to mention the comforting angry blankness of booze and hash and heroin. And the adrenal rush of theft and violence.

Life's a trade, right?

When we got back home I made ham and cheese sandwiches for an early lunch and was settling down to some quiet colouring time with the kids when the doorbell rang. The kids liked colouring time because I encouraged them to go outside the lines on all occasions and at any opportunity. Still, I had to answer the door—Renfield's damn barking ensured that.

"Yes?" I spoke through the crack with the crowbar behind my back. On the stoop outside was a tanned man wearing a dark brown three-piece suit with a dark blue shirt and a muted brown and green tie. He seemed overdressed in the mid-June sunshine and I saw no reason to let him in.

"Mr. Haaviko? My name is Alastair Reynolds and I'm a lawyer ..."

Strike one. I'm not a huge fan of lawyers, unless they're my lawyer. Even then it's pretty much a tossup. The guy kept talking. "... who's representing a client who would very much like to ..."

Strike two. Someone sent a lawyer as a flunky. Not cool.

" ... meet with you."

Strike three. On general principle.

I opened the door to give me more options. "I don't want to talk to you or your boss."

He reached into his right front pocket and I braced myself. The pocket was small but bulging. Enough space for a small semi-auto, like a .22, .25 or .32 or a larger calibre derringer. Also enough room for pepper spray or a folding knife.

I watched. If his hand came out holding something in the palm I'd assume it was a weapon and kick him in the face, hard. Then I'd take him apart properly with the crowbar. If he brought out something in his fingers I wouldn't hurt him. I braced myself and kept the smile plastered in place.

His fingers came out with a wad of bills held together with a money clip shaped like a gold Pacman. He counted out ten bills from the inside of the roll and handed them over.

"One thousand. A grand. Just to talk with my client. Just to listen to what he has to say."

I was still ready to kick but I took the money with my left hand and checked it out. New-model bills, the ones from 2004 when they dumped $100-plus million into the Canadian financial system using the hundreds. If the money was queer it was good queer: the bills had the holographic stripe, the colour shift thread, the see-through number and the watermark. They also had raised dots and high-contrast numerals, which made them easier for the blind and almost blind to read. Prime Minister Borden was still on the front and on the back was a good map of Canada and a canoe.

I smiled when I thought of the joke of the definition of a Canadian; someone who can make love in a canoe.

I figured the bill was real. They were a bitch to counterfeit. I'd tried way back when. I smiled. "I'll get my coat."

Actually I also had to take the kids over to the Kilpatricks'. Mrs. Kilpatrick took them and I gave her one of the hundreds, which made her happy. She immediately gave them a bag of chocolate chip cookies and turned on *Sesame Street* and they zoned out.

Then I went back past Reynolds into my house and changed shoes. The blue and white runners went into the closet and were replaced by the steel-toed oxfords with the reinforced stitching and the good heels. They had been sold as a bartender's shoe and could resist a ninety-pound beer keg dropped from shoulder height easily enough. They made fine thug shoes.

I mean, it wasn't like I didn't trust Reynolds. But I'm not stupid.

His car was parked in front of the house, a nice gunmetal grey four-door sedan. He opened all the doors with a clicker attached to his keys and I got in and made myself comfortable. Then we took off.

#7

In the car Reynolds told me again that he was a lawyer and a warning bell went off in my head. In general and on principle I don't like lawyers, so I told him, "I don't like lawyers."

"Really?" He sounded amused. "Shakespeare, that 'let's kill all the lawyers' shit?"

He drove pretty badly and I looked him over out of the corner of my eye around the side of my sunglasses. Reynolds was well-built, tanned and healthy, and he moved well. If he was a lawyer he didn't work at it in an office under a fluorescent bulb.

We whipped under a train bridge and I answered, "Not Shakespeare. Gibbon. He wrote that men who believe, due to experience, that whatever can be fixed within law is right, or, if not right, then allowable, are not useful members of society. Something like that."

"Ah." Reynolds turned right and down two blocks and then left. "Well, I make sure I'm useful."

Inside my head a little voice said, "Useful to whom?" But I didn't say it.

We got stuck between a pair of idiot tow-truck drivers and construction and I said what I was thinking. "Your car sucks."

"What? It's a fifty-thousand-dollar Lexus sedan."

"It still sucks."

Reynolds was outraged. "What the hell do you know? This car has a V6 engine, heated leather seats ..."

"Still sucks."

"It's got six speeds, an aluminum alloy block, an intelligent throttle control, independent temperature control, satellite radio, ten speakers, bucket seats, ten-way power controlled seats, state-of-the-art information display, power moon roof, auto-levelling headlamps, even coat hooks!"

"Amazing. Despite all that, it still sucks. No power, the seats are uncomfortable and the engine is way too loud."

Reynolds growled at me and then changed the subject. "My client is Mr. Cornelius Devanter. He's a businessman and he owns factories and manufactories all across Canada and the border states. Along with a shipping company in the Caribbean, a trucking company in Alaska, a chain of hotels and so on."

"A rich man?"

"Very."

"I should have asked for more money."

Reynolds just smiled.

Devanter's office suite consisted of the entire penultimate floor of a very old and carefully renovated building right downtown. We parked in a modern garage that had grown like a wart out of the side of the older building and then took the elevator up.

Reynolds was still mad about me insulting the car and told me so at great length.

At the right floor the elevator stopped and my tight-assed chauffeur and guide used a swipe card to open the door. There was a second of waiting and then the doors opened onto a large lobby with a single huge, brushed-steel desk in the middle. Behind it were five doors, three on the back wall and one leading off to each side. The receptionist-secretary-assistant behind the desk was a long-haired redhead with a heart-shaped face and graceful legs I admired openly. As I approached the desk the legs scissored twice and I saw a glimpse of forest-green stockings and garters and then I was too close to admire the view.

"May I help you?" She had a calm, cool voice and she wore a dark green wool sweater and skirt against the cold of the air conditioning. Up close I could see her nose had been broken at least once and I found it an exotic touch indeed.

"We're here," my guide said, "to meet Mister Devanter."

He made it sound like it was a holy mission or something. The woman behind the desk nodded and pressed a button on the computer in front of her. There was a low buzzing sound and the double doors directly behind her opened. "He's waiting."

We went down a corridor, this one panelled entirely in corkboard with dark oak frames breaking it into sections. Hanging on the walls at all heights were an eclectic mix of paintings in differing sizes.

"Mister Devanter," again the emphasis, "is a major patron of the arts."

"Good for him!" I used my happy voice, the one I use to convince the kids I babysat they should do things they didn't want to do. Stuff like cleaning up their messes and peeing in appropriate places.

"Yes. It is." Reynolds sounded suspicious.

Okay, maybe I was trying to goad him a little. He was seriously getting on my nerves. He was an officious little prick who reminded me of too many screws. And way too many embezzlers, dentists, insurance agents, pimps and con artists in various prisons over the years.

He paused in front of a big canvas covered in black, red and blue splotches. "This, for example, is a Riopelle." Reynolds was trying to, a) impress me and b) show me how much money his boss had. And it was, a) not working and b) working.

"Yes, it is."

Reynolds looked at me with some anger. "Do you even know who Riopelle was?"

He hissed. I wondered if they taught hissing in lawyer school.

"Yes. Riopelle was a modern painter and sculptor from Quebec. Classically trained, which is interesting, fucked around with various surrealists in Paris, later screwed around with inks, water colours and other mediums. Big hockey fan. Died in the early 2000's. A piece this big and oil on canvas means it's from his earlier years. What they call a drip painting … maybe worth three hundred thousand?"

"How do you know that?"

I knelt to examine a smaller painting hung at knee level, a gorgeous oil of aspens and birches. The details leapt out at me, the reds and yellows and browns and greens. I lusted after it and tried to read the name. "Oh? Know what? About Riopelles? I used to steal them." I got to my feet using Reynolds's arm and the tips of my fingers confirmed the gun under it. He didn't notice the touch and I went on. "There's a good market for them, even internationally. Most Canadian collections are really poorly protected, the insurance companies have no trouble handing over ransom and lots of collectors want what they want when they want it. I guess that's one of those things that makes them collectors and not dealers."

"You're joking."

"No. If you steal on commission you get maybe fifteen percent of the value. So you'd get forty-five thousand for that Riopelle. If you ransom it you get ten percent of the value generally, which is about the same you get from a fence and there are very few fences out there for Canadian paintings. And the risk is a lot higher."

"Collectors do that?"

"Sure. Scandal adds to value. People always place an extra value on wickedness. That's one of the reasons *The Scream* is so popular—it's been stolen so many times. Same with the Hope Diamond. It's full of history because of the supposed curse, so it's worth more. I even know people who cream over Spanish *onzas* because they were mined by slave Incas. Anyhow, who did this one?"

I pointed at the painting at my feet and Reynolds answered, "Hmmm. Oh. Peter McConville, a local artist. Nice, isn't it?"

"Gorgeous."

It was. I like nice paintings, I just can't afford them. But I do like pretty things that speak to me. I decided if I ever had money I'd pick one up for Claire.

Reynolds stared into the distance and then shook his head. "I can't believe it. You just confessed to a crime to me and I'm an officer of the court. How dumb are you?"

He was looking for an edge, I guessed. "Really? And what crime did I confess too?"

"Theft."

"Know any details?"

"Well ... no."

"Then I confessed to very little, didn't I?"

At the end of the hall there was another set of double doors and, once through them, I got to meet Mr. Devanter himself.

#8

The room beyond the doors was nice, big enough to land a small helicopter. The whole ceiling was cut back to show a loft reached by an old wrought-iron circular staircase. Everything else in the place was new, though; thick windows reaching to the ceiling, inlaid tiles on the floor and ultra-modern black chrome and leather furniture arranged in little conversational spaces. In the middle of the space was a huge desk made out of a single piece of greyish marble supported by steel posts that seemed to flow directly into the floor. Right beside the door we entered was a drafting table and stool.

I looked around curiously.

The walls were covered in different kinds of wood, erratically sized, linked by irregularly shaped plates of bright brass. There were shelves built into the walls holding what looked to be models of ships and buildings, trains and cars and even a couple of planes and what looked like blimps. Overall the place felt busy; chaotic and energized.

Definitely not a place to rest. It was instead a place of

energy, a place to work hard. If there were any extra doors, other than the one I had come in and the one at the top of the spiral stairs, I couldn't see them.

The man behind the desk stood up and came towards me, smiling and showing every tooth he had. I didn't trust him at all.

"So, Mr. Haaviko, thank you so much for coming. So nice of you."

Mr. Devanter was quite impressive. He towered over my six feet by at least six inches and weighed about 300 to my 180. His hair was short, brown with some grey, and his eyes were movie-star blue.

At a guess I put him in his mid-forties. Sometimes a dangerous age for men, when they start to feel the creaks and groans of experience; definitely a time when most men feel powerful. Sometimes an age when a man starts trying new things and trying to make a difference.

His suit was nice, a dark blue pinstripe, quite old-fashioned with a vest and a canary yellow shirt along with a blue tie covered in small designs I couldn't recognize. His tie clip was interesting, though; silver with the design of what looked like two curved knives crossed.

"Shall we sit down?

"Why not?"

We went to a grouping of three chairs around a glass-topped table and Devanter sat down heavily after undoing his suit jacket. It swung open and I caught a glimpse of black leather under his left arm. Then it was gone and he gestured to Reynolds. "Coffee, please, and the Haaviko file on the desk." He paused very obviously and went on, "I'm sorry. Your file says you like coffee. Is that correct?"

"Sure."

Devanter wasn't terribly sophisticated but I liked his bluntness and attitude. He was direct—at least mentioning the file was a hint that he had special knowledge. The file also showed he planned ahead and thought things through, or that's what it meant to me. It was kind of a crude way to manipulate me though.

Reynolds brought the coffee in a heavy silver thermos on a silver service along with small bowls of cream and sugar. I let Devanter pour into thick-sided white china cups and then I dosed it with cream and sugar and had a sip.

"Good?"

I just barely inclined my head. "Very."

"Blue Mountain. From Jamaica."

"Excellent coffee. Very nice island. Great cup."

"Glad you like them."

Reynolds put a manila file into Devanter's lap and I looked around the room some more and let the silence build. When I had finished my coffee I poured some more from the thermos and checked out the tray, which was old and heavy and looked to be real sterling silver. It made a nice contrast to the thermos itself, which was expensive, modern and Italian. It also worked like a charm.

Finally Devanter cleared his throat. "Don't you want to know why I've brought you here?"

"Not really. I'm sure you'll tell me. A thousand buys you me listening."

"I have a file here and you're in it."

I put my coffee cup down on the glass table and held out a hand for the file. Devanter hesitated and then shook his head. "I think not."

"Okay."

"Aren't you worried?"

"No. I'm an open book. An empty vessel."

The silence started to build again. Reynolds took a spot right behind me where he could be menacing but I ignored him and kept my eyes on Devanter. Finally he laughed very hard in a sharp bark. "Mr. Haaviko. I want you to accept that offer made by my good friend Aubrey Goodson. Then I want you to throw the race my way."

I filed the name of Goodson away; it meant nothing. Maybe he was the one who had sent the pair last night. That seemed reasonable. I asked, "Your way?"

Devanter got up and started to pace. "My way. To my good friend Rumer Illyanovitch. He's a good man, although I'm sure you wouldn't think so."

"Why not?"

"He's an ex-cop and former soldier and a hell of a believer in law and order."

He sneered and I turned my head from side to side following his movements. "You want me to betray my employer?"

"Yes." He stood in front of me and put his hands on his hips. "Although he's not your employer yet. I want to hire you to betray him before you're actually hired by him."

"You want me to throw the race. And you'll give me lots of money if I do so?"

"Yes."

I walked to the window and looked down at the centre of the oldest part of the city, old roofs covered in pipes and pigeons. On the streets cars crept along, avoiding movie trailers hosting crews shooting the city doubling for Chicago or Dodge or Kansas City or wherever else anyone could imagine. I raised my eyes and saw a beautiful girl about 200 metres away working at a computer with one hand supporting her black-haired head. She was on the sixth floor of a battered building sitting in the middle of an intersection, and between us was a park that had trees around the edges and was mostly dug up.

I raised the coffee in cheers but she didn't see me and so the gesture was wasted.

Then I turned back to Devanter. "How much is lots of money?"

"Quite a lot."

I changed the subject. "Why do you have a gun?"

He looked startled and glanced down at himself. "You can see it?"

"Sure. Fire your tailor. Why do you have a gun?"

His smile was grim and tight. "I have enemies."

I walked back to the thermos and refilled my cup. Then I went back to the window and leaned against it, looking back into the room. "Am I one?"

"No."

"Then lose the piece."

He didn't argue, just stripped it out from under his arm and put it carefully on his desk before holding his hands out all open. "So, I am unarmed."

"Completely?"

"Completely. Now, can we do business?"

Out of the corner of my eye I saw a quick smile cross Reynolds's face and then it was gone. He did not reach for his gun, no, not him. Maybe he thought I didn't know it was there. I wondered if they both thought guns were fashion accessories.

"Of course. What are you offering?"

"Ten thousand dollars to throw the election. Twenty five hundred now, twenty five hundred at the halfway point, five thousand when Rumer is elected. Fair?"

"Not really." I put the coffee down on the desk beside the

gun and, without stopping, walked towards the doorway and in the general direction of out. Reynolds crossed quickly to block me and I turned back to Devanter and said, "First off, even if I throw the election there's no way I can guarantee your boy will win. So take that right off the table. I'll think about the rest of your offer though. Can you have Reynolds let me leave? He's really scaring me."

I said it mildly.

Devanter's voice boomed, "If this is your way to raise the price it won't work." He was being aggressive and loud and I wondered if he was trying to overwhelm me. "I will drop the condition that Rumer wins though. You dropping out of the race at an inopportune time for Goodson would be sufficient."

A deal is only a deal if both people agree and agreement cannot be forced. I learned those lessons when I was just a little thug out bruising knees for lunch money.

And if you intend to deal honestly with someone you do not bring artillery. That's a basic rule of life everyone should understand.

When I was close to Reynolds he reached out with his left hand to put it on my shoulder and stop me.

When his hand touched my shirt it became assault.

And then the shit really hit the fan.

And it felt good.

#9

I like to fight. I try to argue with that truth every day of my life, but I like to fight. I like to challenge myself. I enjoy how it feels to take a shot and to deliver one. I try to pretend I regret the violence but there's a certain unholy glee every time.

It's an awful truth to admit, but I like hurting people. If they deserve it.

These two men resorted to violence too quickly. As though they didn't really understand what it was and what it was for. Their tactics were probably effective enough against businessmen though.

My open right hand came up as quick as could be and hit Reynolds's hand off my shoulder and up. His eyes locked on mine as I rocked back on my left foot while his right hand reached under his jacket. I lashed out with the tip of my steel-toed shoe and tagged the outside of his left ankle right through the side of his blood-red oxford.

Behind me I heard something break. A china coffee cup maybe?

I think something shattered in Reynolds's ankle and suddenly his face went slack and he started to wobble a little. That gave me time to drive my open left hand (slightly cupped) into his ear. That drove a packet of air into his ear and probably blew his eardrum out; if you do it with both hands you can permanently deafen someone. Doing it to one ear only really wrecks someone's balance. Theoretically you can kill someone by doing it but I've never succeeded yet.

The blow made Reynolds scream and propelled him to the floor and, as he went, I reached into his jacket and helped him pull his piece. It was a nice little stainless steel semi-auto that looked and felt like a Walther PP. I thumbed the safety and kicked off Reynolds, tucking into a roll as I went tumbling across the floor.

On the other side of the room Devanter had reached the desk and was raising his pistol, holding it in both hands like they teach you in gun school. He was in the Weaver stance, legs wide and braced. He looked thoroughly competent.

I wasn't worried. He had one eye closed to squint down the barrel and his tongue was sticking out of the corner of his mouth.

They don't teach you that in any gun school I've ever heard about.

I landed on my left shoulder and kept rolling. Thank God the furniture was scattered far and wide. Else it would have been messy and loud and painful; as it was, it was just loud and painful. Those tiles were hard; give me a carpet any day.

As I rolled I worked the slide on my borrowed gun and a bright shell jumped into the air, which meant that Reynolds had been carrying it cocked and locked.

Interesting; he had been anticipating trouble. Or he was an idiot. Either/or or maybe both.

A second later I hit the wall. A model of a plane smashed to the floor beside me as I aimed down the barrel and centred Devanter's chest in the three white points that made up the gun site.

Neither of us did anything.

About twelve feet away Reynolds tried to get to his knees and puked something fierce as his weight shifted on his ankle.

"Put ..." Devanter's voice broke and he tried again. "Put the gun down!"

A cop technique. A direct order designed to promote an immediate and instinctive reaction. An absolute demand with no discussion or options offered, refusal was not even an option. Results of failure would be left to the imagination of the threatened.

But Devanter hadn't had any practice doing it.

"Nice piece." I looked it over while keeping it pointed. The gun was a Sig-Sauer P230, an expensive small-frame pistol from a German/Swiss combine. On the street I could get five bills for it easy, probably less than I'd get on the legitimate market—thugs and thieves never knew quality.

The gun was a little longer than six inches, five inches high and weighed maybe a pound. From the markings on the side it was chambered in .32, not the biggest calibre in the world but a pretty fast round and good enough to kill someone with.

Devanter's nostrils were flared and his hands trembled. I marked that away for future use. Maybe he was more used to boardroom violence than this kind. Maybe he didn't like hurting people. Who knew? Maybe he had never actually had to shoot a real, live, human being before.

I got to my feet by bracing myself against the wall. "Call

the cops. Reynolds attacked me, Cornelius. I was trying to leave and he grabbed me and pulled a gun on me."

"What?" It was not what Devanter expected. Reynolds must have heard it because he muttered something with a question mark and then puked some more as his eyes rolled up into his head.

"Call the cops."

Devanter remembered his training and barked out, "Put the gun down. Now!"

Nice technique, still very familiar. Order and imperative. But the bad guy response is ingrained in me, and that's to escalate, so I switched targets and centred the white dots on Devanter's crotch. I tried to imagine what a nice little .32 would do at this range as it dumped maybe 110 pounds of energy over a third of an inch into his family jewels.

I imagined it wouldn't be pretty.

He flinched when his eyes followed the trajectory.

"Cornelius ..." I used his name to personalize the experience. "Cornelius. Call the cops or I will shoot you in the penis. It won't kill you. Then I'll call the cops."

He flinched again and then got bold. "You don't want the cops. You'll be arrested."

That amused the shit out of me. "Been arrested before."

He absorbed that and went on, "It'll be my word—our word—against yours. Who will they believe?"

He was getting confident and he squared his stance, although he turned a little to try to take his penis out of the line of fire.

"You. They'll believe you. Then they'll find the holster on Reynolds and probably his fingerprints on the magazine and on the bullets. And then they'll find the piece on you. Then they'll find the nine $100 bills on me and the $100 bill on my neighbour. And then they'll check the parking records and find when the Lexus was parked. And then they'll canvas the neighbourhood and find someone who saw Reynolds park the car. Then they'll check your security tapes and find me coming in. Then they'll check the O'Connell in the hallway and find my fingerprints there. Then they'll find my fingerprints on the coffee cup."

Devanter's face went slack and I went on, "Then who knows what they'll believe. They'll come up with something that makes them happy. They always do and they'll polish the shit out of their idea until it shines. Sometimes, just sometimes, cops decide to not like rich people. Just saying. Sometimes rich people just piss them off. It's a class thing, poor vs. wealthy."

His eyes squinted and, at twenty feet, I could see his pulse throbbing on his neck. I gave him a three count, slow, and then gave him another option. "Or I can walk out. And think about your offer—which is now twenty grand, by the way, as a penalty for the violence of your employee—and then call you. And you can get Reynolds to a doctor and get him stitched up; I blew his eardrum and probably broke his ankle."

Outside a cloud passed by and the room got dark and then light again and I went on, "To do that, Cornelius, you have to put your gun down on the ground. Not the table, the ground. And you have to do it slowly. And back up. Then I take both guns and walk out ... I'll leave them with your secretary outside. What's her name, by the way?"

"Gwen. I think I'd rather call the cops." He was getting aggressive again.

"Go ahead. Like I said, I've been arrested before and know what to expect but, trust me on this; it'll cause you a hell of a lot more pain. The fingerprinting, the photographs, the media, it'll be unpleasant for you. And if you call the cops I'll never

work with you. Right now I probably will. I just don't negoti-
ate under the threat of a gun. It's a rule of mine."

He thought about it and put the gun down and backed
away.

#10

In the foyer Gwen was reading off the computer screen and making notes on a pad of legal paper. She turned to face me when I came in and she tried very hard not to react when she saw the two guns in my hands.

"Do you have a sink or bathroom here?"

"Yes." Her finger moved towards a small panel of buttons inset into her desk and I said, "No." Loudly. Then I smiled brightly, "Don't press anything. It makes me nervous."

"Sorry, I wasn't thinking." She was trying to be as calm as possible and her voice carried it off. However, I was up close and could see the flush down her sweater and on her cheeks and I could smell a sharp whiff of sweat. I also couldn't help noticing that her nipples were as hard as diamonds.

She swallowed noisily. "The top left button on my desk opens a panel in the wall. There's a sink in that space along with a fridge and coffee maker."

"Excellent. A little showy and strange but excellent. You may press it now."

She did and the panel slid aside. While the sink was filling I kept an eye on her. "Your boss is fine but Reynolds is a little battered. He tried to shoot me. In any case neither of them wants you to call the cops. But check with them after I've left."

Gwen nodded and I saw the sink was taking a ridiculously long time to fill. "So, have you worked here long?"

She was perplexed. "Three years ... What are you doing?"

"Filling a sink and making small talk. Never mind, I'm lousy at small talk." The sink was full and I tipped both guns in after putting their safeties on.

"Have a great day!"

And I left. I wasn't an idiot though. I took the stairs. Just in case Devanter had the elevator under remote control, which is easy to do. And just in case he changed his mind about how to deal with me.

Two blocks from the building I made a series of random turns and found myself in a pawn shop owned and operated by a young, nervous man with glasses and bad skin. Everything was locked away in racks and on glassed-in shelves. I was examining a display of telescopes and binoculars when the clerk came down to me. "Find everything you're looking for?"

There was a pretty nice-looking Simmons 1209 telescope, with tripod. Maybe nine inches long and about three pounds. I tapped the glass above it and asked its cost.

"$75."

I looked at him, astonished. "Uh, no. It's what, twenty years old? How much?"

"Really? That old? Look at its shape; it's in great shape, isn't it?"

"I'll give you $30."

He haggled me up to $40. and I paid it with one of Reynolds's hundreds. The owner ran the bill under an ultraviolet light and pronounced it real. He gave me change made up of some of the dirtiest money I've ever seen. Then I left, carrying the scope in a plastic bag from Safeway.

I soon found myself at the strange triangular-shaped building I'd seen from Devanter's office. It was called Artspace and was full of strange organizations and a few ad firms along with magazine and book publishers. No one said a word to me or tried to stop me and the elevator worked (badly) and took me to the sixth floor, where I got off and faced a hallway going left and right. I went right and passed by studios and organizations and ended up back at the elevator.

In my head I had a map of the building, so I figured the office I was interested in was in front of me and to the left, as close to the corner of the building as possible. There was a door there in roughly the proper position. I knocked on it and heard a woman's voice say, "Come in!"

Inside I found a large office space broken up with bookshelves and partitions. In the centre of the room near the far wall and the windows was a pretty young woman with short black hair and piercing green eyes. I recognized her from looking out of Devanter's window.

"May I help you?"

There was a trace of both an accent and attitude. I gave her my best smile. "Yes. Actually I just want to look out your window with a telescope. Do you mind?"

"Why?"

I had lots of options. I could lie or I could lie even harder. I chose that one. "I'm a spy."

"Oh. Then go right ahead."

To get to the window I had to pass behind her desk. On it was a picture of a young boy and piles of invoices.

The woman pushed her chair back from the desk as I knelt down and took the scope out of the bag.

"What's that?"

"A telescope. Twenty-five power. So it makes things look twenty-five times closer than they actually are. Which is handy if you're a spy."

I set it up on the windowsill and focussed it at Devanter's building and then started counting floors. At six I stopped and found I had a pretty good view of the whole glassed-in monstrosity that was the office. The view wasn't perfect, not by a long shot, but I could certainly identify Devanter and Gwen, both standing, and Reynolds, sitting in a chair with a towel pressed to his ear with one hand. With the other one he clutched his ankle.

Someone came into the office behind me and gave a large package to the green-eyed woman. She signed for it and started to make happy noises. I turned to find her admiring brightly printed catalogues.

Back through the telescope I could see Devanter on the phone and I looked down and checked the ground floor for ambulances or police cars but could see neither.

The phone beside me rang and the woman took complicated notes about percentages and dates.

I did math in the back of my head and decided that I'd left Devanter's office forty minutes before. Forty minutes. So if he'd called the cops they'd have arrived already. Cops may be slow if you report a residential break-in or a loud party at 3:00 a.m. on Friday night/Saturday morning but they're pretty fucking quick if you're a millionaire reporting an armed gunman and assault and battery on a lawyer at noon on a Monday.

This meant that Cornelius Devanter and Alastair Reynolds and Gwen, no last name, hadn't called the cops. I leaned back on my heels and bit my lip while thinking.

"Find what you wanted?" The woman was sitting back down at her desk.

"You bet!" I packed the scope back into its bag. "Thank you so much."

She had a nice smile. "You're welcome."

"I love the fact you're not asking me all sorts of questions."

"Would you like me too?" She seemed genuinely interested in my response.

I still couldn't place the accent so I just shook my head and told her, "No. I'd just have to make up a lie."

"That's what I thought. Have a good day."

"I will. You too." And I left.

#11

I took my trusty telescope for a walk south, heading towards the Millennium Library, which sits in roughly the centre of the city. As I walked I saw posters on lampposts and walls for the Red River Exhibition and more for something called the Fringe Festival, which apparently involved plays. There were other posters for the Folk Fest, which involved music, and Folklorama, which involved many, many cultures.

None of them seemed familiar and I wondered if they were unique to Winnipeg or if every city had them. Maybe I'd just never noticed stuff like that in my earlier life, being so involved in theft, drugs and general anarchy. I couldn't really come up with an answer so I just kept moving and thought about other things.

I love it in the movies when the hero needs to know something and he, or she, of course has immediate access to a newspaper reporter, a friendly snitch or a whore with a heart of gold—some kind of expert on any subject needed.

In the real world reporters almost never tell you things

because their jobs are to gather news, not to spread it around all indiscriminate like. And snitches require payment and are very, very, very unreliable. They also have the lifespan of some elements on the south side of the periodic table. That's because bad guys don't like snitches and snitches need to be around bad guys in order to make any kind of money at all. So snitches HAVE to be attached to bad guys and bad guys HAVE to crush them down whenever they can.

And whores rarely, if ever, have hearts of gold. They are individuals who rent out their equipment for the pleasure of others so they see the worst of people at the worst of times. It makes them bitter, and rightly so. In other words, they may know but they will never, or almost never, tell.

So I had to make myself an expert as needed. In stir I had read Ian Fleming's original James Bond series and found a common thread where Bond's boss would send him off to learn about various subjects as needed. If he needed to learn about gold, he would go to the Bank of England. If he needed to learn about diamonds, DeBeers would lend samples and a loupe. And if Bond needed to learn about guns, then Q, the quartermaster, would come and give an expert opinion.

Unfortunately I did not have the Bank of England on my side, nor did I have good relations with DeBeers and I had no Quartermaster named Q. So I used libraries, lawyers and bartenders to learn about whatever was necessary. Libraries would fill in many answers through back issues of newspapers and magazines. Lawyers could tell you a lot more, if you asked them nicely, especially if you were their client. And bartenders, the right bartenders, could generally fill in everything else, and they liked to talk. Most of their life involved listening, so talking was a nice change.

None of that was really an option, so I decided to head

to the library, and five minutes' walking got me there. On the fourth floor I went through the white pages looking for Devanter, Cornelius, Reynolds, Alastair and Goodson, Aubrey. I struck out on the last two but found that Devanter's address matched the building downtown. Then I signed up for an Internet-enabled computer and used it to run searches on those names, plus variations. That got me a listing for Reynolds as a lawyer in a city law firm, apparently a partner in Reynolds and Lake. It also mentioned that he had written a piece for the University of Manitoba school newspaper back in the early nineties. The same search gave me eleven articles about Devanter in the *Free Press*, the Toronto-based conservative *National Post* news rag and something online called *Canadian Business*. Goodson showed up only once as a major donor for a museum that dedicated itself to aircraft and the history of flight in Canada.

I marked down the dates and pages of the articles and checked out the business site to find that the article was basically a puff piece about how much Devanter was worth, over $100 million, and how much he donated to good causes. I logged off and went up to where the periodicals were kept and filled out the request forms, three at a time, as the librarian instructed me. When they came they were in microfiche and I went over to the nearest machine and started reading.

Basically Devanter was a business man. A successful one. He had started with a small company building airplane components, mostly engine controls. That had been very successful. With that money he had diversified into other businesses, buying up a series of cheap hotels across the country and linking them together under one name. Then he'd staffed them with students just out of hotel management schools he ran in British Columbia. Later he had gotten a gigantic contract

with the American government to build bits and pieces of unmanned drones used to blow up people in Afghanistan and
Iraq early in the wars.

But there were some controversies. According to a union
press release, the components his company claimed to have
made had in fact been made by another factory and shipped
over to augment the stock—just before a buyout was attempted
by a conglomerate from Luxembourg. The value of the company had thus been augmented considerably and Devanter
had avoided the buyout offer (which had been "anaemic,"
according to officials) and then borrowed against the factory
and stock. Then he'd gone to work with that money buying
this and that.

And the drones he'd built hadn't been terribly successful ones. However, they'd been backed by a fierce and senile
United States senator from a state that started with a vowel.
So the drones had kept flying even when they'd become famous for catastrophic engine and equipment failure.

And the hotels he'd bought hadn't been a chain, as the article had implied. Instead they had been seized by banks, mom
and pop places that had failed in dribs and drabs over the
years. The banks couldn't dispose of them any other way so
they'd been a cheap, fire-sale buy for Devanter. As for his hotel
management school, it had gotten into some serious trouble
with the Chinese government for overcharging students, but
that problem had vanished when a certain official had been
demoted for incompetence in Beijing. Over the next year most
of the students had been hired by Devanter, not at terribly
high wages, but they'd been happy enough to get the work.

These days Devanter was mostly into real estate in and
around the city. And he pumped a lot of money and attention into civic causes, enough to keep his name in prominent

view. He built hotels, mini-malls and condos, and spent a lot of time organizing the demolition of older buildings. His interest in the police commission was well known, although no one seemed to know why.

I did another search and got three articles about the commission which confused me even more.

The commission was new. An idea the mayor's office had arrived at after consultations with experts.

One expert in the paper mentioned how strange this was because the mayor never listened to experts unless they agreed with him.

The board was an elected one and there was one like it in every other city in Canada (except Montreal). It dealt with citizen complaints and budget issues and generally provided oversight to the police force, basically ensuring that the police department was accountable to the public. In theory it helped build trust and respect.

Another article pointed out that the commission concept did two bad things for the police: it removed control of its budget from a purely political process, and it allowed citizens a clear view into the operations of the force. The same article noted that the boards had no real ill effects for citizens.

The commission was going into operation early in the next year and it had a board of six consisting of a president and five voting members. The president was elected from a cross-city election and each police district in the city elected one commission member as well.

The police, through their union, were resisting the commission strongly and were regularly publishing articles about what a bad idea it was and how it would "tie" the hands of the police.

They were unclear on what "tie" actually meant.

The last thing I did was go online and find Reynolds's article in the University of Manitoba newspaper. It was a brilliantly reasoned piece on the history of execution and the importance of returning to a system of capital punishment.

It was titled, "Arthur Ellis, Where Are You?" Arthur Ellis had been the official name of the hangman in Canada back when we did that kind of thing, a pseudonym chosen to permit a degree of anonymity on behalf of the executioner. Reynolds started by listing the history of executions, going back to Babylonian times and reasoning that executions were part of what made a nation civilized. He talked about the Egyptians, the Greeks, the Romans, the Italianate states, the French approach, the English and Scottish angle and the humane executions of the nineteenth and twentieth centuries.

It was all shit but it was kind of fun to read.

My own feelings on executions were somewhat more pragmatic: I had no desire for the state ever to have more power than it was willing to give the individual members who made up that state.

Even Rome, that notoriously brutally beautiful civilization, had known enough that the carnifex was not allowed to live within city limits.

And Reynolds wanted to bring him back? To give the power of life and death to a faceless and anonymous cypher?

Back home the phone was ringing as I went in. I picked up and the voice on the other end of the line sounded furious as soon as I said hello.

"Who is this?"

The voice was frail, kind of reedy and petulant but I answered anyway. "Monty. I could ask you the same thing."

"Put Claire on!"

"No. As a matter of fact, I will ask you the same thing you just asked me: who is this?"

The voice sputtered and whined and finally hung up on me and I stared at the phone in bemusement before replacing it in the cradle.

Lots of strange people out there.

#12

A message showed up with a couriered package the next day. It read, "I'm so very sorry about last night ... I just lost my head. I hope this doesn't change things between us, please consider this a sign of my contrition."

Claire looked at me and we both said, at the same time, "Weird."

I looked the paper over. It was strange stuff, coarse and un-even and quite discoloured. And the ink was odd too, a faded green that lay strangely on the page. Claire looked closely at it and then leaned back, stumped. "There are two almost cuts on the sides of each line of each letter with less ink between them."

She took the box in hand and shook it gently to hear some-thing weighty shift within. She handed it to me and I looked it over but seemed like a normal box. Cardboard and heavy but just a little gift box like you'd buy from a bargain store.

"So," Claire said, "what's in it?"

I was paranoid but that was okay, former professional

criminals have many good reasons to be paranoid. I opened the package slowly, feeling for resistance that would hint at a trigger wire or a friction fuse. I also listened for any clicks or buzzes that might indicate a firing pin being engaged. And while I did that I used my nose and sniffed for any interesting chemicals like nitrates, acids or petroleum products.

Eventually though the box was opened safely and Claire and I ended up admiring the contents, a massy gold bracelet irregularly studded with a variety of small stones, lying on a bed of white cotton. I looked closely at the stones and saw white ones and reddish ones, grey ones and dark blue ones. They were arranged in no pattern I could recognize and the effect was quite beautiful.

Claire picked it up. "Look at the gold; it's made into mesh links."

"Like chain mail armour?"

"Yes. Like the gloves my dad used." Her dad had been a butcher and I remembered the gauntlets he'd worn, but I was thinking more of knights and dragons. Claire looked closely. "I think that," she touched the dark blue stone, "is lapis lazuli."

"Really?"

She shrugged and her breasts moved under her shirt. I never got tired of that. "I think. I never dealt with that stone much. The best comes from Afghanistan and Siberia."

Claire was running a curio and relic shop when I met her. I'd been shooting an ex-partner at the time and it had been love at first sight for me. As for Claire, she'd hated me but had gotten over it. After a few years.

Okay. After many years.

Anyhow, she'd had lots of experience with semi-precious stones, fossils and other strange items. So I believed her when she named a stone I had only heard about yet never seen.

I touched the grey stone and felt a slightly greasy surface.

"That's an uncut diamond ... I think."

"You're not sure?" she said dryly.

"It's been a while," I admitted. "I stole a half tray of them in Vancouver ten, maybe eleven years ago."

My mind drifted. I remembered the chaos of that day in the Chinatown shop. I remembered the smell of cordite as I dumped two rounds of #6 shot into the ceiling to get everyone's attention. I remembered the howls of the customers and staff and the shrilling of the alarms.

It had been a messy robbery but we'd gotten away with two trays of unset stones—diamonds, rubies and some emeralds. Also sixty grams of gold in tiny bars and a double handful of Bulova watches. I remembered the whole experience in snapshots. There was Jimmy Brunswick standing tall and walking the manager into the back room, he moving fast because of the long-barrelled .22 in his ear. And in the corner there was Jarrod Black cracking display cases with a roofing hammer and picking through the debris with inhuman precision.

Two minutes later we were all in the car with Sally Leiter driving the speed limit. Behind us four army surplus smoke bombs spewed orange and filled the road with even more chaos and then we were gone. As we travelled Sally passed me a Steyr Mannlicher Classic carbine in .222 and I worked the bolt to put the first of four rounds into the breech and flicked the safety off. Sally laughed like a bell and I hoped and prayed that no cop would show and that no citizen would decide to play hero.

Because if anyone did, I'd have to kill them, because I was the only decent shot in the car.

And we'd gotten away clean with two million and change, which a Seattle fence had bought for a quarter mil. Which was $55,300 and change each after the expenses were covered.

And I couldn't remember where the money had gone.

I vaguely remembered cocaine and whores in Quebec City and I remembered a meth-fuelled brawl in a strip club in Hull. I remembered a long poker game in a Kansas City steak house with a waitress bringing drinks and wearing only high heels and a smile. I remembered coming down from a heroin-fuelled lost weekend in Saskatoon on a farm rooftop with a teenage girl telling me she really, really loved me. I remembered believing her.

Sally and Jimmy and Jarrod.

All of them gone.

Sally beaten to death when the love of her life turned septic in a suburb outside Quebec City.

Jarrod pulled from a wrecked semi after a cigarette hijack near Victoria. The cop had been over-eager and had twisted while pulling and Jarrod had ended up a bag of dead meat from the neck down. That had lasted until he'd managed to chew through his tongue late one night in the hospital while the guard was pissing in the bathroom sink.

And Jimmy, spiking on PCP and meth, had his face punched in by eleven rounds from a cop's forty calibre in a Saskatoon back alley.

I touched the stone again and shivered. "Yeah. It's a diamond, and I think the white stone's a pearl. I've never seen an irregular one like that though."

Claire touched it. "Well, it's gorgeous."

"It is that. Let's go to bed."

That night we fucked until I'd said goodbye again to all my ghosts. Claire seemed to understand.

#13

First thing the next morning Reynolds's Lexus sedan pulled up out front and a red-headed woman got out. For a second I didn't recognize her and then I realized she was Gwen, Devanter's secretary/receptionist. She was wearing a brown leather coat and green slacks, and she carried a thin metal briefcase under one arm as she got out of the car. Then she took a deep breath and walked up the sidewalk to my house with a determined stride.

I asked Claire to open the door and she did, saying warmly, "Yes?"

Gwen's voice was soft and calm. "I'm looking for Montgomery Haaviko."

"You've found him. Come in then."

She entered cautiously and I came towards her wiping my hands on a dish towel to imply I had been in the kitchen. I was in my robe, and Claire and I still smelled of sex. Gwen noticed and her nose wrinkled and she smiled.

"Mr. Haaviko!"

She offered her hand and I shook it and introduced her to Claire and she said, "Pleased" with far more warmth. Then she turned back to me, opened the briefcase and handed me a sheaf of stapled papers.

"Let me guess. Alastair is suing me? And you got stuck serving the papers?"

Gwen smiled. "No, it's a contract. Space for you to sign. Mr. Devanter has already signed."

I took it and read it. It was simple. I was contracting to provide unnamed services for an unnamed period of time. It was very open and very vague and very full of legal crap. I read it and looked at Gwen. "There is mention of an initial payment of $5,000. Do you have it?"

"I do."

She gave it to me from out of the wallet, a thin sheaf of fifty new hundreds so crisp I cut a thumb. I counted it and checked the serial numbers for repeats but the bills were either real or such good queer I could pass them painlessly. Reynolds and Devanter were definitely paying their way.

So I signed the contracts and the receipts and kept one copy of each and then showed Gwen out. As I closed the door Claire said, "Nice girl."

I fanned the money and said, "Not really."

Claire looked thoughtful. "A natural redhead? I wonder."

I shuffled the money and handed her five bills. "I got another five if you can find out."

"It's a deal."

After Claire left I thought for about ten seconds. If you pull a gun on me I will distrust you. So I distrusted Devanter and Reynolds. I thought for another ten seconds and then I called Dean Pritchard. "Mr. Pritchard? This is Monty Haaviko. I've thought about your offer and I'd like to accept. Could I meet whoever hired you? Who would be the person who wants to hire me?"

He was speaking on a cell phone and his voice came in scratchy. "Certainly. Let me give him a call and we'll set something up. Can Brenda and I meet with you today though? There's not much time to get all this organized."

We made a date for six at a restaurant and bakery I know and then I wrangled children for the rest of the day. Since it was hot, my wrangling consisted of turning on a sprinkler in the backyard and letting the kids rampage. As the grass also needed watering I felt this was an effective strategy. For supper I made spaghetti and sauce with a recipe from an Italian lady whose three sons played with my kids occasionally. She had given me not only the recipe but also eight tomatoes from the greenhouse she had built on top of her garage.

When she told me that I was amazed. "You built a greenhouse on top of your garage?"

She was slim and prim and looked maybe nineteen. She always sat in the corner of the parks, in the shade, knitting and watching her kids with her dark eyes and a slight downturn of her mouth as though she disapproved. The sound of her clashing needles had first drawn me when we'd originally met that spring. Later she decided she could trust me a little and when I asked about the greenhouse she looked at me with round eyes. "Of course! Store tomatoes taste just awful."

The next day she brought the recipe on an index card along with the tomatoes in an old, creased paper bag and so I made spaghetti. And it was a tremendous success, which had nothing to do with my skills as a chef.

By quarter to six I was at the commercial bakery on Main that I liked; the one run by the Greek family. It had five round tables under an awning around the side, which made it a good place to meet.

When I'd first come to town I'd visited the place and fallen in love with the coffee and the pastries. Me and the owners had gotten along fine until a psycho cop named Walsh had tried to run me out of town. But that had been more than a year ago.

There were two other patrons at the place, an old man sitting by himself and drinking a small cup of coffee beside an aboriginal child, maybe eleven, wearing designer jeans, eating a cream horn and reading Carl Jung's *Psychology and Alchemy*.

I sat down and a fattish young man with dark, curly hair, blue eyes and a silver stud in his eyebrow came out holding a menu. He was wearing white overalls and an apron and tucked into his apron was the worn wooden handle of a hammer.

"I thought we told you not to come back."

"You did."

"Yet you come back." He sounded amazed.

"I do. Fancy that."

"You are a crook." He said it flatly and the old man looked up and so did the kid. Their faces were blank and the kid carefully put one finger down on his book as though to mark an idea.

I kept facing the waiter. "I was. Now I'm meeting some people. Can we be friends?"

"No."

"Okay. Can I meet some people here?"

"No."

I got up to leave and the waiter watched me. Before I could reach the sidewalk he said, "You didn't threaten me."

"No. Why would I do that?"

"I thought you would."

It made me laugh. "No. I told you, I want to sit here and have coffee and Danishes for which I will pay you. And I'll even tip you. While I am here I want to meet some respectable people. Basically I want to smooth over the damage done by Sergeant Walsh last year when he called your family and told all those truths to you. Threatening you would not help me do any of that."

"You say Walsh told the truth?"

"Yes." Walsh had gone around to every business in the neighbourhood when I'd first come to Winnipeg, telling everyone about my criminal past while trying to drive me out of the city. The fallout from that monumental fuckup never seemed to end.

"So you are a bad guy?" He probed and the old man and the kid kept watching.

"I was one. Maybe I still am. But right now I want to have coffee and Danishes here and meet some people. Even bad guys have to drink coffee and eat Danishes and meet with people."

The man glanced back towards the bakery and I saw a huge fat man filling the doorway. He was maybe six foot five and easily 400 pounds and looked like the guy in front of me at 150 percent magnification. His head descended once abruptly and he went back in.

"You can stay." The waiter was magnanimous.

"Thank you. Could I get a large coffee with cream and sugar and a cheese Danish?"

I ate it with hunger and licked the tips of my fingers and drank some coffee which had improved a little since the last time I was there. Someone had told me that Muslims licked their fingers when eating because they never knew what part of the food held God's blessing. I did it because I liked the taste.

And, deep down inside, I was never sure of the next time I would eat.

A little after six Dean Pritchard and Brenda Geraghty showed up in a dark-blue, low-end BMW sedan and came in with huge smiles on their faces. They each carried slim leather briefcases with brass fittings and Brenda wore a narrow fanny bag around her thin hips as well.

They said, almost in unison, "so glad you accepted!"

They ordered coffee and biscotti and were somewhat ticked over the absence of espresso, lattes, chai or imperial cookies (I concealed the knowledge that I had no idea what an "imperial cookie" was). As they dosed their coffee I watched them and wondered which one had ratted me out to Devanter, because it pretty much had to be one of them. When they were comfortable I started. "You want me to run for the position of chief of the police commission?"

"Yes." Dean spoke and both he and Brenda had notepads of canary-yellow paper out with mechanical pencils ready to go.

"So, I guess we need a contract between us ensuring you'll cover the expenses. However, please, explain to me what exactly it is you want me to do."

Brenda spoke up and made boxes on her sheet of paper. "Okay. The way it currently works is that the mayor is in charge in the city. Beneath his office is an appointed cabinet— I guess cabinet is the best word—who are elected and who support him no matter what and beneath that is the city council, also elected. The mayor orders the specific departments who report directly to him, however, not to the council or the cabinet."

She looked at me expectantly and I nodded understanding. "The new plan is to have a police council put in place. That would provide oversight to the police department specifically and deal with budgeting issues, complaints, staffing and so on, anything having to do with the police."

"Winnipeg doesn't have this already?"

"No. Most cities do though; we're not reinventing the wheel. We're copying an existing system and putting it into place."

I thought about it. "Okay. Currently how are the police responsible to the city?"

"Through the mayor. They also have a union and massive grass roots support, so they can bring considerable political force to apply through any elected official whenever and however they feel it is needed."

She said it blandly and I could imagine the network of politics in city hall with all the authority ending with a single individual. It didn't sound very pretty. "Who proposed the police council?"

"The mayor."

I wondered why. The current setup had all the tools in the hands of the mayor's office; he had absolute control over the police force, so why would he want to give any of it up? My dead friend Smiley had said, "This is the truth: Some people like to fuck. Some people like money. And some people like power."

Politicians liked power; it was pretty much in their job description. So why give it away?

I filed the question away. "So there is going to be a police council, suggested by the mayor and elected by the populace."

"Right. To enhance the accountability of the police force and to prevent crime."

She said it straight-faced and I checked Dean but he wasn't smiling either.

"Okay."

"The mayor is having special elections to choose six people for the board. five regular members and one chief commissioner. The regular commissioners were supposed to represent Districts 1, 2, 3, the East District and District 6. However, that has ..."

I stared at her. "You made that up."

Dean answered, sounding puzzled. "No. You're in District 3 but the chief can be from anywhere."

I interrupted. "The City of Winnipeg Police Department is divided into districts numbered 1 to 3 consecutively. Then an East district. And a District 6. Is that right?"

They both answered, "Sure."

I ordered another Danish and more coffee and Dean gave me a thumbnail sketch of the history of the force. "Originally there were thirteen separate forces in the city as it expanded. They all started being incorporated in 1874. In 1972 they began to be amalgamated into one force, and this was finished in 1974. Right now there are 1,682 members of the police force with a chief, a deputy, superintendents, inspectors, staff sergeants, sergeants, patrol/detective sergeants, constables and a variety of non-sworn members."

"How many wear uniforms or carry guns? Or both."

Brenda answered, "1,326. 1,142 men and 184 women. 1,109 Caucasian, 142 Aboriginal, 24 Black, 5 Filipino, 26 Asian and 20 others. To cover a city of 653,000 with a racial demographic of mostly white with 64,000 being aboriginal, 14,000 Black, 37,000 Filipino, and 38,000 assorted Asians with a post-tax median income of around $23,000, with women generally bringing in around $3,000 less."

Dean listed things off on his fingers. "There's a bicycle unit, a SWAT unit, a canine unit, a horse-mounted unit, the whole schmear—even a river patrol unit. No aerial unit though. That's been a bone of contention in the past that can be engaged as needed by any politician to gain support by the police. It's a pretty extensive force."

Brenda smiled sweetly. "We're going to put together a package about your district—individuals, incomes, race, sex, employment—and then the city as a whole. Then we'll talk some more and get this whole thing started. Districts vote for individual commission members but the chief gets voted on by everyone and Dean's going to put your name in today. All you have to do is sign."

I swallowed and realized this was one of those key weird moments in life where things would change. I also realized I had no idea what to do. That's why I said, "Fine."

Dean produced the required legal forms, all filled in, and I signed where necessary. Then they told me that they'd set up a date to meet my benefactor, paid for coffee and everything else and vanished softly away.

I made sure they tipped well. A good Danish is hard to find, after all.

#14

Two days later I went to a tiny jewellery store off a side street in Saint Boniface. It was an old-fashioned store with a grill just outside the door to give your name and business and then a holding space with another door to open before you could get into the business proper. Inside there were long counters holding rainbows of gems and dozens of ounces of gold and platinum, fashioned into rings, necklaces, brooches, bracelets, earrings and some things I didn't recognize.

There was good stuff on display—worth a half million easy—and the security was first rate. Steel bars on the windows to back up heavy plastic windows which were visibly alarmed for vibration and breakage. Radar alarms in the room itself, one in the front of the store and one in the rear, both backed up with cameras in slick Plexiglas domes. There were separate alarms on the jewellery cases and a smoke projector in the centre ceiling, designed to fill the room with impenetrable fog if an alarm was tripped. That alone was enough to stop most thieves, it being damn hard to steal anything if you couldn't see your hand in front of your face.

I was impressed. And I was even more impressed by the jeweller himself. He was an old white man who looked middle-European, with piercing blue eyes and long white hair gathered in a ponytail. He wore a black suit and tie with a starched white shirt and constantly polished a pair of rimless spectacles with a silk handkerchief monogrammed with E.G.

"You wanted an appraisal, sir?" The 'sir' came out slowly and softly like an afterthought. His speech had an accent that was almost scrubbed clean and he looked at me dispassionately, weighing my value and my potential to cause trouble and finding me wanting in both categories.

"Yes, for this."

I put the bracelet on the counter and the man picked it up with his right hand while his left exchanged his glasses for a monocle. He checked it over carefully, inside and outside and then said, "Interesting."

He was smiling as he put the bracelet down on a green felt pad that lay on top of the counter and stepped back. The smile stayed on his face as his left hand dipped into his vest pocket and came out with a black, flat-framed pistol. The gun looked like a toy but probably wasn't.

"You'll freeze."

And I did. The old man looked serious and the gun didn't waver at all. I checked distances by eye and came to the conclusion that he and his gun were out of my reach.

"All I want is an estimate. Nothing more."

The old man nodded. "You'll be silent."

He reached into his front pants pocket and came out with what looked like a television remote. Without taking his eyes off me he pushed two buttons and I heard the doors lock loudly behind me.

The remote went back into his pocket and the old man said, "You'll be calm. The cops are on their way."

I relaxed a little. There was nothing I could do, not without risking a bullet. And I could maybe convince the cops but there was no way I convince a bullet and so I waited. Ten minutes later the cops showed up and one knocked loudly with the butt of his skull-buster flashlight. The old man brought the remote out and opened the door, and while he did that he made the pistol disappear. He kept watching me, waiting for me to do something but I just waited too.

When my hands were cuffed the first cop, a dark-skinned, middle-aged man, asked, "So. Mr. Grim, was that a gun I saw?"

The old man, Grim, I guessed, looked offended and horrified. "Of course not! Carrying a firearm is a felony."

The cop nodded. "So you wouldn't mind if I searched you?"

"As long as you have a warrant. In which case I'll call my lawyer to read it for me. My eyesight being so bad, after all." He smiled sweetly at the cop. "Shall we do all that again? I got no problems dancing to the same tune if you don't."

The cop and his partner, a younger white guy whom I recognized, looked at each other and then shook their heads in unison.

"Fine then." The old man looked a little relieved.

The younger cop was staring at me with a furrowed brow, trying to remember. His name was Halley and he had been one of the first cops to arrest me when I'd come to town. Realization started to dawn and his partner asked, "Now why did we handcuff this nice man?"

Mr. Grim gestured at the bracelet. "He brought that in; it's one of Redonda Paris's pieces."

Halley looked blank but his partner was startled. "Are you sure?"

"Positive."

After that it went fast and I ended up in the back of the Crown Victoria sedan while Halley talked urgently to his partner outside. Inside the shop Mr. Grim looked at me impassively and something must have showed on my face because he finally stepped back into the interior darkness away from me.

The side door opened and the darker cop leaned in. "You Monty Haaviko?"

"Yes." My first words.

The cop nodded. "Enzio Walsh was a friend of mine."

I stared at the cop. Just fucking great. Walsh was the cop who had tried to frame me, kill me and run me out of town. By the time the dust had settled he was no longer a cop. He had been forced into retirement and I was still there.

The cop waited until I said, "My lawyer is Lester Thompson."

The cop nodded and I gave him Lester's number. I seemed to spend a lot of my life giving cops the name and phone number of my lawyer. The cop slammed the car door and we took off.

#15

The screw pulled the heavy iron door on the holding cell open and pointed with his chin and so in I went. For a few minutes there was silence in the jail cell and then the noise started again. I stood there and it hit me, washed over me and dragged me back in time.

In the corner there was a Black kid who sat on the concrete floor and leaned his forehead against the cold steel bars. The toilets were in the other corner, open to the room, and a dark-skinned Aboriginal man vomited endlessly into a porcelain bowl. And in the centre of the room there was low-keyed screaming from a white teenager who had crammed his sweatshirt into his mouth to muffle it. All that and an FM Rock radio station on one side and a Christian evangelical television show on the other. And everywhere the muttering, coughing, swearing, talking.

"Home again, home again, jiggety-jig." I said it under my breath and inhaled the smells. Old sweat from the guy on the steel picnic table bolted to the floor as he did sit-ups.

"One thousand and six ..."

There was the musk of urine and semen from the guy sitting beside the crier as he jerked off into his boxers. And from two Asian men wearing leather and silk clothes suitable for night clubbing there was the faint aroma of pepper spray. And the thickened reek of dirt and shit off the crummy and crumbling old man asleep on the floor.

And in my ears was the sweet ever-changing flow of lies and bad advice echoing off the concrete and the steel. "You gotta teach them bitches respect, right? If she ain't scared then she ain't loving you the right way. So you use a wire coat hanger, a wire one, you hear me ..."

"So you got a good case for wrongful incar-cer-ation which means muy dinero, my friend ..."

"... and he just kept getting up ..."

"... but you want sharp, real sharp, you got to go ceramic, walk right through a metal detector, man ..."

"Well. I had me a Mustang with a sweet eight cylinders just as slick as a pussy ..."

Home.

One of the guys got up from his seat and came over towards me. He was a little taller and a little heavier than me with blond hair cut short and violet eyes.

"Do I know you?"

He was wearing jeans and a sleeveless t-shirt that advertised that the wearer was "badgerous." I wondered what badgerous meant and decided it meant something unhappy.

"You look like someone I know ..."

"No ... I don't think you know me."

"Yeah, I know you."

There's always some asshole who thinks they know how prison works. Some moron who thinks you have to prove to the other guys how bad you are, generally by beating the shit out of someone else. The truth is most cons are pretty polite. If you're not polite, someone will pour a bucket of cleaning solution into your cell when you're asleep and toss a match. Which a friend once called "bake and shake," because the body keeps twitching for a long time, even after the fire dies down.

Or you'll get a visit from two or three guys with shaved broomsticks and ground down files. Or something worse.

So cons are pretty polite.

So I looked at the guy and shook my head.

"Nope."

He was coming closer and I did the math. The guys in the cell were backing away; there was no loyalty, no solidarity in the place, because a holding cell was exactly that, a place to keep people, which meant there were petty crooks in along with mutts like this guy. Which meant no one would interfere; they all wanted to be entertained.

Also a fight might lead to charges that could be used by a snitch to get out of their own troubles.

The other prisoners made a circle about five feet across for the two of us. Since it was a short-term holding cell it meant that Mr. Badgerous probably didn't have a weapon, he wouldn't have had time to make or buy one. Which left us with fists and feet and my imagination, if things got physical, which was good, 'cause I was probably better than he was.

"Fuck off."

His face got red and he started to say something but I didn't let him finish. "I've been in the system for most of my adult life. I'm guessing you haven't. I have been in Drumheller and Kingston and Atlantic and Port-Cartier and Millhaven and Kent and I have seen things and done things that you cannot even imagine. This place isn't the real world, so listen to me;

walk soft or you will get hurt. And especially leave guys like me alone."

He stared around looking for backup but no one said or did anything and finally he opened his mouth. "Sounds like a threat."

I was fighting a losing battle. I do not look impressive. I am slightly over six feet tall and about 180 pounds with very pale skin covered in old scars. My eyes are pale grey and my hair is dirty blond and cut with a razor. I do not look scary enough to avoid fights, at least to some people.

"No, it's not. I am having a bad day right now and I would love to take it out on you but it's not a threat. I am giving you information you should have before you do anything."

"Fuck you, pal; I've got a green belt in Goju-Ryu Karate and am a second-degree black belt in Hapkido ..."

I yelled, "Fire!"

It was a universal call. Much better than yelling "Rape" or "Murder." Claire had told me that years before, if you yell "Fire" people look, if you yell "Rape" they might decide not to get involved. She had learned that lesson from a self-defence teacher at the Banff Community Centre.

When the screw arrived ten seconds later everyone else in the cell was minding their own business, especially Mr. Badgerous.

"Who yelled fire?"

"Me."

It was a girl screw, blond and plump and breathing hard. She looked around. "Where is it?"

"I must have made a mistake. Any chance I can get a private cell?"

She snorted and I leaned towards her and whispered, "I feel like maybe I don't belong here. You might wanna talk to one of the cops who dragged me in about that. They might want me moved."

The screw was confused and stepped back to think about it. After a while she took me out and put me in a different cell block where everyone left me alone.

And time passed.

Jail's good at making time fly.

Two hours later my lawyer Lester came onto the range with a fat sheriff who unlocked the iron door and let me out. Up close Lester was rumpled and smelled of vodka and his dandruff was still amazingly bad. He had been my lawyer when I'd first been arrested in Winnipeg and he'd done a good job dealing with three charges of murder one plus drug possession and assorted other things.

He'd also done a good job getting me freed later that year when I'd been arrested for bank robbery.

"Monty!"

"Les! Am I free?"

Lester looked at the sheriff and then back at me. "Sort of. Not really. It's complicated."

He took me by the arm and off a few steps down the hallway to where there was some privacy. "Monty, some detective wants to talk to you about the bracelet."

"No charges? Just questions?"

Lester shrugged and a rain of flakes fell to cover his shoulders. "None. Just questions. They're willing to let me sit in. They've even apologized."

That made me pause. Cops never say they're sorry. I was still puzzling that out as I was escorted through the old cell blocks and then down two floors to Major Crimes, which had its own office. My stomach twisted as I entered but the first person to come towards me had a huge smile on his face and that made me pause as well. When cops smile it's generally bad for me, I've learned that over the years.

"Mr. Haaviko?" The cop was a thin man with a skull face and black hair cut short over warm brown eyes that looked friendly and sorrowful at the same time. "So sorry about the arrest. You'll understand when we've explained a few things though."

Lester nodded like he knew what was going on and it crossed my mind that he might be drunk. Then I figured probably not.

The cop went on, "I'm Sergeant Osserman. The reason this has taken so long is because we were waiting for Inspector Atismak."

He turned and Atismak got up from a desk and came towards me, a big man in an expensive suit who moved well. He was Royal Canadian Mounted Police and not city and he didn't seem to be in his jurisdiction here. It pissed me off; the whole situation pissed me off, none of it made sense. Atismak was very much a pro and had cut me slack when I'd been dealing with Walsh which meant, I figured, that I owed him big. He'd also interposed himself between Walsh and my family and that meant I owed him even more.

We shook hands grudgingly and he looked me straight in the eye as he did it. He was smart, I knew that. And Osserman bringing him in to deal with me meant he was smart too and so my respect for him went up a notch. He led the way to a boardroom with windows overlooking the city's tiny but vibrant Chinatown and we all sat down around a wooden table big enough for a dozen fat men.

"Okay, Mr. Haaviko, let me explain." Osserman spoke fast. "The bracelet you brought to Grim's was hot. Stolen sixteen years ago. So." He smiled and it looked like a fresh knife wound. "Where'd you get it?"

I turned to Lester who just shrugged and then at Atismak and Osserman in turn.

"Okay, I know what you want. And I know you want me to answer. Honestly and quickly which is why you are laying your cards down. Finish it off; show me the file. I want to know you are not jerking me around."

"Why?" Osserman's voice was flat and mean.

"Because I don't really trust you. This wouldn't be the first time a cop lied to me. And the story doesn't make sense—this much heat on a sixteen-year-old robbery? No. So explain to me what exactly is going on."

Osserman looked me over and I shook my head. "The fact you're even thinking of showing me the file means something."

Osserman nodded. "It means some of the crimes that are dealt with in the file occurred when you were in prison. It means you are not a realistic suspect."

"Prove it."

Osserman started to get mad and Atismak silenced him with a raised hand. They went outside and spoke quietly with their backs to the doorway. Then Atismak came back and said, "One minute."

He sat down and Osserman took off. Twenty minutes later he came back with a legal-sized manila folder two inches thick. He slid it down the table to me and both men waited while I went through the typed pages, photographs and drawings. As I finished each page I passed it to Lester. When I handed him the photos he gagged suddenly and vomited into a garbage can.

Mostly.

Everyone ignored him.

When he was finished throwing up Atismak pushed the can outside and let Lester go find a bathroom to clean up.

I finished leafing through the photos, and then I tapped them into place and slid them into the folder again. The smell of vomit was sharp in the air but it didn't really register. When I spoke I could hear the exhaustion in my voice.

"I see."

Osserman nodded. "Yes."

Atismak stood up and said, "Mr. Haaviko, nice to see you again. I take it you will help the sergeant?"

"Certainly. Can I call my wife though?"

"Of course. Here."

He handed me his cell phone and I dialled. While the call went through I memorized Atismak's number and then Claire was on the line. "Yes?"

"Monty here. Everything's fine. I should be done in an hour or so. Lester's with me."

"Well ... that's good. Is he drunk?"

I looked over at him and said no into the phone. Atismak gestured with one finger and I told Claire to hold on. Atismak said, "Tell her hello from me. Tell her I remember the coffee and doughnuts fondly."

When Atismak and the RCMP had searched my house Claire had laid out doughnuts and coffee to greet them. He was smiling as he spoke and I repeated the message. Claire said, "Say hello back. Atismak is RCMP, right? What's he doing there?"

"No idea."

We were both silent and then she said, "Come home soon."

"Of course. Love."

"Love."

She hung up and I flipped the phone to Atismak who put it away. "Thanks, Inspector."

"Think nothing of it."
Then he got up, rotated his shoulders and left.

#16

When Lester came back Osserman started to speak. "It was a burglary at Redonda Paris's jewellery shop. July first, 1992. As far as we can tell the perp broke in, triggered the alarm and hid in the crawlspace above the ceiling tiles in the back. Ms. Paris arrived after the cops and checked the place over with our men. They found nothing."

Osserman ran his thin, spatulate fingers through his hair. I could see them tremble slightly.

"The cops left. Then, we believe, Ms. Paris sealed the broken window with lumber from her back room. At that point we believe the perp came out of hiding and took control of the situation."

I listened and heard Lester swallow convulsively. Osserman kept talking.

"We estimate, and the RCMP concurs, that it took the perp five or six hours to finish. Ms. Paris was probably alive up until the last half-hour or so."

I flipped the folder open and looked at some of the photos. "I see."

Osserman exhaled loudly. His voice was very cold. "Do you? Interesting choice of words. Ms. Paris was raped. Thirty-seven bones were broken throughout her body. More than fifty bite marks were inflicted on her body; those were the ones that broke the skin. Before she finally died she was taken apart with a chipped flint or glass blade about four inches long."

Osserman paused, took two pills from an inner pocket and dry swallowed them. "She died alone. When the killer was done he cleaned up in her bathroom and then cleared out her stock of custom jewellery and maybe $200 in cash. Then he left."

Lester fidgeted in his chair and Osserman marked off points on his fingers. "We have DNA from semen. We have hair samples from the floor around her and from off the remains of her clothes. We have skin samples from under her fingernails. We have blood from where the FUCK ..." his voice cracked, "bit his tongue or cheek. We even have fingerprints. However we do not have a suspect. So when jewellery made by Ms. Paris shows up we are very interested indeed."

Lester looked pale and so did the cop. Even I was feeling green.

"So," I started, "you sent pictures of her jewellery to all the shops in the city. Pawn shops, jewellery stores, and so on?"

"Yes."

Osserman was getting impatient and I stared at him.

He was lying. Con rule: if a cop is talking and not asking questions then they are lying. None of it rang true. I thought it through again. A murder sixteen years ago and the cops were still keeping it active? That wasn't right. The city averaged twenty to thirty plus murders a year which meant that there would be 300-plus corpses between now and Paris. Not counting rapes, assaults, child abuse cases and all the rest of the nightmare shit that was a cop's life; no way would they be able to keep a single crime in the forefront. No matter how gruesome.

I stared at him and wondered why he was lying to me.

But the pictures were real or incredible fakes and sometimes you have to balance everything out and make a decision. Most of the time making a decision, any decision, was better than waiting.

So I made a decision and told Osserman to get a tape recorder. When it came in I told him everything, including finding the package, the roses, the note, everything I could remember. Nothing I supposed or suspected. When I was done a uniformed cop brought me my belt, wallet and pocket knife and Lester and I went downstairs to the street. He gave me a lift home in a beat-up Volvo he kept in good working order himself on the weekends, when he wasn't playing softball or getting juiced.

He drove badly for about five minutes and finally pulled over, took a slim flask from his briefcase and swallowed convulsively as the sharp stench of peppermint schnapps filled the air.

"Jesus. Sweet Jesus Christ."

It was dusk and dragonflies were filling the air, part of an environmentally friendly assault on mosquitoes. Those vampires were one of the biggest drawbacks of Manitoba as far as I was concerned, so I watched the predators flit around and thought about what I'd been told and what I'd seen in the cop office.

In prison you run into the occasional minor-league psychopath. More often you'd find the sociopaths, but Ms. Paris had encountered the real deal—a full-blown sadistic sexual psychopath. And those did not go to prison; those end up in asylums mostly. Occasionally I'd run into them out on the streets or working their way through the court system. On the street they generally slipped into crime because they couldn't function in society and they didn't last too long, as they didn't have great control over their needs and urges.

In the court system they generally tripped warning signals along the way and were escorted into solitary cells so cons didn't spend much time with them.

Once or twice though I'd found them or they'd found me. There'd been a pimp in Edmonton who liked to turn out young girls, younger every month, until he was putting ten- and eleven-year-olds out on the street to service businessmen going to work to sell oil or coming home after a hard day buying oil. He kept his girls in perfect control and they were known for their willingness to do absolutely anything. Finally one of the girls got friendly with another streetwalker, who found out the girls were all from the same town up near the Yukon border, a place called Hazard. The girl had told the other hooker something else too, something she hadn't told anyone else, not ever.

The next day the hooker found me in the bar I was propping up and traded me an eight ball of coke and two hours of sex for a chopped and channelled Iver Johnson .30 calibre carbine I'd been intending to keep for myself. She put it in a shopping bag and the next morning she unloaded on the pimp as he walked out of his favourite corner store eating a drumstick ice-cream cone.

She'd opened fire from thirty feet away and kept walking towards the man as the small-calibre bullets kept him upright and twitching. At about ten feet her magazine had run dry and she'd reloaded with another thirty-round magazine and finished him. Then she'd dropped the gun and walked away.

The coroner had pulled forty-nine soft-nosed surplus World War II lead bullets from the body.

They'd never caught the hooker.

Over time the girls the pimp had brought left. Just melted away into the street and were gone.

Another time I'd run into a guy in prison who thought that bugs were eating his nervous system and the only way to keep them out was to make little cuts on his arms and legs to let them out. The cops caught him for public indecency—he'd masturbated on the window of a downtown Montreal restaurant—and had put him into remand while awaiting trial. In remand he hadn't been able to get his hands on a knife so pressure had built up.

At least I think that's what happened.

When they'd given him a job in the kitchen though he'd been happy as a pig in shit and had lasted all the way to lunch when he'd gone out of his way to sharpen a medium-sized skinning knife. That clued the prison cook finally, because he was making vegetable soup (opening cans anyway) and grilled cheese sandwiches (white bread with Velveeta and margarine). None of which really required a knife to make. When the cook had looked for the guy though it had been too late, he'd already cut off six fingers and was most of the way through his wrist. The guy bled out while the alarms filled the fucking place with sounds of panic and excitement.

In the car Lester wasn't doing too well.

"Sweet Jesus Christ." Lester repeated himself and I shook my head and took the flask away, capped it and put it into his briefcase.

"No, Lester, Jesus has nothing to do with any of this. Take me home."

Outside of my place I thanked him and got out, and then I leaned back in. "Lester? What do I owe you?"

His face was haunted. "Oh. I'll try to run it by the Legal Aid system. They should cover it, if they don't I'll run it by the crown—you were helping the cops so they might have a little coin. Glad I could help. If no one can cover it then I'll send you a bill, 'kay?"

"Definitely. I'd still be in there if it wasn't for you. May I make a suggestion?"

He got defensive. "About my drinking?"

"No. Drink yourself to death if you want. It's your choice. No, I wanted to suggest you do something nice for your wife. It'll help. And then she might have sex with you. And that is a sure cure for this kind of shit."

He snorted. "That doesn't happen. Not anymore."

"Suck it up, buttercup. You've just gotten a big mouthful of death and the best way to wash the taste of it away is through life."

"What makes you an expert?"

I looked Lester in the eye until he turned away, then I said, "Experience. Make love to a women you genuinely respect and like. If not your wife then someone else. Just make sure you like and respect her."

He drove away and I went inside to where Claire was waiting, drinking coffee at the dining room table with the crowbar and bayonet in front of her.

She kissed me when I came in and followed me to the phone in the kitchen without asking any questions. Lester's home number was in the book and I called it and spoke to his wife, Elizabeth, whom I'd met two or three times. She was a nice lady but tense. When you're married to a drunk you get tense.

"Elizabeth? This is Monty."

"Is Les all right?"

"He's fine. He saw some gruesome photographs and heard a pretty bad story today. He's on his way home but he's shaky."

Claire's eyes asked questions and I kissed her again as Elizabeth asked, "How drunk is he?"

"Pretty drunk. But he's not handling it very well. He's shaky."

She snorted into the phone. "It's an excuse ..."

"No, Elizabeth, he saw thirty-four eight-by-ten glossy colour post mortem photographs of a young woman who was raped and tortured to death over a six-hour period."

"Oh." Her voice got small.

"I have no idea why he drinks in general but right now he has a reason to do so. I just thought I should tell you so you're ready."

She said "oh" again and then waited in silence before asking, "What do you think I should do?"

"Me? I'd make him a stiff cup of coffee, lace it with Viagra, pour it down his throat and then fuck his brains out. He's feeling dead right now."

Claire's eyes got wide and Elizabeth laughed harshly into the phone. "You assume a lot."

"Yep. You can tell me to fuck off if you want. It's okay, you wouldn't be the first and I might even do it for you."

She thought about it. "Is Claire there? Put her on?"

I handed the phone over and listened in as she said, "Claire, make sure your idiot husband can't hear."

"Sure, Liz. He's in the other room." Claire held the phone at an angle so I could hear better.

"Okay, hon. Did you hear what he said? What do you think?"

"I think," my wife smiled and unzipped my pants with her free hand, "you should go put on that little dress your husband likes, you know."

Elizabeth sounded concerned and serious. "The one that lifts and separates?"

"That's the one." Claire pulled me out of my pants and started to massage me. She'd learned a trick from a gay friend of hers in Edmonton and she was doing the one with the wrist twist that worked really, really well. Despite myself I was responding. Claire spoke brightly into the phone, "Then fuck his lights out."

"What about you?"

Claire winked at me. "I'm going to do exactly the same thing. Only I'm going to wear the birthday present I bought Monty. I told you about that."

"Right. Oh, happy birthday Monty."

I couldn't help myself, I was supposed to be in the other room but I answered anyway. In my defence, I was distracted. "Thanks, Elizabeth."

She laughed, only this time it was lower in her throat. "Stupid Monty. Really stupid. I'm amazed you got away with being a thief for so long."

Claire kissed the phone wetly and hung it up. We put Fred to bed and then Claire showed me my birthday present. Then she did two things we only do on special occasions and that cheered me up so much I forgot I wanted a drink and I did three things in return that I generally save for making points after I've made serious mistakes.

#17

The next morning my joining the race for the police commission was in the news and I had to unplug the phone because every reporter in the universe wanted to talk to me. I did however listen to the news and found out I was the only one running against Rumer for the position of chief commissioner and that eight people were running for the remaining five seats.

At two I got a phone call from Dean telling me a lawyer named Virgil Reese would call and set up a meeting with the man who was paying my fare. I said that would be nice and called Claire to come home but I got her partner instead, a woman called Vanessa Rose. She was young and intense and smart, a brunette who rarely wore a bra and who hid her brains behind perpetual cheerfulness.

"Monty? One sec, Claire's going in for the kill ..."

She laughed into the phone and it sounded like running water and then she chanted a rhyme under her breath, "Sign, sign on the dotted line and everything will be just fine."

"And how are you and your boyfriend? You know, what's-his-name?"

She laughed again. "I traded him in on a friendlier and healthier model ... and, she's done it. The paper is signed and the deal is done and I'll go deal with buyer's remorse and you can talk with your lovely wife."

Claire came on. "Just sold a big house to a nice couple."

"Sweet."

"You bet. What do you need?"

"You to come home. I've got a date with a man to talk about being chief commissioner."

"'Kay. I've made like $9,000 split in half anyway so far today, so I can take a break."

I hung up and tried to figure out why I had ever begun robbing banks in the first place—it could not have been for the money.

Fifteen minutes later a man phoned and told me his name was Virgil Reese and that he'd like to pick me up and introduce me to my employer. I told him that would be fine and he was there thirty minutes later, pulling up in an older-model four-door car I couldn't identify immediately. Before I could go to meet him he got out and came to the front door carrying a brown paper package which he handed to me. "For your wife."

I looked at him, surprised. He was in his fifties and wore a black silk suit and canary-yellow shirt with a string tie that emphasized his thinness and pallor. His politeness and poise were otherworldly.

"What is it?"

"A bottle of Benedictine. A smart liquor for a smart lady. And a voucher for the Kai Ping restaurant in the south end—they deliver and their lo mein is fantastic. I'm sorry to say I'll have to take you away for most of the evening so I figured I should bring your wife dinner as partial recompense."

Claire came to the door and accepted the package and the man actually kissed the back of her hand. "Virgil Reese, lawyer. You're a good real estate agent. May I send some clients your way?"

"Certainly. As long as they pay."

Mr. Reese smiled thinly. "If they didn't they wouldn't be my clients."

"How do you know I'm good?"

"I do my research, ask questions, analyze, consider and think. You have a good reputation."

Claire put her forefinger on her lips. "Thank you, and keep Monty as long as you want."

He smiled thinly and handed her an embossed card on heavy stock. "Enjoy the Benedictine. It's made from a 500-year-old secret recipe of twenty-seven separate herbs, known only by a small number of monks."

Claire gave her best smile. "I will. And you enjoy my husband. He's not 500 years old and I'm pretty sure no one knows how he was made."

Sometimes my wife is a real comedian.

I took the bottle from him and brought it into the kitchen before looking it over. No drill marks on the glass that I could see and the foil on the cork looked pristine. I closed my eyes and ran my fingers over but found no imperfections at all, which meant it probably wasn't poisoned.

I dumped it down the sink anyway.

Upstairs I pulled on my black denim thief's jacket that I'd had custom made years before by an understanding tailor. It had extra pockets sewn into the reinforced inner lining, steel chain mail around the left arm for dogs and knives and a hidden pocket in the back with a Gem razor blade. I also made sure my pocket knife was in the right pocket and my steel-toed shoes were on my feet. The last thing I did was pocket a little digital tape recorder from Office Depot with new batteries. Then we left.

In the car Mr. Reese waited until I had buckled up before starting the engine which made barely any noise.

"Where are we going?"

"To my employer's home. It's up near Riding Mountain National Park, about three hours away."

"Ah."

"However, it will give us a chance to talk and I had a secretary pack us a lunch so we won't be hungry. It's in the back."

I looked and there was a real wicker picnic basket right out of a Yogi Bear cartoon on the leather seat behind me.

"Okay, Mr. Reese. Sounds fine."

A block away from my house Mr. Reese asked, "Have you ever been to Riding Mountain Park?"

"No."

"It's fascinating. An escarpment—a mountain almost—rising up from the prairie with unique wildlife and vegetation. Lots of elk and deer and all looming over the fields and prairies. It's the closest this miserable little lake-bottom province gets to an actual mountain."

I checked and he was smiling.

"You should take the kids. However, there is a long hike listed on top of the, quote, mountain, and it is a nightmare. Close underbrush. Mosquitoes. Biting flies. Elk. And at the end of it a view of nothing because the trees haven't been cleared in decades. Skip it."

The car ride was smooth and finally I asked him what he was driving. He patted the dashboard with every appearance of affection. "A Bentley Flying Spur. Not very common. English and very well bred."

We drove in silence out of the city and headed west and north. Reese set the cruise control at 110 klicks and then spoke again. "Do you know the name of our client?"

"Aubrey Goodson."

"Excellent. How do you know that? I know Dean and Brenda would never have told you."

I had turned in the slick leather seat and was watching Mr. Reese carefully. "A man called Cornelius Devanter approached me energetically to betray Mr. Goodson."

"You agreed?"

"I did."

He pursed his lips in thought. "I see."

"No you don't. He offered me ten grand to throw the election to his good friend Rumer Illyanovitch. After bargaining the offer went up to twenty."

Mr. Reese stole a look at me and nodded. "You have no intention of following through on the agreement?"

"The term 'throwing' the election is a slippery one."

He nodded. "True."

"I can 'throw' and he can avoid 'catching' and the deal is still met. So I want to see what Mr. Goodson offers. You see, Mr. Devanter and his lawyers pulled guns on me. I hate that. So, what does Mr. Goodson have on the table?"

Mr. Reese looked unconcerned at the mention of guns. "Well. To start he offers to finance your election entirely out of pocket. Once elected, the income of the chief commissioner is $21,000 per annum."

"That's not much."

"Can you pour me some coffee? It's in the thermos back there."

I did and tasted it and it was good. "Timmie's?"

"Yes. Tim Horton's finest. Let's break that down: the $21,000 is paid for attending eighteen meetings, each roughly three hours long. So fifty-four hours of work. Plus homework, say ten hours for each hour in a meeting for a total of 594 hours a year, which makes for an hourly wage of $35.35 for four years, the term."

"But there's no guarantee I'll get elected?"

"True. So make me a counter-offer."

He drove and we ate small fresh whole wheat buns, slices of Thüringen sausage, ripe black olives, chunks of Gouda and black cherries. And while we travelled I thought and then I made an offer. "Okay. Guaranteed election expenses, including covering house expenses I'd normally contribute—roughly a thousand a month—plus one-year salary to be banked in case I lose. Plus you let me take Devanter for the twenty grand."

Mr. Reese smiled. "Make it six months' salary and it's a deal."

"You don't have to talk to Mr. Goodson?"

"No. Not about this. He pays me for my decision-making ability."

Hours had passed and we were approaching a slowly rising chunk of land off to the right.

"Almost there."

"Fine."

Mr. Reese drove without effort and finally opened his mouth. "What's your definition of a fanatic?" He seemed genuinely interested in my response. I leaned back in the seat. Two responses quickly came to mind and I considered them both before pitching them into the abyss.

"A fanatic," I said slowly, "Is someone who has only read one book."

Reese's mouth narrowed and tightened. "That's hardly original."

"Let me finish. Someone who has only read one book and who has had that same book explained to him at length by someone who agrees with them."

Reese turned his head quickly and then back to the road and we swerved a little as he answered, "Ah. Well, Mr. Goodson is not a fanatic. He's the opposite of a fanatic."

I wondered what that meant and we turned left off a secondary highway to a well-gravelled road that snaked through brush. Above the entry off the highway was a wrought iron sign that read "Goodson Ranch."

#18

I trust my fellow man to fuck things up. I'm generally right. It's kind of a business and life principle for me."

The old man was strangely compelling; he had stayed up on the wide cedar porch that surrounded the three-storey wooden house when we drove up in the late afternoon. We'd walked up the steps to meet him where he sat on a rocker hand-made out of antlers, with a red wool Hudson's Bay trade blanket tucked over his lap. Around us were thick stands of trees.

His first words had been a formal hello and his second had been about how he expected men to fuck things up.

I stared openly at him and didn't answer. He was old, in his seventies, maybe older, and he looked like he'd been awake for every second of it. The man's face was thin and sharp with patchy white hair and his brown eyes were set deeply into his skull. He wore a grey wool long-sleeved shirt buttoned to his neck with yellowed bone buttons and faded jeans that ended above his ugly, twisted toes sticking out of a pair of battered leather sandals.

"Look there." He pointed at a heavy-barrelled rifle and a scratched metal case beside his chair. I reached down and picked up the rifle by the butt. It took my breath away.

"It's gorgeous."

"It's a drilling. A three-barrelled rifle/shotgun. That one's Nazi German, issued by Goering to German Luftwaffe bomber crews in North Africa in case they were shot down and decided to survive. The aircrew were expected to be shot down and they were expected to survive. That gun reminds me of my rules that people fuck up."

I took the weapon out. The blueing on the barrel was slightly faded and the walnut stock was scratched but beautiful. I could still make out "J.P. Sauer & Sohn Suhl" on the butt plate. On the right side of the butt was an eagle carrying a swastika and the pistol grip was finely checkered.

Bringing the weapon to my shoulder I found there was a selector switch on the receiver. I moved it to the centre and a folding site rose automatically graduated out to 100 metres. On the side of the barrels was written Krupp-Luftstahl and 9.3x74 R in one place and 12/65 Eagle/N in another. I looked up at the old man. "The calibre?"

"Ya. I have to hand load them but that's not hard, just painstaking and precise. I can't do it no more so I pay a smart Filipino in Brandon to do it for me."

I put the weapon down and looked at the case. It had a leather handle and two locking latches and held a wooden cleaning rod with brass fittings, some bore-cleaning brushes and boxes of shotgun and rifle ammunition.

"Beautiful gun."

"Thank you. Very old. Very accurate. I brought it out to start the conversation, better than many other things like a whore or cigars or a fine wine, don't you think?" He gestured to the west. "Over there I've planted different kinds of grasses—timothy, orchard grass, clover designed to grow at different times so something is always young and tender, which elk like best. There are also patches of raspberries and blackberries for bears and deer. Then I go shooting."

"Off-season?" I said it mildly.

The old man shrugged. "Shooting. Not hunting. I kill for the pot. I feed the animals and the animals feed me."

"What about the game laws?"

"All this land is mine for twenty kilometres every which way. I don't normally let the game wardens onto it. What do you think of my habits?"

"Not very fair."

The old man kept his eyes locked on mine. He was trying to tell me something very bluntly. "Not interested in being fair."

"Then you have a good system."

"Ya. Sit down." He gestured to another chair made out of antler pulled up against the side of the house. I dragged it out and got uncomfortable in it while Mr. Reese leaned against the split log railing that ran around the porch.

Mr. Reese started. "Mr. Haaviko would like the election expenses, his home operating expenses and $11,500 banked against the chance he loses. Call it roughly $40,000 total. He's also been approached by Mr. Devanter to accept $20,000 to throw the election towards Rumer Illyanovitch." He turned his head towards me. "Is that about right?"

"Yes."

The old man kept his head poked forward and nodded. "You accepted the deal, Mr. Reese?"

"I did, on your behalf."

"Then you are an idiot. I have no desire to pay for a campaign that will benefit that prick Cornelius."

I cut in, "My agreement with Devanter is for $20,000 to throw the election towards Rumer. Nothing else."

He scratched his head. "Those are the terms? To throw it towards Rumer? No guarantees? And he accepted?"

"He did."

"You did not guarantee victory for his candidate?"

"No."

"Or that you would lose?" His face was tilted to the side and he was thinking hard.

"Exactly."

"Now why would the dumb prick accept that kind of deal? Wait a minute; are you smart enough to make it happen? Or are you jerking me around?"

"Yes, I'm smart enough. I don't like the idiot so I'm motivated."

The old man laughed until he choked and, when he recovered, said, "Good." He thrust his hand towards me. "Good to work with you, Mr. Haaviko. With the help of Brenda and Dean we'll beat Devanter's bum boy like a drum."

We shook and I kept hold of the hand. "Two things. First, the money?"

Goodson was amazed and astounded at my distrust. "The money? The money? Mr. Reese will provide that as needed, have no fear of that."

"It's always easier to pay someone in promises. That's like rule number 601 in life and it's served me well, just like yours. The money up front, please."

"That's insulting."

"They're my rules."

He argued, wheedled, cajoled, bitched, whined and whimpered while Mr. Reese and I watched and I, at least, admired his technique and stamina. When he was done he got up and went into the house and I noted that he had a thick felt pad on the sharp, uncomfortable antlers that made up the seat of his chair.

After about ten minutes he came back with a well-used manila envelope. Inside it was $40,000 in fifties and hundreds, all old bills, all used, none consecutive. Both men watched as I counted it out and then dealt it back out of sight.

Then Mr. Reese spoke again. "You said you had two things, what is number two?"

"Number two is a question. If you lie to me then I will keep the money and hand the election to Rumer or quit, whatever will cause you the most pain and suffering."

Both men looked amused and the old man said, "Ask."

"Why do you want to win the election? Why is it important to you?"

Goodson looked uncomfortable and squirmed around for a few seconds. I felt sorry for his ass until I remembered the felt pad and then I didn't feel so bad.

"It's," he looked at his lawyer who shrugged almost imperceptibly, "... complicated."

"I've got time." My ass was numb so of course I had time. If I tried to stand up I'd probably fall down.

"All right then. I don't want to win, I want Devanter to lose. There's a difference. I knew Cornelius Devanter's father back in the sixties when we were both wheeling and dealing all across the west. We fought for timber rights in provincial parks when all we had were a couple of pickup trucks and we fought over flight times and hangar space when we were bringing in supplies to mining camps. We fought over liquor licences for bars and distribution rights for outboard engines and we fought over women and staff and customers."

The old man picked up the drilling and broke it open to

check that it was unloaded. He did everything slowly and, when he was done, he continued, "Basically we fought. Anyhow, the old bastard finally died in the early 1990's, his heart blew out while he was trying to convince a client of mine to file a lawsuit over some transformers I was late delivering. But his son, Cornelius, now he's something special. He just picked up the feud and kept going—but hard, you name it; class action suits, criminal complaints, civil judgements, patrimony suits, blackmail, low balling, industrial espionage, localized sabotage, injunctions and so on. He just goes like a fucking bunny."

The old man looked at me and there was a kind of twinkle in his eye, he was enjoying it. "Now he wants this asshole Rumer Illyanovitch as chief commissioner of police—no idea why. So I want someone else in place."

"You really don't know why Cornelius is backing Rumer?"

"Nope. No idea at all. The position can't appoint anyone. It doesn't control a bureaucracy. It doesn't have a budget. The only thing it has any kind of influence over is the police force. And it doesn't have much of that."

I stared at the old man and had to agree.

"Anyhow, I figure the friend of my enemy is my enemy and that the enemy of my enemy is my friend, so I picked you. I got Dean and Brenda to start looking for someone to counteract Rumer Illyanovitch, backed as he is by Cornelius's money. Rumer's got star power and influence and ability."

"And what do I have?"

"The freak factor, the unknown, the x. You are a walking example of the biblical quotation 'Set a thief to catch a thief.' You will get everyone's attention and that will sway a certain percentage of the vote. My weight and Brenda and Dean's skill will help as well."

I stared at him and didn't bother telling him that the thief quote wasn't in the bible.

"Now," he said off-handedly, "you might want to find out what kind of plan Cornelius has for Illyanovitch."

He said it oh so casually but I shook my head. "Nope."

"Nope?" He was slightly pissed I'd say no to him.

"Yep. Nope. If you want me to find out I'll try but it's a lot of extra work. It'll cost you another $5,000."

He cursed and whined and bitched and again Mr. Reese and I watched him and finally he agreed. We talked over how to explain the money and the old man came up with the idea of claiming it was a wager between me and him over cards. I agreed and Mr. Reese noted that since it was a wager for pleasure, as opposed to professional reasons, it was untaxable.

When we were done I got up to leave but I needed to know one more thing. "Quick question: do you put visitors in that abomination of a chair on purpose to make them uncomfortable and put them at a disadvantage in their dealings with you?"

The old man nodded, "Yep."

"'Kay. Just checking."

We left. When I got back home it was past midnight and there was a written note from Elena that she had to see me the next day at 2:00 exactly (she had underlined it twice) at the Greek coffee house.

#19

The next day I got Claire to watch the kids. Then I went to the café where Elena was already sitting. I sat across the table from her and we ordered cheese Danishes and coffee and they came quickly.

"You get your order a lot quicker than I ever do."

Elena looked preoccupied and said, "Hmmm?"

"It's probably the gun."

"Probably."

She was in full cop regalia: uniform, body armour, radio, pistol, collapsible baton, Taser, spare ammunition, handcuffs and attitude. Every few minutes her radio growled and she'd hold up a finger and listen.

Elena didn't know where to begin so I started. "Look. You wanted to talk to me. Here I am. Like you asked."

Elena nodded and suddenly shook her head in exasperation. "Okay. I have a problem. I have a big problem. And it involves you and Claire." She sounded very concerned.

It took me aback. "Should I call a lawyer?"

"No. Maybe. I'm not sure."

She examined her fingernails and I saw they were bitten down, something I'd never seen. Finally she took a deep breath. "Okay. Claire got a present in the mail, right? A bracelet?"

"Yes."

"And you went to get it appraised and got arrested."

"Pretty much."

She ordered more coffee and leaned in. "Osserman lied to you."

"Cops? Lying to me? Never."

Elena wasn't amused. "They told you that Paris was the first? That was true. But they didn't tell you about the others."

My blood pressure surged and I felt a tight band around my forehead. "Others?"

"Others. Since 1992 there have been seven women that we know of. Each received some of Paris's jewellery as a gift. There has also been one husband and one son killed. The pattern is the same in each case; the women receive phone calls, flowers, letters, dinner invitations, etc. All from a secret admirer. The tone of the communications gets progressively more strident and finally the women vanish and are found later, tortured, raped, mutilated and murdered."

"Jesus."

Elena stared at her cup. "We missed any connections between the first woman and the second one and we couldn't find any connections between the second and the third."

She took a bite of her Danish before grimacing. "The force was going through a rough time. A whole changeover of major crimes personnel, a new chief, dissent in the union, disagreements with the RCMP and so on. In 1996 someone found the connectors—the jewellery all the women had and complaints they had made to their neighbours about being stalked. Two had even called the cops and filed complaints against 'Persons Unknown.' Not that any of it helped them."

I reached out and grabbed Elena's hand. "Is Claire in danger? Right now?"

"No. She's covered. We've got cops everywhere, watching and waiting. We've brought in RCMP plainclothes and, well, she's covered."

I wondered about the other women and whether they'd been covered. I also wondered how rusty I was getting not to notice cops around my house.

"Okay. Go on. So you guys found out you had a serial killer."

The term sounded ridiculous. It was something out of Hollywood, the boogeyman, the new monster of the time.

"Yes. So we set up a system to flag any of the signs we were seeing—complaints, stalking accusations—but there were a lot of them, still are."

I nodded and she went on, "We also started to get the pawn shops and jewellery stores to watch for the stuff that Paris made. It was unique, after all. Finally, in 1998 we found a necklace being cleaned. By the time we got to the woman's condo though, she was gone."

She stared into the distance.

"Dogs found her remains on the banks of the Assiniboine. We told the public she had been run over by a boat. You see ..."

I realized she was pleading with me. Her mouth opened twice and then she said, "We didn't want to panic anyone."

My mouth froze open and I just stared at Elena. When I could speak my voice was low and vicious, "Panic anyone? You didn't want to panic anyone?"

Elena touched my hand and I drew it back out of her reach.

"Yes. When the Nightstalker was killing in California more than thirty people died as vigilantes and scared civilians panicked and opened fire, thinking the murderer was creeping up on them. Most of the people who died were innocent spouses and children. Lots of cops think some wives and husbands used the opportunity and the fear to get rid of unwanted spouses."

Somewhere I had heard that but the rage was still very strong inside me. "Panic. Okay. So you kept it quiet."

She nodded, "Yeah. We found more of the jewellery. Some turned up in estate sales. Other pieces we just ran across."

Elena looked off into the distance. "We call the killer the Shy Man. Sometimes he sends letters but they never get mean. Other times he sends a single piece of jewellery and that's it. Other times the letters build to a crescendo and then stop and nothing happens for months, even years. Then the woman vanishes."

I rubbed my forehead. "How many more dead?"

"Paris, we think, was the first one in 1992. Followed by a woman in 1995 who ran a flower shop in Saint James. We found her in an abandoned house, in the basement, pretty late and the coroner fucked up and claimed she had died of natural causes and that the damage had been caused by rats and insects. She was the one we didn't catch until 1998 with better DNA testing. In 1997 there was a woman lawyer we found mutilated in her cabin in the Whiteshell. Her husband was beside her with a bullet hole in his brain and it looked like a murder/suicide. In 1998 there was a part-time model; she was the one we found in the Assiniboine. In 2001 there was a waitress we found in a minivan parked where kids neck sometimes near the zoo."

Elena shook her head. "In 2003 we caught on to a case

before the murder happened. It was an accountant, a nice woman, dated a provincial sheriff. She went to a cop Christmas party with one of Paris's brooches and a sergeant noticed it. We went to her directly and set her up as a decoy—full coverage, all the time. Nothing happened."

I was watching Elena. It looked like this was hurting her.

"Then, in 2005, we caught another one in time. She was a bank teller and we pulled most of the coverage off the accountant to cover her. Which was a mistake, because in the summer of that year someone broke into the accountant's house, shot her ten-year-old son to death and took her apart. In 2006 the bank teller went on vacation to Mazatlán. There she was kidnapped from the beach and murdered on a rented catamaran a mile off shore."

"Jesus."

Elena smiled. "You said that. So. We know the Shy Man sometimes kills and sometimes doesn't. And we know he can 'date' his ladies for up to forty-one months, that's the longest we know about. And we know he's Caucasian, probably, and right handed, probably. And we have finger- and footprints and DNA samples and so on."

She smiled brightly. "Claire is probably safe."

"Sure."

"So don't tell her."

"Of course not." The lie rolled off my tongue easily.

"I've got something for her though. Come with me."

There were tears in her eyes as she paid the tab and took me around to the back of the café where her police issue Crown Vic was parked. She walked around to the trunk and opened it. Inside were neatly racked tools, a shovel, a big first aid kit and a towel, neatly folded, from a Holiday Inn. Elena opened the towel and showed me what was inside.

"They're throwdowns."

I knew what that meant. The three pistols she had in the towel had had their registration filed and burned off. They were meant for cops to drop if they shot an unarmed person and didn't want to go to jail or answer a lot of stupid questions.

"Take 'em."

She was serious. I looked at her face and then back at the guns. Two semi-autos and a revolver. I leaned into the truck and picked them up one at a time and examined them. Finally I kept the Beretta Model 21 and the Taurus revolver in .32 long.

"You can keep the Star. I'm not sure about the firing pin."

Elena nodded and closed the trunk as I put the guns away in my pockets, first making sure the safeties were on. They were loaded with eight .25 rounds and six .32 rounds respectively and just having them made me nervous. For an ex-con those two guns, illegal, unregistered, restricted weapons with no serial numbers, represented about six years of prison.

I went home in the cop car to tell Claire my good news.

#20

Claire took it better than I expected.

"Really? Me? Being stalked by a serial killer?"

"Yes."

We were walking around the neighbourhood and pulling Fred in his red wagon. Claire stopped and turned her back to me to examine a cancer growing a boll on an oak tree. I respected her privacy and when she turned back I went on.

"I wanted to tell you outside of the house. There's a fair chance the cops have it bugged."

"Ah."

I couldn't read her face. "Elena gave me two pistols for you. A .32 revolver which is fairly big and a .25 calibre Beretta you can carry on your person."

She ran her fingers across the bark of the tree. "In my purse."

"Never in your purse. I'll rig something up for you. Frankly, the gun's so damn small you can slip it into a pocket or into a wallet and no one will notice."

"Is there an 'or' here about this whole situation?"

"Sure, there's always an 'or.' In this case it's 'or we can run.' The only problem is we'll never be sure we've gotten away with it. He's hunted the same woman for more than three years before. He might do it again."

"Ah." Claire turned back to me and I saw something very angry in her eyes and I was glad that it wasn't me who started it this time. "Any suggestions?"

I thought about saying it diplomatically, then punted that idea and went for the truth. "We figure out how to antagonize him. How to make him react emotionally. We figure out what makes him tick and then we press those buttons hard. Then, when's he's really angry, we make him come out and play. Then I kill him."

She smiled.

That night we pulled the drapes closed and I took some remnants of canvas and heavy thread along with a six-foot length of six-inch tensor bandage and made a holster Claire could wear all the time. It fit at the base of her spine, under her pants or skirt, and it was almost unnoticeable as long as she always wore her shirt out. Since the Beretta was so small (less than five inches long and less than an inch thick) and light, it was easy for her to get used to it.

When the holster was ready I got her to strip to underwear and a bra and put it on. Then I made her practise drawing it quickly, right hand and then left. Over and over again.

Actually, it was kind of sexy to watch.

When we had to talk we wrote it down on scraps of paper, just in case the cops had the place bugged.

While she was practising I took the opportunity to rip some seams out of one of Claire's favourite leather jackets and insert a ten-inch plastic knitting needle down her spine. The brass tip stuck out just behind her neck and she could draw that with either hand but other than that it was unnoticeable. Since it was plastic it bent with her movements and it was flexible enough to slide easily between ribs as needed.

When I was done we headed down to the basement. We went into the corner where I filled a garbage pail with water from the tap and had her stand on a chair over it. When she was ready I had her pull the gun and fire a single shot straight down into the water.

Crack.

It was an insignificant noise and the bullet went into the water maybe a foot before losing momentum and drifting the rest of the way.

She wrote, "*It works.*"

"*Any problems with the recoil?*"

Claire just shook her head. She had fired rifles and shotguns with her dad over the years so she was no stranger to guns. I handed her the revolver and she fired that as well.

Bang!

Much more authoritative.

She holstered the gun and I gathered up the spent shells and bullets and put them in my pocket for disposal. Upstairs I wrote her a note to remind her, "*The Beretta is always double action so squeeze and that's it. Seven rounds left, which is more than enough.*"

I checked Claire's purse. She had a Mini-Mag flashlight (useful to find door locks in the dark and to give weight and a rigid surface in a punch), a nice Gerber Guardian Back-Up knife sewn into the side (great for opening letters and slitting throats as needed). She also had a whistle and a can of pepper bear spray but those were obviously for defence.

Claire watched me closely as I checked the house. Doors, windows and locks. Upstairs I turned on the internal alarm I'd built when Smiley, an ex-con friend of mine, had lived with us. If anyone came up the stairs it would trigger a light display which I put on my side of the bed.

Then I took the door off its hinges from Fred's room and used two pieces of thread to tie it into place on the stairs. If anyone came upstairs quickly they'd break the thread and it would make a hell of a racket as they went skiing away, not lethal but loud and disorienting. Claire took Fred and his mattress into our room and put him in a corner nearest to her.

I looked around and froze, standing there. Finally Claire put her hand on my arm and led me to bed.

I didn't dream that night.

I'm not sure I even slept.

#21

The next morning I phoned Mr. Reese. His secretary had a slightly nasal east-coast accent but put me through to him as soon as she heard my name and the first thing he said was, "Call me Virgil. What do you need?"

"Thanks, Virgil. I need to quit, actually."

He was silent and then laughed and it was kind of cold and amused. "You can't quit."

"I have to. I have a serious personal problem that I have to deal with."

"What's the problem?"

"I can't discuss it over the phone."

"Are you serious?" He answered his own question. "Yes, you are."

I started again. "Yes. I have to quit ..." and he interrupted me, "I'll be right over. Thirty minutes. Please wait."

He made it in less than twenty. On my way to the door I kissed Claire and she showed me the gun at her back and the Gerber knife tucked behind her neck under her hair. It made me feel better.

I sat down and wondered whether I trusted Virgil. My reflex was to say no. But the whole situation was so complex, it didn't feel like a setup. Everyone wanted something—Virgil wanted to help Cornelius, Devanter wanted to win, Cornelius wanted Devanter to lose.

None of it added up to Virgil being part of the Shy Man problem. And he might be an ally—if he kept paying me then I'd have the money to help deal with the Shy Man. Even run, if we had too.

I wrote it out on a pad of paper and showed it to Claire and she nodded.

When Virgil came in I showed him the paper on which I had written, "*The cops have the place bugged.*"

He nodded and sat down.

And we started to write copious notes back and forth.

Claire and Fred sat in the living room while I "talked" to Virgil. Claire read over our shoulders and Fred kept himself plugged in via earphones to the television watching a thirty-three-year-old recording of a *Muppet Show* starring ballet dancer Rudolf Nureyev.

When I had explained everything Virgil shook his head and said out loud, "I'll be honest. I thought maybe Devanter had gotten to you. Offered you more money or something."

"No." I wrote down the rest of my answer. "*If that had happened I would have strung you all along with copious quantities of bullshit and lies, collapsed my campaign at the last moment and collected from both sides.*"

He stared at me and so did Claire. Then he said slowly, "You are a very corrupt individual."

"You mean neither of you thought of that?"

"No." They both answered and I felt pretty bad about myself. But then I had never claimed to be a gentleman.

Virgil closed his eyes and patted the dog. After six or seven minutes he opened his eyes and said slowly, "Do you have a dollar?"

Claire did. I tossed the gold-coloured coin to him and he put it into his watch pocket. "You're my client now. So everything you tell me is confidential. This is my advice; the cops are watching the house, right?"

"Yes."

"And you want to hang around and help your wife?"

"Yes."

"*If you're in the race you're in the public eye.*" He wrote quickly. "*That fact might keep the killer away. The race will also provide you with money so your wife doesn't have to work. Lastly, if you win you can pressure the police to do more.*"

I spoke out loud. "Okay. All that sounds legitimate."

"However. If you're not in the race then ..." He wrote, "... it's you against the Shy Man with limited resources. Mano a mano." He turned to Claire and said, "Your decision."

It surprised me. "How is it her decision?"

"It's her life. So that makes it her decision."

Claire stared at me unblinkingly and I just stood there immobile and she finally nodded. "Stay in the race. It seems to give us more options that way."

Answers, complaints raced through my head but I didn't say anything. The bad guy part of my brain stepped back and let me look at the problem dispassionately. She was right and he was right and if they were wrong then I could still dump the race and follow my instincts.

"'Kay."

I was supposed to work on my campaign but I phoned Dean and Brenda and left that in their capable hands while telling Virgil to come shopping with me.

I took Claire and Fred to Buttes, the local archery range where I work sometimes, and dropped them off there with Frank, who's a nice guy, albeit a little screwy. The lanes were full of a Christian boys' and girls' club and I felt both Claire and Fred were pretty safe.

While Virgil drove I thought.

We stopped at a big-box hardware store, where I spent $600 of the old man's money. Then we went to a sporting goods store and I blew another $300. After that there was a hobby store, a gun store that dealt primarily to cops and lastly I hit a libertarian natural food store in the south end.

When everything was loaded I looked around and said, "Ouch."

Virgil looked at me over the top of a soft-serve ice cream cone he had bought from a vendor. "What?"

"Spending money hurts. Especially when you've earned it instead of stolen it honestly."

He slapped me on the back. "You'll get used to it, princess. Are we done now? Because I have clients who pay more than a dollar a day waiting ..."

After dropping me off in front of my house with my purchases, he took off. Once all the stuff was inside I went back to Buttes and collected my wife and son.

When supper was finished I went to work with the decorative iron grills I'd bought, each two feet high, four feet long and made up of one-inch round wrought iron bars. Once I'd sharpened the ends properly (and illegally) with a file I used the recommended hardware and used them on the inside of the windows. Four covered the front window, three more covered the windows on the side of the house and more went on over the spare bedroom and kitchen windows. Then I did the same for the windows upstairs and the ones in the basement.

I hooked up radar alarms in each room of the house. They ran off attached nine-volt batteries and would trigger a foghorn if anything bigger than a mouse moved, and I set them to run from eleven at night to seven in the morning. Keeping the dog Renfield under control would be a pain but not impossible—he generally liked to sleep in the same room as us anyway.

While I was working with some six-inch lengths of iron pipe my eyes started to droop and I had to go to sleep.

The next morning I used the new Dremel multi-tool I had bought and finished with the pipes, attaching butt plates, cutting an L shape through the surface into the cavity and installing heavy duty springs and sliding metal bolts at the same time. The hard part was getting the handle into the bolt while it was in the pipe, but when it was done I had five simple-looking zip guns. Each looked vaguely like a pen and could reliably fire a single .32 calibre shell with a twist of a thumb.

I spray-painted them silver and put them aside to dry while I finished testing the last couple of gimmicks I'd bought. Then I invited Claire down to the basement where I was working and showed her the tool bench.

She looked at it all and shrugged theatrically. Then I wrote out my notes and took her through the items, one at a time.

First up was the lighter I'd taken from the assholes at the fair. It didn't look very prepossessing, a three-inch by two-inch rectangle made out of a dull grey metal. She took the paper from my hand and wrote, "*Looks like a lighter.*"

I answered, "*It is!*"

She looked disgusted and I jotted down that it was a butane lighter with an electric ignition and burned at 2,500 degrees Fahrenheit, hot enough to melt steel, hot enough to fire a crematorium and reliable enough to light in a rainstorm. I wrote that if she ignited it and touched the flame to anyone they would quickly become interested in other things.

Claire looked impressed and put the lighter in her purse.

I showed her the rest, a plastic vial of pills a couple of inches long, and wrote *speed* on the paper and that she should take it if someone drugged her. It was ephedrine, from the ma huang plant in China, an appetite suppressant, a decongestant and a fairly powerful stimulant. I had no idea how the Shy Man kidnapped his ladies but if he used drugs then he probably used a narcotic or hypnotic. Amphetamines worked really well at overriding both of those and the pills were legal in Canada. Ephedrine and pseudo-ephedrine were also the base ingredient of crystal meth.

As a recovering drug addict I really wanted to take them instead of giving them to Claire but I resisted.

There was also a copy of a Smith and Wesson police handcuff key in case the Shy Man used handcuffs. And there was a single-edged razor, to be hidden because I knew he used ropes. I let Claire think about where to put those where they'd be most useful. I normally sewed them into shirt and pants cuffs but that was me. If I needed them I could pick the threads free with my fingernails and then I'd be free. As Claire was a better seamstress than me I was sure she'd have a better idea.

Claire took two of the zip guns that looked remarkably like fat pens now that the silver paint was dry. She balanced them for a few moments and then put them in her purse as well. Then she kissed me and went to make supper. Afterwards she phoned all the parents whose children we babysat and made sure they understood she'd be doing it for awhile.

Most of them sounded relieved when they heard I was out of the picture. But they got really panicky when they found out I was running for police commissioner. I'm not entirely sure why they felt more nervous about me as a public official than as a babysitter.

Then Claire phoned Veronica and explained that she was housebound and to ask her to deliver some paperwork for her to keep up to date while Veronica concentrated on selling. Veronica hemmed for awhile but agreed when Claire offered an extra week of vacation.

While she was doing that I sat there thinking about how to get my brain thinking like that of a monster.

#22

The next morning we campaigned, Brenda and Dean and I. We went from door to door and generally got them slammed in our faces. Brenda or Dean walked first, knocked, talked and then waved me in or away, depending on the response.

I was wearing my only suit, an expensive pale grey two-piece with a black shirt, grey tie and the pair of steel-toed shoes, good for crunching up a kneecap without breaking a toe in case of debate. It was my go-to-trial suit, so old that it was almost back in style.

I looked pretty good so I got waved in more often than not and I'd walk forward confidently to shake hands and start to talk.

"Good morning! My name is Monty Haaviko and I'm running to be the chief commissioner of the new police board. I want your vote on September 13."

Sometimes they'd say yes. Sometimes no. Sometimes they asked questions like, "What the fuck is the police board?" or

"Why do we need a police board?" and sometimes, "Why are you bothering me?"

I got pretty good at some standard answers. "The police board is a citizen-run board that oversees the police department on issues like citizen complaints, public inquiries, criminal investigations and budgets."

I said that a lot. About the same amount of time as I said, "The police board provides an extra element of oversight of justice and security in the city. It is impartial and supports the police mission."

And for the "Why are you bothering me?" I just started to apologize and say that I believed it was time for a change here in the city and that things had gotten out of hand.

Between houses Brenda and Dean briefed me on my responses and made suggestions. At first it was annoying but then I realized that their input was helping, it made me more comfortable with questions and responses.

Dean had overheard me at the first house, "Okay, Monty. That was good. Three things to hit though: A) Mention citizen complaints first. In the city most of the complaints against cops come from this district so that'll make you friends. B) Mention criminal investigations. Lots of people would love to know what actually goes on in a police room so it's a kind of tease, a hint that someone they know might know something secret. C) Mention budgets. Most voters have a strong response to that issue—either there's too much money or not enough."

Brenda agreed. "And watch the voter. If their eyes narrow when you mention the complaints, they're probably anti-cop, so run with that. Watch their hands; if they clench them they're feeling strong emotion. Watch their feet: are they being defensive? Watch them and tailor your message."

And much, much more. I learned a lot from both of them and I learned more when we stopped for lunch at a greasy spoon six blocks from my home. Over acid coffee and kielbasa sausage in a kaiser bun with the best french fries I'd ever had we talked. And then the two of them took the entire electoral district apart verbally and on a map they laid out on the table.

Benda ate tiny bites while she talked. "District 3. Basically the northwest corner of the city, wealth in the western part, poverty in the centre and south. Lots of crime to be concerned with. It's the second most crime-prone part of the city after the city centre. Some shootings, lots of break and enter of homes, lots of car thefts, lots of graffiti, lots of marijuana grow operations. So it's a crime-prone area. However, lots of complaints against the cops over the past ten years. So it's not an ignorant area. They are aware of their rights in general."

Dean had finished his lunch and ordered three slices of pie chosen at random. "Right. Mostly a masculine district—lots of families, lots of immigrants, lots of self-created businessmen working out of their homes or in small businesses. The immigrants are mostly from Asia and two factors work with them in our eyes: A) They have a cultural history of distrusting cops. And B) Immigrants generally vote to support the powers that be. Not sure how to handle that."

He dealt the pie to all of us and I found I could eat it, to my surprise; normally I wasn't all that fond of desserts. But the politicking was hard work and so I ate the pie and was still hungry.

Brenda cleared her throat. "You were fine today, Monty, just fine. But remember, you only have a few seconds to be memorable and you have to be memorable. When you meet the voter look them directly in the eye and think positive thoughts only. Imagine the voter is beautiful and powerful and believe that."

Dean polished off his coconut cream and said, "Let's roll."

And we were back at it. At one house I received a copy of the *Watchtower* from an ecstatic young man, a Jehovah's Witness who assured me it was full of good news I wanted to hear. I agreed to read it if he would consider voting for me and he felt that was equitable.

At another house a four-year-old shot me with a water gun through the screen door and Brenda wordlessly produced a disposable towel about one foot by two from her purse and let me clean myself while Dean talked to the mother.

I handed her the towel when I was done. "Nice."

"Isn't it? A Lightload towel. Disposable."

"What else do you have in the bag?"

"Everything. I believe in being prepared."

"A Boy Scout motto."

"Yep. I used to date them."

"When you were younger?"

"No." She turned a bland face towards me and I decided I liked her. Which made me hope she wasn't the one leaking information to Devanter. Dean came back from the house and said, "She'll vote for you and isverysorryfortheactionsofherson."

He said the last quickly and we kept going.

Near the end of the day one of the last houses we came to was a small-framed one where the young woman, maybe eighteen, who opened the door, listened to my spiel and said: "Fantastic. I'll vote for you if you speak me the truth to the following question."

"Okay."

"Would you like to see my breasts?"

Nothing was going to shock me today but that was close and I just stared at the woman and finally said, "Sure."

She showed me and they were very nice and I told her so.

After a minute she pulled down her shirt and closed the door and I went back to Brenda and Dean.

They started to say something and I said, "Enough."

They agreed. After fourteen hours I was ready to collapse but they were still going strong as they dropped me off at my home. Brenda took their car and went off to compile data at their office and Dean walked away on foot towards Main Street. When they were both out of sight I pulled off my jacket, put on a dark green windbreaker and trotted off after Dean, keeping a half block back.

He never veered, just headed straight towards Main and then took a right. He also never looked back or around and finally turned into a sports bar. I followed a minute later and found him with his arms around a tall, good-looking blonde beside the hostess stand. She resisted him for a second and then kissed him passionately and I faded back and out.

In a nearby bowling alley I used a payphone over the racket and roar of the pin setters and the balls on the hardwood floor. I had the number of the local right wing flake radio station handy and I got through to the night talk show.

"Hi, Jim? This is Action Jackson, you remember me. Long time listener, regular caller. Just wanted to drop a line supporting Rumer Illyanovitch. He's running for chief cop commissioner. He's solid, a good egg, and he can take care of the chinks and niggers and kikes. He knows where they all stand and where they should go! Anyhow, great show!"

Then I hung up and went home.

#23

Nothing happened about the Shy Man and I kept campaigning, answering phone calls, doing interviews and otherwise being a good political animal. In between I polished the security of the house until it was practically perfect and worked at spotting the cops around our house. At the same time I was always trying to find the Shy Man.

I found the cops, a rotating series of six men and women working in pairs. One pair on the street in a car, one across the street and down the block in the church tower (they were probably very hot because the church did not have air conditioning) and one across the back alley in a rundown bungalow that no one had ever rented or bought. I knew what the surveillance rooms would be like. Lawn chairs and coolers, microphones and tape recorders, telescopes and newspapers, paperbacks and notebooks, and everywhere piles of pizza boxes and take-out containers. In the past I had broken into those kinds of rooms two or three times, just to find out what the cops really knew.

I imagined I found the Shy Man everywhere but I was never sure. I imagined him in the face of the paper delivery boy, in the jogging fatness of a man trying to recapture his youth, in the tired stride of a meter reader and in the shifty glances of an erstwhile car thief who gave up when he spotted the cops staked out at street level.

I felt the criminal's paranoia start to seep into my skin and I welcomed it reluctantly. Everyone was against me and Claire and Fred and that was okay. I like long odds and my bad guy optimism buoyed me. But that was psychotic so I stopped thinking that way and went back to watching everyone and everything around me.

And when I had down time I kept trying to get my mind into that of another kind of killer.

On Wednesday, I spent the day campaigning, talking and arguing, absorbing facts and thinking. Then I went home and made roast potatoes, corn and a leg of lamb I'd bought from a butcher. I hadn't wanted the leg of lamb but it was the only way he'd let me put up a poster in his shop and I'd charged it to the campaign.

At 7:00 we got a package from a delivery company. It was handed to me by an angry woman in her mid-thirties who accepted my signature balefully and then ruined the effect entirely by wishing me a cheery good-night.

Claire and Fred watched as I went into the backyard under the street light just in case it was a bomb. I had shot the street-light out (okay, Claire had) with a blowgun the year before but the city crew had replaced it and it gave me some light to work with. I also had my pocket knife, a pair of needle-nose pliers and a 6 D cell Maglight flashlight I had bought while shopping with Virgil. The machined aluminum flashlight was shock and water resistant and pumped out 57,000 candlepower with the xenon bulb, which basically made it an x-ray machine. It also weighed three pounds, was nineteen and a half inches long, about two inches in diameter and made for a handy club—as most cops could attest.

With the light in hand I went over every inch of the package and decided it was wrapped in strange brown paper, tied with strange brown twine and weighed too little to carry anything really dangerous.

When I opened it I found a cardboard box with a bouquet, but not a normal bouquet. There were garlic bulbs, big orange fleshy flowers, long sprigs of tiny pink flowers I couldn't identify, some walnuts and holding everything together were twists of fresh grass. It was bizarre and while I was staring at it Claire called, "We got another one."

The package had come from a different delivery company and I opened that one the same way and stared some more. In the box were more dark red roses, but along with them were sprigs of waxy leaves and bright white berries that looked like pearls, red and pink flowers with long yellow growths in the middle, red and white big-headed flowers that looked to be the same species and some pink flowers with very long thin petals. Wrapped around everything were sprigs of dark green plant that smelled like pickles.

I showed it to Claire and she didn't understand either. Then we both locked the house up tight and slept uneasily.

The florist up on Main the next morning was young and pretty and looked at me like I was an idiot, so I repeated myself. "What are these?"

"Orange lilies. And the long pink flower buds are amaranthus. And that is garlic and the others are walnuts. While this," she held it up for me to see, "is what we call grass."

"And these?"

"Roses. Hybrids. Mistletoe, a nice specimen. Japonica flowers, not terribly common. Chrysanthemums, very common. A spider flower, not terribly common and then dill. Used in pickling."

"Thank you. Do they mean anything to you?"

"Nothing at all. Very strange bouquets. Someone with an odd sense of humour?"

"Thanks again. May I put up a poster?"

"For you to be our police commissioner? No, I don't think so. You're kind of weird."

"But I am cute and charming."

"True."

"And what if I buy some flowers?"

"Then sure, you can put up a poster entirely because of your cuteness and charm."

"Thank you."

I bought a bouquet of twelve white roses with baby's breath and sent them to a TV news reporter named Mildred Penny-something. She had huge breasts and was given many, many scoops by cops who apparently liked her lisp. I, personally, liked her large breasts.

#24

In the evening there was a debate scheduled between me and Rumer at a nearby high school gymnasium. Because of that my minders let me stop early and go home to shower and get ready.

As they dropped me off I turned to Brenda. "You have to understand, this is as pretty as I get."

She smiled. "Try harder. So what are you going to do?"

"In the debate? I'm going to attack very hard on the corruption of the police and their inefficiency."

Brenda looked surprised and I thought about what I had said and dismissed it. Attacking the cops directly would never work; I'd just alienate half the audience. But I had no better idea so I said it and decided to come up with something else.

Brenda stopped and I went inside and took a nap and a shower. Afterwards I went out and looked through a file of photos and notes that Brenda had provided of Rumer speaking at events—in one he wore his police dress blues, in another he wore a dark blue power suit, in another he wore a kilt, in another he wore a black suit. In all of them he looked sober and respectable and a member of the power structure.

I thought about my own image and decided not to shave.

When I was clean I went through my closet and picked my clothes with care. Rumer always looked professional, competent, respectable and reliable, so he would probably go for the same kind of look again. I wanted something to contrast—I wanted smart, streetwise and rebellious but I did not want to look scary. For that reason I put on freshly pressed black dress slacks, black oxfords, a dark blue dress shirt and a very old-style battered brown leather jacket that retained a certain class despite its age. Which was only fair since it had cost me $3,000 new ten years before.

I wanted to look hep, smart, Joe everybody, someone you might want to have a beer with.

When I was ready I gathered up my notes and walked downstairs where Claire was watching Fred and the kids and talking business with Veronica. Veronica whistled when I came in and Claire muttered, "Down, girl."

I charged Chinese takeout to the campaign and we all ate, after which it was time to go to the gym. Veronica stayed and worked on accounts while Claire, Fred and I walked to the high school.

Because of publicity, news reports and general curiosity the gym was already crowded when we arrived. Claire looked at me nervously. "Are you doing okay?"

"I'm just fine." My teeth were gritted and I realized how stressed I actually was. I didn't like crowds. Crowds meant an absence of anonymity, and danger. I took a deep breath and faked calm as we moved to the front where three podiums had been set up. A thin, colourless man in a pale blue suit that matched his eyes introduced himself as Jim something, the moderator, and showed Claire and Fred to two chairs right in front.

"Mr. Haaviko. You have the podium on the left. Mr. Illyanovitch has the one on the right. I hope that's all right?'

"Wonderful. Thank you, Jim—may I call you Jim?"

"Certainly. Now we start with a brief announcement from me. Then you both make general remarks. Then we start. Each of you will have an opportunity for rebuttal. At the end the audience can ask questions."

"Who speaks first?"

Jim looked uncomfortable. "It doesn't matter, not really."

I climbed up on the stage and looked down at about 100 grey metal chairs that were slowly filling with middle-aged men and women. I'd come early on purpose to get a moment with Jim so I turned to him slowly and reasonably. "Well. If it doesn't matter can I go first?"

Jim hesitated and then nodded and I knew everything was going to be just fine.

Within twenty minutes the rest of the gymnasium filled up with reporters with cameras and microphones taking polite spaces in the back. With ten minutes to go Rumer Illyanovitch himself showed up, a six-foot-two-inch man with wide shoulders and waist and a delicate step as he moved through the crowd. His wife came in beside him; a slightly shorter brunette in a plain black dress, and behind them came Alastair Reynolds with his foot in a cast and a cane in his hand.

Rumer's wife and Alastair sat down near Claire and then Jim went forward to speak with Rumer and lead him to the microphone. On the way Rumer spoke intently to Jim and he nodded slowly and then faster. When Rumer was set Jim came towards me. "Mr. Haaviko? Mr. Illyanovitch would like to make the opening remarks. Is that all right?"

"No."

That made Jim pause. "No?"

"No. I would really like to go first. It's important to me. Mr. Illyanovitch has spoken on many occasions to the public. I have not. He has expressed his message. I have not. Also, to be petty and juvenile, I got here first and you said I could go first."

Jim looked pissed but turned and went back to Rumer to tell him. Then he went to his microphone, tapped it and announced, "Good evening everyone, we are here to listen to a debate between Mr. Montgomery Haaviko and Mr. Rumer Illyanovitch. Both men are running for the position of commissioner of the new police commission and this is the first in a series of debates they, and other candidates, will be having prior to the election on September 13."

Rumer looked stunning in a dark blue suit and brilliant white shirt, he looked professional and competent and trustworthy. His skin was tanned and carefully maintained and his hair had a slight wave. The nails of his hands peeked over the edge of the podium and were buffed and slightly polished.

I took a deep breath and started to talk into the mike.

#25

Good evening everybody, thanks for coming. My name is Montgomery Uller Haaviko. I have also been known as Sheridan Potter, Igor Worley, Gerry Timmins and Samuel Parker in the past. I am an ex-thief and former criminal."

The whole room was silent and then someone coughed.

"I've been arrested for assault, arson, uttering threats, theft, breaking and entry, smuggling, possession of weapons, dangerous driving, resisting arrest, fraud, possession of controlled substances, sale of controlled substances, attempted murder and murder amongst others. In the past eleven years I've done eight of them in prison."

I waited but no one said anything. I knew Dean and Brenda were in the audience and I wondered what they thought of my spiel. I had not checked it with them at all.

"I've been addicted to alcohol and drugs of all sorts, from heroin on down. You name it and I've tried just about every vice imaginable."

I looked down. Claire was in the front row with a slight

smile. She caught my eye and nodded slightly and I went on, "Now I live in your city. I have a wife, a son and pets. I have a home. I have a life. And I would like to be your police board commissioner because I can tell you from personal experience that the current system does not work. It is time for a change."

There were a few murmurs of agreement.

"Our current justice system puts people in prison at a phenomenal rate. And they come out and nothing has changed. Then they look around and go back to being bad guys because that is what they know. Even if they wanted to change they cannot. And they come out with a profound contempt for the legal system and the police. And that contempt has to change as well."

That got some applause. I checked my notes.

"Between 2003 and 2007 the number of men, women and children in Manitoba prisons increased to over 1,800 from over 1,400. Right now there are over 2,100 men, women and children in a prison system designed for 1,600. Manitoba has the second highest rate of incarceration in Canada with Saskatchewan beating us. Yet we continue to feel afraid."

There were fewer murmurs of agreement to that. There was also some grumbling.

"So we can make a change and we can start with the police force, because it does not work. And we can make it work in a way to make the streets safe. We can make the police more effective and more efficient."

That got a much stronger response.

"So vote for me. It's time for change."

Rumer Illyanovitch waited until the applause died before he started to speak. "My opponent is very passionate," He paused to let it sink in and then went on, "and very WRONG.

Crime in this city is out of control! Gangs deal drugs to our children, an incompetent justice system gives house arrest to killers and our mothers and wives and daughters are no longer safe to walk the streets. And my opponent wants to limit the powers of police? We should be expanding them, not curtailing them!"

He glared at the audience and then visibly got control of himself. "A vote for my opponent is a vote for anarchy. For chaos. A vote for me is a vote for law and order. I will make the police stronger. I will make the thieves and rapists and drug dealers hide. I will make the city safer."

The applause was deafening and Rumer started in on me. "You state that there is a problem with the police force?"

"Yes. I'll go farther than that. I'll state that the people don't trust their police."

Rumer looked across at me and narrowed his eyes. "And how do you explain the fact that the number of complaints to the Law Enforcement Review Agency about the police dropped in 2007 compared to earlier years?"

That was an easy one; Dean had fed me those facts and figures. "Simple. 2006 was a bad year for the police. The police got into a feud with a group of bicyclists during their annual protest ride over cycling safety and those bicyclists complained. It's that simple. In 2007 the police did not confront the bicyclists and so the bicyclists did not complain about the police. The result was many fewer complaints."

Rumer swelled with anger but I raised my voice. "Most Winnipeggers have given up on their police. They no longer believe they are accountable for their actions."

Rumer was dismissive. "The system worked. Public inquiries are called when the people complain."

I pointed a finger at Rumer. "Public inquiries are called

when the police and the Crown make mistakes. And Manitoba has more public inquiries than any other province and the majority of them deal with the actions of their police."

I let my words hang in the air and turned to the audience. "That is what I mean when I say the public does not trust the police."

Rumer tried to interrupt and I just got louder again. "People don't TRUST the police. We, the people, expect our police to be professional. We expect our police to be honest. That's pretty much it. We're not getting either honesty or professionalism and so the people do not trust their police."

The moderator was gesturing to me to shut up and finally he cut off my mike but I just raised my voice some more. "And that lack of trust is a goddamned shame! That's just wrong. We should trust our police. And we don't. So we need to change what's happening. And we need to change it at a grassroots level!"

My voice echoed in the auditorium and then I was silent. Down front Claire nodded and Fred clapped.

Jim said sternly, "Mr. Haaviko, there are rules to debates and you are required to follow them."

I looked at him and imagined breaking his kneecaps, and then I lowered my head. "Sorry. I'm new at this."

He was satisfied and turned to Rumer. "Sir. Your turn."

"Thank you. I would like to say that most Winnipeggers do trust their police. I would say that my opponent is repeating lies and falsehoods."

I raised my hand and said calmly, "May I speak?"

The moderator was surprised; I guess he was ready for me to rant. "Why?"

"Mr. Illyanovitch is making a mistake. I wish to correct it."

Jim looked blank and finally said, "Certainly."

"Thank you. Mr. Illyanovitch, I am not telling a lie. I am giving an opinion. There's a difference. Let me ask you something: do police officers rely on each other?"

"Yes. With their lives."

"That requires trust."

"Yes. Absolute trust."

"Absolute trust. Good term. Now, do the police ever break the law?"

"Certain bad cops have been found in the past, yes, but it is rare."

"And who turned them in?"

"Who turned them in? Other cops."

I had the paper in front of me memorized but I looked at it anyway. "Three decades ago a woman was murdered here in the city and a man was arrested. The man went through three trials and four years in prison before being cleared of the murder and paid $2.6 million in compensation. The report criticized the unfortunate acts and omissions of some police officers. Two decades ago a man was shot to death by a police officer. The police department cleared the shooter. An official inquiry did not. Two decades ago a man was murdered and another was arrested. An official inquiry found flaws in the actions of the police and the Crown and paid the imprisoned man $4 million in compensation. Shall I continue?"

"What do those have to do with anything?"

"Simple. There is a pattern. Inquiries found miscarriages of justice in each case on behalf of the police and the Crown. Yet the police did not catch any of the miscarriages prior to the inquiries."

"Those were unique circumstances. And justice was done in each case."

"True. I would argue that three unique circumstances form

a pattern that should be examined. But I digress; no charges were ever laid against any police officers, right?"

"None."

"Why?"

"Why what?"

"Why were no charges laid? A miscarriage of justice occurred in each case but the police, the investigative branch, could not investigate. The police could not determine who should be brought to trial and that is not right."

Rumer held up his hand and the moderator stopped me. "Mr. Illyanovitch. You wanted to say something?"

"Yes. The police are professional, thoughtful, respectful and brave. They take care of dangers to society. They enforce the law of the many and protect the rights of the few. You obviously don't understand that the role of the police commission should support the police, not hinder them."

The moderator turned to me and I responded, "Exactly! That is what I am supporting and what you are fighting."

Rumer was surprised and his hands fluttered to the pages in front of him. I went on. "Police are doing an impossible task and must trust each other implicitly all the time. Yet we expect them to investigate each other. To effectively spy on each other. We sow dissent by doing that. We make it impossible for them to do their job."

I looked over the audience. "It is a legal principle that a husband cannot testify against a wife or a wife against a husband. And the relationship of the police to each other is possibly equally strong—we always hear the term 'brother' used by the police, for example. And one purpose of the commission is to oversee an independent investigative system so the police will never have to investigate themselves again."

Rumer spoke up. "That's ..."

I let the moderator shush him and went on, "After all, there seems to be a pattern here. When will it stop? The strength of the police, their traditions, their loyalty, precludes them from watching themselves. Yet Mr. Illyanovitch comes to you from a police background and wants to be chief of an organization designed to moderate the police. Yet he is a police officer and he will still treat the police as brothers. He has to do so. He is a police officer; he will always be a police officer. The police are his brothers and deserve his loyalty."

I paused. "How could he ever be fair when his brothers are threatened with arrest? You see how hard he fights to protect them here and now. The loyalty that makes him a great police officer makes him a lousy police commissioner. This is why you should vote for me. Because that vote is a vote for change."

#26

Pandemonium ensued and I had a drink of water. Rumer waited it out and clenched his fingers over and over again on the podium. From where I was I could almost swear he was growling.

Jim turned to Rumer and said, "You may begin."

"You started young." Rumer held up a sheet of paper and gestured towards me.

"Yes."

"As a criminal. AS A THIEF."

His voice echoed but I just nodded politely. This whole thing was kind of like a court case and I was used to listening instead of participating. It was kind of fun to be an actual participant. Rumer had apparently wanted me to react in a more aggressive fashion because he looked unhappy and then went on, "When you were sixteen you robbed a pharmacy and attacked the pharmacist with a hatchet. A year later you stabbed a female police officer with a screwdriver while selling her ecstasy."

He stared at me and waved the paper. "Should I go on?"

"Sure."

"You were a member of Los Apaches, a street gang in Vancouver."

"No."

"You were a ... what?"

"I was never a member." I turned to the audience. "I didn't make it all the way to being a full member. I was a prospect. But I got kicked out for disobeying orders. They felt I didn't show enough respect."

There was silence and then some people in the room started to laugh. I turned back to Rumer. "Where did you get that information?"

Rumer just grinned tightly and I turned back to the audience. "Mr. Illyanovitch is holding a list of crimes I committed while I was a juvenile. That information is sealed by court order to allow the juvenile, in this case me, to start fresh when they become an adult. So Mr. Illyanovitch is holding something the courts will be very interested in. I, myself, cannot access that file. So how is it that Mr. Illyanovitch has it here and now?"

I waited but Rumer had nothing to say so I turned back to the audience. "However. What he said is true. I was a violent man and a violent child. I was a thief and many other things, most of them bad. Now I am not."

I held my hands out to the sides. "All that is in the past. Let's leave it there. Consider the future, consider this: police make mistakes sometimes, that's a fact. If you or I make a mistake the damage is limited but a police officer making a mistake, breaking the law or looking away, can do an awful lot of damage."

Rumer tried to speak but I just kept going.

"And other cops are forced to watch and stay silent because of loyalty. A loyalty that they must possess in great measure in order to do their job properly. And never forget that their job is to arrest people and provide a good case for the Crown to prosecute. Make no mistake that their job is very hard, almost impossible."

I glanced at the page in front of me.

"I'm going to list some names. These are people convicted of murdering children."

I named them and there was silence in the room. I waited a few seconds and went on, "All convicted due to the flawed testimony of a pathologist who was later discredited in a public inquiry. For years police knew there was something wrong with the man but they kept referring cases his way because it was a quick, reliable way for them to do their jobs. Which was to arrest people and send them to trial and prison. This happened in another province but it shows a pattern."

Rumer quieted down and the moderator waited for me to finish.

"There are other people, some convicted forty years ago because a cop didn't like hippies. Another convicted two years ago because a cop didn't like Indians. I could go on."

The moderator said, "You should wrap it up, Mr. Haaviko."

"Certainly. I want the police commission to watch the police so they can focus on being police. And the police commission cannot do its job if Mr. Illyanovitch is in charge."

I waited but Rumer still had nothing to say.

I turned and addressed the gymnasium. "Something is wrong. We are not getting justice now. Something has to change. It's time for a change and this commission is the start. And, if you vote for me, I will be the agent of that change."

Some applause and a few boos and catcalls and then it was

Rumer's turn. He stepped out from behind his lectern and faced the audience with his hands clasped behind his back.

"My name is Rumer Illyanovitch. I was a Canadian soldier wounded twice in Somalia and the Balkans and I left the forces with the rank of lieutenant."

He brought his hands in front of him. "And I was a police officer who retired with the rank of sergeant."

He brought his feet together. "I have always protected the people of Canada and the people of this city. If you elect me as chief commissioner I will continue to serve and protect."

He lowered his voice. "That is all that I ask."

The applause was deafening. Hell, I almost joined in myself.

#27

Down on the floor Claire gave me a hug and a kiss and then whispered, "That man is going to kick your ass."

"Wanna bet?"

Her eyebrow went up. "What's your wager?"

I whispered a complicated obscene act that was patently illegal and required a high degree of organization. She nodded. "'Kay."

"The bet is that he won't win."

Claire narrowed her eyes. "You're betting that Rumer won't win?"

"Yep."

"In exchange for ..." She repeated the act with a questioning inflection.

"Yep, that's the one."

We shook hands and turned to the small crowd who were pressing forward. Dean and Brenda had appeared as well. Both had notebooks in hand and looked thoughtful, which I assumed meant they were going to chew my ass off.

I ignored them and turned to the rest of the people who wanted to talk to me, three men and two women. Behind them were a television reporter and a camerawoman along with a man with a tape recorder in one hand and a fancy camera around his neck. I ignored the press and talked to the women first and then the men. In each case I shook their hands with both of mine while meeting their eyes directly and smiling broadly.

The smile I had been practising since I'd started the campaign and the handshake as well. Shaking someone's hand with both of mine gave me control of the person if necessary. It may have looked warm and friendly but it allowed me to move the person along with a little arm pressure if needed. And staring into the person's eyes allowed me to gauge them.

The first woman was middle-aged and middle-class with a wide mouth and a nice smile. She wanted to know more about my criminal past. "So did you do everything you mentioned?"

"Pretty much. Plus other stuff. But I did all my jail time plus some extra so I feel pretty good about myself."

She was puzzled. "Extra?"

"Sometimes extra charges and extra time get added. It's how things get cleared up."

"You're not angry?"

"Oh no. Not now. So can I expect your vote?"

She pushed her head forward. "I think so."

The only other person who wanted to talk to me was a blond man in his early twenties who looked very familiar. As I was placing the face Dean swayed past me and said, "Be gentle. Cameras everywhere."

I kept my poker face. The blond man came in front of me and jutted his jaw out. "You're a piece of shit." He said it loudly and it made heads turn.

My hands were already in front of me and my feet were

braced so I kept the smile in place and said, "And you're an asshole. Will you vote for me anyway?"

The reporters and Claire laughed, but no one else did. The blond man flushed red, balled his left fist and leaned back to swing. I let him and it was the slowest, softest punch ever. I just stared at it. There were maybe six blocks I could use and two counter-blows and two ways to avoid it entirely. As it travelled towards me I saw Dean's face was painted with a slight smile and so I chose to step forward and let the punch pass under my left arm.

Up close the blond guy smelled like good aftershave and expensive soap. When my face was an inch from his I said, "You wanna stop this?"

He didn't and I wrapped my left arm around his right, going under and over and then I had him in a shoulder lock a drunk lesbian had used on me once. I braced and forced him backwards towards the ground. Before he could hit I slipped my left knee under his back.

When he hit my knee he grunted and I smelled spearmint mouthwash.

Again I leaned down. "I can break your back or your arm from here. Stop. Please."

The stupid smile was still on my face and the blond man stopped fighting and held up his other hand, open.

"Hey, it's cool."

"It is. You gonna behave?"

"Yeah."

I let go of his arm and let him fall while I stood back. Two cops had appeared from nowhere and stood over the man. "Is there a problem?"

"No." I looked at the man on his back. "Are you having a problem?"

"No." I finally recognized the young man and helped him to his feet. Dean had talked to him for twenty minutes this morning outside the lunchroom where we were having coffee during canvassing. I repeated myself, "No."

The cameras had caught the whole thing and I saw Dean out of the corner of my eye and he smiled just a little more.

That stunt had attracted a crowd and the camerawoman and reporter came in. I recognized her from the fairground and smiled. "Good to see you again."

"Mr. Haaviko. Can we ask some questions?"

"Certainly. What is your full name, by the way?"

She was tiny and tough and her smile was cold and I quite liked it,. "Candy Sawchuck."

The camerawoman must have been set up already. She planted her camera on the tripod and started filming. Candy turned to me immediately. "We're talking with Mr. Montgomery Haaviko, ex-thief, currently running for the position of chief police commissioner. He's made some dramatic claims about the dysfunctional state of the police."

She waited but I had nothing to add and she had to ask, "So how would you change the system?"

"I would eliminate the Law Enforcement Review Agency because no one should be tried twice and that's what LERA does to the police. It's not fair. It's a provincial organization but we can start there."

Rumer had wandered over and was listening but he didn't react. The agency gave a get-out-of-jail-free card to the police but it was a damn hard thing to defend to civilians. So Rumer didn't do anything but stand there smiling.

Candy nodded and I went on, "I would also propose the

establishment of an independent organization to review claims of wrongful imprisonment like they have in the UK."

Rumer couldn't stand it and blurted out, "That would never work!"

Candy held her mike to him and made him repeat himself and then I answered, "It's been around since 1995 in the UK. It's received more than 10,000 submissions and has referred about 400 to the courts. Sure beats the hell out of all these justice inquiries going one at a time, don't you think?"

Rumer was quiet so I went on, "I would also arrange to have every single police interrogation on film, and in fact I would do that for every single police/civilian interaction. As a society we seem to be willing to put cameras everywhere so I'd put them on the police as well. Then there would never, ever be a question of who said what, when. Those are the places where I'd start and those we could begin immediately and cheaply. The cost of one public inquiry would pay for all the hardware."

I turned back to Rumer. "And what would you do?"

He didn't have an answer.

Candy waited for awhile and then shut down the camera, thanked me and left. Claire and I had to wait though and shake hands and smile.

When everyone had left Dean handed me an envelope. "A present. Take tomorrow off."

"Can I speak with you?" He nodded and we went into a corner and I went on, "Your idea about the blond guy?"

"Uh-huh. I thought of it this morning and just went with it. What did you think?"

"It worked. Warn me next time."

"You bet. Now take tomorrow off."

So I did.

#28

Claire and I spent most of the next day in bed.

When we weren't fooling around we babysat, played with Fred, made shepherd's pie and played cribbage.

When Fred fell asleep we made love until Claire fell asleep.

#29

I still couldn't sleep.
  Wired on fear, waiting for the Shy Man.
  Watching my family.
  Waiting.
  And, in some strange way, enjoying the sensation of being
absolutely and totally alive.

#30

The next day I was back on the campaign trail with Brenda and Dean. Claire was at home watching the kids and doing real estate paperwork with the doors locked and alarmed. I had also bought each of us a disposable cell phone so we could keep in touch no matter what, and that helped reduce the stress level. Of course the dozens of cops around helped too.

I had about three hours of messages to deal with the next morning and I listened to them all with a pad of paper handy to take notes and doodle. The calls were mostly from radio stations and reporters asking for sound bites and bits of brilliance along with anything controversial. However, I had very little brilliance in me and so I just listened and made notes. Then at nine I went with the flow, which consisted of heading out with Dean and Brenda. Once I was in the car they told me they had decided it was time to hit another electoral district.

They had chosen the eastern district so that's where we went, and as Dean drove, Brenda filled me in.

"Okay. We are heading into a nice residential area but, overall, this district is rough for us. It is mostly very conservative, at least that's how they vote federally, provincially and locally. Most of the residents are blue collar and they have a low crime rate. They also have a low rate of police complaints and a low rate of civic involvement in general. This is Rumer's stronghold, along with the far south end of the city, but this district might be able to be turned. There is considerable unhappiness having to do with the economy and job loss. That means the residents are starting to distrust the powers that be that got them into this mess in the first place."

"Ah?"

I sat in the back seat and thought, then borrowed a pen from Dean and made some notes on the back of one of my pamphlets and came to a total of $9.1 million, which I doubled and then divided by $38,002.28, the starting salary of a fourth-class police constable. The final number I got was 479. I circled that and we started in on a street of well-maintained single-level bungalows.

The first thing I noticed was the large number of garage sale signs everywhere. The second thing I noticed was how few people actually wanted to talk to me. For the first fifteen houses either no one was there or else no one answered the knock. Dean marked streets off on his map as Brenda went up to try another door, moving carefully up the sidewalk because no home owner wants to see their lawn despoiled by an unwanted visitor.

Dean looked up. "So few people. Kind of sad, really; these are the working poor. Both man and woman have to work full time to support a house they never visit and kids they never see and then they wonder why their life is shit when they finally stop working and retire."

It was more philosophical than I'd expected from the man and I glanced at him sideways as I pulled off my jacket and tie. He noticed my look and shrugged. "Sorry, Monty, it just gets to me sometimes. Everyone hustles and no one gets anywhere. The sad-ass lie in the centre of the system."

"Yeah." I stared at the rows of houses. "Let me tell you a story. Guy I knew was from a little village in Jamaica, a couple of miles from Kingston. He used to haul garbage away from the excavation of Port Royal, the pirate city that got drowned for its wickedness, and worked other part-time jobs like that, but he also fished and sold shit to tourists. He had it pretty good. He wanted to make his million, so he came to Canada and did bank robberies and insurance scams. He always talked about home, how peaceful it was, how cheap the rum was, how pretty the girls were. Someone asked him, so why are you here? And he said, to make my million and retire."

Brenda found someone and waved me up but I bent to tie an already tied shoelace. "Anyhow, someone asked, retire where? And he said, Jamaica, back to where it's peaceful and the rum is cheap and the girls are pretty. And we said, you're nuts, you leave paradise to make money so you can go back to paradise which doesn't cost to live in."

I stood. "And it was like a thunderbolt. He just stood up and walked out of the safe house and got on the next flight home and that was it."

Dean nodded. "Yeah. That's the lie. Work to get what you want. Not enjoy what you've got. Oh well, give 'em hell."

At the door was a thick-bodied white man with his left arm in a sling.

"Good morning, sir."

He ignored my hand when I offered it and I pulled it back.

"Morning. Wanted to see you in person but I got no intention to vote for you."

"Well, thanks for seeing me anyway." I turned to walk away and he called me back.

"Aren't you going to try to convince me of why you're the right person?"

I shook my head. "No way. You're a busy man. You've made up your mind to vote for Rumer, right?"

"Yes. He's a cop, you're a thief. He's honest, you're a liar. No offence."

"None taken. Hmmm. Can I ask you one question and tell you two things?"

The man was solid, with layers of fat on top of muscles, there were bags under his eyes and his fingers were thick with yellow calluses He nodded reluctantly. "Sure. But my mind's made up."

"All right. First, are you safe here?"

"Safe? What do you mean?"

"From crime."

He laughed loud and hard. "Fuck no! Little punk shits spray crap on my garage, my van got stolen last year and my daughter got groped by some perv downtown last month. Crime is a fucking problem and Rumer can deal with it."

"Sure. Rumer is a cop, through and through, and always will be. In the past twenty years there have been three public inquiries because of cop and prosecution mistakes. That's cost the city and province $18 million."

The man nodded. "Shit happens, so?"

"That $18 million would have paid the annual salary of 479 policemen. But we had to have the inquiries because shit happened. That's what this commission is about, stopping shit before it happens and stopping it cheaply and fast. Now why should we have a cop in charge of cops? We already know they can't govern themselves."

"Because they've got experience ..."

"Wasting $18 million? Yes, they do. How many chances do you want to give them? I think we should try something new."

The man shook his head. "And that's you? That's putting a fox to guard the hen coop."

"So vote for someone else, not me. I don't give a rat's ass. But don't vote for Rumer. Or we'll keep wasting money. And if we don't have the money, there will be fewer cops on the streets. Which is where they do good."

The man stared at me and started to say something and then changed his mind and said casually, "So how much does a cop make?"

"To start? $38,002.28 is the starting salary of a fourth-class police constable after thirty-seven weeks of paid training. But in eleven years they can become a first-class constable, which pays $73,081.30. Plus overtime and benefits."

The man's face tightened. "How much?"

I told him again and he swallowed and asked, "But they have education, right?"

"The thirty-seven weeks of training, yes. But all they need is a high school degree. Or a general equivalency degree. And you can retire at fifty."

The man swayed and closed his eyes and looked pissed and I went on, "Look. You decide. But you said crime is bad. The system we currently have sure hasn't helped solve that problem and Rumer is all about keeping the course. And the course doesn't look so hot to me."

The man's hand came up slowly and I shook it and looked him straight in the eye. "And have a great day."

On the sidewalk Dean and Brenda were both smiling. We kept walking and she asked, "And how did that go?"

"Fine. I think I understand these folks."

She seemed surprised. "You do?"

I told them what I'd told the man and they nodded. "He's a working guy. Probably with a good paying job that he fought for. Probably with a union backing him up and making salary increases of 1-2 percent per year, increases he has to threaten to strike for every year. Probably a job he started out with as a journeyman apprentice or trainee making very little. And I'm telling him about a job that pays $20 an hour to start and goes up two, three bucks a year until it reaches $40 an hour."

Brenda and Dean looked at each other and I asked, "Do we still have the police recruiting pamphlet?"

We did and I read it as we walked and by the next house I was ready with some more numbers and data. I may not have convinced anyone to vote for me but I sure made a few dozen people start to think in a new way.

When I got back home that night there was a package between the screen and patio doors—I opened it standing there. As I did so I stared into the distance, feeling for anything odd or heavy in the brown paper parcel. Sniffing deeply for anything chemical, listening for anything clicking or whizzing or chirping or preparing to explode. And as I opened it my eyes roved and I saw movement in the car way down the street where the cops were and I saw a shadow appear in the loft above the church.

So I knew the cops were watching and it didn't bother me. It even made me feel safer.

Inside the package was a ten-kilogram box of chocolates from Mordens, a Winnipeg institution and one of the best candy makers in Canada.

They were called Russian Mints and they were delicious. I ate one slowly and looked around.

There was nothing else with the box, no message or note or anything, so I put the box under my arm, took the garbage with me and went inside.

#31

A few days later Brenda and Dean and I were at the University of Manitoba at my insistence.

Dean had been nonplussed when I'd suggested it. "Why are we doing this? The students aren't well known for showing up for civic elections—federal yes, civic not so much." Brenda had agreed and I'd taken Dean aside for a minute.

"We're going for two reasons; it'll get good press and it's a weak spot for Illyanovitch. He has no attachment to the young, educated voters."

Dean had agreed grudgingly and then went about getting permission and spreading the news of my presence on campus far and wide.

While he was gone I told Brenda, "We're here for two reasons; it's not something that Illyanovitch has on his radar and the students are already furious because he supports the cops and the cops raided the protest bike ride two years ago."

She went off to start rounding up students and dragging them to me as I stood in the centre food court near the bookstore.

To my surprise the students had lots of questions and informed opinions and they were enthusiastic. Apparently the cops were a tender spot for them; who knew? For them I kept the idea simple. "Hire me, who's outside the system, to watch how it works and to keep it honest. The cops will watch me intently, so I'll be honest, and I'll watch the cops intently, so they'll be honest." The students and professors liked that.

One professor even quoted someone by saying that kings should have nooses around their necks to keep them upright.

When we were done I told my minders I had to pee and then hit the bookstore. In the anthropology section there was a copy of *Hunting Humans* by Elliot Levin, an anthropologist from Newfoundland, who'd studied serial killers as social phenomena. The book had been recommended to me years before by a wannabe serial killer. I bought it for cash and tucked it down my pants when I went to pee.

Ten minutes later Brenda and Dean and I were headed north.

That night Claire and I were expected at a "Greet the Chief" meeting in Wolseley. I didn't know the area well so I asked Brenda and she said, "Granola country. Hippies and hippy wannabes."

We parked Fred with Veronica and took a cab to make sure we'd arrive on time. In the cab Claire leaned close to me and whispered in my ear. I responded in my best prison yard speaking voice, which meant my lips were motionless. Just in case the cabbie was listening.

"Monty, did you call the candy company?"

We crossed the giant rail yard that sits to the north of centre in the city. Dozens of tracks and strings of red and black boxcars stretch for miles to the east and west. The bridge soared over it all and I could feel the warm wind through the open window and smell a hint of rust and diesel fuel.

"Yes. They received cash and an anonymous order. It was dropped in the main office mail box overnight. That's it. They also told me they produce one ton of Russian Mints every three days from October to December."

"That doesn't help us. So, a dead end?"

I hugged her with one arm. "Maybe not. The cops will follow up on it; they saw us get the package. They can order copies of all the surveillance tapes of all the buildings around the head office. They might get a good picture."

"Might? So the odds aren't good?"

"No. Not at all. Question here: why did Veronica want to watch Fred?"

Claire giggled and the noise broke the solemnity of the moment. "She's taking him to the mall with her. She trolls with him."

I looked at her to find out if she was kidding. "Trolls?"

"Trolls. She says that men keep an eye out for single mothers sometimes and look for a woman with a baby but no ring. She says the men think that single mothers are ... ummm."

"What word are you looking for?"

"How about, not shy?"

"Good choice, but a mall? Won't she get mostly eighteen-year-olds?"

"Yes. But she says you can date two or three of those at the same time and it's not too bad. As long as you don't talk to them. And as long as you don't mind the smell of Axe cologne."

We arrived at our location, a huge, four-storey home, and I didn't have to answer.

Inside we found out that the party was not just to meet me but also to deal with community problems, which took a lot of pressure off me. The festivities stretched into the backyard where people had laid out potluck dishes on folding tables under Chinese lanterns. A tall, thin man with a black Vandyke beard and a patch over one eye came up as soon as we arrived. He wore a red velour smoking jacket and introduced himself by saying, "And you must be Montgomery Haaviko, the reformed thief."

"I must, and this must be my wife Claire."

He shook my hand and hers and led me off to meet strange people whom I quite liked.

Lots of great conversation and some fantastic food. Homemade chocolate and roasted pine nut clusters made with all organic ingredients. Tiny cheeseburgers made with bison meat spiced with cinnamon and jalapeno Monterey Jack cheese from a place called Bothwell's. A pomegranate and saskatoon berry punch laced with Indonesian arrack liquor for the brave and with Schweppes ginger ale for me.

The history of Wolseley told by a fat, unhappy woman. "Yes. It all used to be regular homes but then everyone left in the seventies and eighties and it turned into a district of rooming houses. Then a whole new brand of owner started to come in and rebuild a pride in the neighbourhood ..."

The mechanics of crime by a young man in a leather bomber jacket. "And so, crime, real crime, is a reaction against the chains of authority and the morality of the rich ..."

I nodded and agreed and the night went on and more people arrived and left and the food changed to desserts and free-trade coffee and teas that were not from tea but from South African and South American bushes. Plates of tiny cupcakes with cream cheese icing, cranberry/apple butter tarts and thick two-layer brownies sandwiched around fudge.

Claire stopped me while I reached for a brownie and I complained, "Hey!"

She spoke slowly. "Two things. One. It's not on your diet. Two. It's laced with hash. The woman who brought it told me to go easy."

"Ah. Thanks."

She wandered away and I went back to a crowd listening to a young girl reciting T.S. Eliot's poem *The Wasteland*. As the girl was only six, the effect was unnerving. When she was done I applauded and she bowed from the waist. The girl thanked us all for listening and then left to play badminton. I talked with her father, who owned six news websites.

"Well, Mr. Haaviko. What do you think should happen next?"

"Mr. Rhine, the police should not be necessary but they are. They wield a great deal of power in society and deserve the greatest possible oversight. Mr. Illyanovitch would receive their support so I am not sure he would ever be able to treat them with the correct degree of irrespect and doubt."

Rhine smiled and I saw three other people nearby, listening. He gestured broadly. "What do you mean?"

"The essence of our legal system is conflict. The prosecutor attacks to the best of his ability and the defence attorney defends to the best of his ability. In that struggle, with the help of a judge, the truth is supposed to emerge. Yet Mr. Illyanovitch will not fight with the police, he will cooperate. And there will be no judge; Mr. Illyanovitch will hold that position as well."

Mr. Rhine nodded reluctantly and I finished, "So how can there be justice?"

"I see your point. I may not agree, but I see your point."

"A second factor is that I being on the commission will attract intense scrutiny. No one will try anything funny with me being there because of that scrutiny."

"Including yourself?"

I looked at Rhine in amazement. "Me? I'm an ex-thief sir. I'm like a cockroach. You shine a bright light on me and, I assure you, I will behave."

He laughed and I went looking for Claire. We got coffee and took a look inside the house.

Claire linked her arm in mine and we looked at the photograph on the wall above the old fireplace for a long time. It was made up of six separate black and white pictures of a dark-skinned man leaning against a cave wall. He wore a long, flowing robe and his hand rested on the hilt of an ornate dagger tucked into a sash at his waist.

My wife turned to me and frowned. "Just because they call it art and give it the respect art is due does not make it art."

I stared at it for a long time. "I know what I like."

Claire's frown stayed in place. "And?"

"I hate it. It bores me. I hate being bored."

"This is true."

I touched the glass covering the images with my knuckle and Claire sipped some pretty nasty dark roast. I knew because I was drinking the same stuff. Then she asked, "What do you get from it?"

"Hate and disrespect. The subject is minimized and marginalized. He's out of place and out of time. He's wearing a dress. He's living in a cave. He's a fetishist, fondling the hilt of his jambiya."

"Jambiya?"

I touched the image with my knuckle. "The dagger. The

Arabic name for dagger is 'jambiya.' The sheath is curved at the bottom to keep it secure under the sash, the blade itself is actually fairly straight. The hilt is traditionally made of rhino horn and the quality of the hilt defines the status of the owner, the more ornate the better."

"Really?" Claire sounded amused and I turned to catch her smile.

"Really. So we have an image of a man, out of place and out of dress."

Claire drank some more coffee. "So we hate it?"

"Yep."

We went back outside and traded the coffee for more punch. The party had livened up and three teenagers were standing in a patch of grass throwing bowling pins to each other. Which they caught and tossed back to create an intricate pattern amidst laughter and polite applause.

#32

I listened and listened and listened at the party. About problems with gangs and problems with hookers. About meth labs and marijuana grow operations and police arrogance. About the corruption of big business and the intolerance of the wealthy.

So far maybe 100 people had come through the party and I overheard some interesting conversations. Like one between two businessmen wearing tie-dyed t-shirts and ragged cut-off Levi shorts.

"... and then I get an email cease and desist. Can you believe it?"

"No! Wow. So what did you do?"

"I foreclosed on the little shit. Called in my loan approval and cancelled his insurance."

They exchanged fist bumps and I wandered along, thinking. A cease and desist order was a legal paper telling someone to stop doing something or some specific penalty would be enacted—generally a lawsuit. A preventative injunction, for example, would stop the person from doing a single specific thing and a restraining order would keep someone away. Both worked in theory.

I sat on a park bench under an elm, stared up into the sky and watched a few late dragonflies wheel around. As I watched a few darker shapes emerged—bats, I guessed. I knew about injunctions and I couldn't remember the last time I had received one. The conversation between the two men had reminded me of a quote by a guy named Anatole French to the effect that the law forbade the rich as well as the poor to sleep under bridges and to beg.

I had always liked that quote although I disagreed with it on several levels, so I sat there and rested my feet and thought about the conversation. Finally I realized that I had been unaware you could send a cease and desist order by email.

That seemed important, so I filed it away and went back to wandering.

While I was listening to a discussion about shoplifters Claire came up to me again. "You should hear this."

I excused myself and went to a medium-sized woman with a very nice smile in a dashiki printed with gold flowers. She introduced herself as Mrs. Godiva Lightly and laughed. "My father, bless him, had a sense of humour and a profound love of James Bond films and novels. That's how I got my name. People either love it or hate it, no middle ground."

I smiled and she went on, "I was talking about the language of flowers and your wife said that you would want to hear this."

Claire looked at me flatly and sipped a coffee and I turned to Lightly. "Yes. I would love to hear about, what did you call it?"

"The language of flowers. I teach history and language at the University of Winnipeg and the language of flowers is part of one course—it's a Victorian curiosity, earlier actually, but the language was perfected by them in the English world at least. They believed that each type of flower had a meaning so you could send a bouquet promising sexual ecstasy or retribution with some degree of secrecy. Until everyone knew the language, that is."

"Was it common knowledge?"

"Eventually, yes. Books and treatises were written on the subject. It provides fascinating glimpses into what made the English culture tick."

"And what made it tick?"

She gestured. "Profound dissonance in the society. Apollonian prudishness on one hand with piano legs being covered and cliterodectomies being performed if a wife dared to climax while performing her middle-class duty with her eyes shut. And Dionysian excess on the other hand, with a quarter of the female population of London fucking for money, mass abuse of arsenic, cocaine, morphine and hashish, and a superabundance of nipple rings in the sweaty teats of wealthy dowagers."

"Really?" I absorbed what she had said and then asked, "What do Apollonian and Dionysian mean?"

"Apollonian refers to the Greek sun god—it's a kind of chaste, respectful love. Dionysian refers to the Greek god of wine and excess—physical lust and so on. This was the culture that gave us the proud Dr. Frankenstein, the vengeful Miss Havisham, the foreign Count Dracula, the enigmatic Moonstone and the illustrious Mr. Hyde. They are the peoples who raped India, invaded Afghanistan, allowed the Irish potato famine, created concentration camps in the Boer War, got involved in the Zulu wars, tried genocide against the Kalahari Bushmen and so on. All at the same time maintaining a high degree of civility. Two sides of a coin; the proper English culture and the conquest of half the world."

"Fascinating. What about ..." I closed my eyes and remembered the girl in the flower shop and the way she held her head while she recited. "What about orange lilies, amaranthus, garlic, walnuts, grass, red roses, mistletoe, japonica, chrysanthemums, spider flowers and dill?"

Lightly shrugged. "Those are easy. Orange lilies means 'I hate you!' Amaranthus means 'You've got no balls.' Garlic means evil, to be warded off, and walnuts mean stupidity. Red roses sing of love, the darker the colour the guiltier the love, however. Mistletoe means a kiss, of course, we still see that at Christmas but it can also ask for a quick lay. Japonica means sincere love and chrysanthemums mean the same. The spider flower is a request for eloping and dill means pure, sweet lust."

Lightly stared off into space and then cheered up. "Oh! And grass means 'You're a practitioner of the French vice,' which was what the Victorian English called homosexuality. Of course the Victorian-era French called it the English vice."

She beamed as though she had accomplished something. Claire and I thanked her, made our apologies and excuses and finally fled into the late night.

While we waited for a cab Claire leaned against me. "Wonderful. The Shy Man wants to make love to me and he hates you. And apparently he speaks flower."

I hugged her close. "Could be worse."

She looked at me suspiciously. "How so?"

I had no answer so I finally just said, lamely, "I'll come up with something but something could be worse."

Claire bit me and while I was getting her fingers out of my arm I figured out how to really annoy Mr. Devanter and his lovely lawyer.

#33

I slept for about an hour beside Claire and then I went downstairs and brewed coffee and drank two while sitting at the dining room table with the book about serial killers, a pad of paper and several pencils. When I was comfortably awake I lit a candle and put it in front of me, focussed on the flickering light and listened to the sounds of the house.

Thor, the mouse, rustled in its shavings a few feet away. Programmed to be nocturnal by millennia of being the smallest thing on the block, prey to pretty much everything. Crickets outside, carnivorous and delicious to many things but forced by the need to breed to rub legs together and sing. They balanced fucking and breathing together and the loudest bug got the most girls but also had the greatest chance of being eaten. The hum of electricity and gas and water in the walls of the house, the sounds of what amounted to a living entity: breathing, eating, maintaining a constant temperature and excreting. The buzz of cars outside. The soft press of the wind on the house, rushing across the roof and sighing away, the physical manifestation of the atmosphere and the fact that the planet spun in space at less than 1,000 miles an hour and around the sun at 67,000 miles an hour.

Motion compounding motion and sometimes conflicting.

The truth was old planes with their weak engines could stay motionless relative to the ground by flying into a strong wind. And that explorers racing to the North Pole might travel south if the currents picked up the ice sheets they were on. And that an undertow could drown a man if he wasn't careful and didn't understand the rules.

I wrote that down and underlined it.

Then I read the book, skimming it at first and reading in detail where necessary. A crazy cannibal motherfucker (literally) in California, an angry Black man in Texas, an angry preppy extrovert, and others. Each unique. All the same.

I poured some more coffee and thought about the Shy Man. The cops thought he was Caucasian because he preyed upon Caucasian women and because most serial killers were white.

I considered it and decided that they were probably right.

The Shy Man was probably white. I wrote it down and underlined it.

The cops thought the Shy Man was a male because of the rapes and the semen and I thought they were right about that as well. A woman could be a serial killer, although it was rare (like Eileen Wuornos), and a woman could fake the rapes with a dildo, although I hadn't heard of it happening except in bad fiction. And a woman could introduce the sperm from someone else, although again, I had only heard of it in the cases of bad fiction.

So the Shy Man was probably a man. Underline.

The cops thought the Shy Man was solitary because they had never found signs of a second killer. I thought about pairs of killers and ran them through my mind, the Bernardos in Toronto, the Moor Killers in England, the Hillside Stranglers in Los Angeles, a few others. But in those cases the killers had all left traces and there were signs of only one killer with the Shy Man killings.

· The Shy Man was probably one person.

I knew that some serial killers involved a woman; they acted like a lure to bring the victim in close and lull suspicions. The Shy Man though had attacked without subtlety, so no lures or lulls were needed that I could see.

The Shy Man was probably a man.

The cops thought the Shy Man was probably in his forties. He had started killing in the early nineties and most serial killers don't start until they're adults, which meant he had been in his early twenties when he started. I thought about that and agreed.

The Shy Man was probably between thirty-five and fifty.

I poured more coffee.

So the cops had a pretty good image of the Shy Man. An early-middle-aged man, white, and who worked without a partner.

I thought about the city and the notes and statistics that Dean and Brenda had given me and I realized I was talking about somewhere around 50,000 people just inside the city. And maybe another 10,000 within an hour's drive. Way too many suspects.

From the book I knew that most serial killers had similar childhoods. They wet the bed until quite late, they started fires and they tortured animals. And I knew, from personal experience, that most serial killers liked cops and frequently had a kind of fetish about authority, so you could find them as security guards, cops, soldiers and so on.

None of that helped.

For a few seconds I wished I believed in profilers and all that other crap the television and movies feed citizens. The idea that someone could know what goes on in a psychopath's head was ridiculous when you realized that most psychopaths didn't know themselves. Not to say psychopaths didn't have patterns, everyone had patterns. But there was no magic to finding those patterns.

And I wished I believed the police could actually investigate a crime.

But that never happened. Most crimes were solved because of confidential informers or cash rewards or drunken confessions or sheer, unbelievable stupidity.

A solitary psychopath like the Shy Man would be immune to most of those factors. He wouldn't talk to anyone because of his very nature which meant there would be no confidential informers and no one to be attracted by cash rewards. In addition the citizens didn't know a serial killer was out there which meant that there was no one looking for him. There would be no Jimmy Stewart looking out his rear window and no brother to rat out the Unabomber.

In the back of my mind I wondered about telling the press about the Shy Man. Laying everything out and letting the cards fall as they would. It was an option and I filed it away. That kind of chaos might help the situation.

The Shy Man wouldn't confess and he wouldn't make a single dumb mistake because he was enjoying what he was doing. He was having fun. He was planning and plotting and taking his time with his victims.

More coffee, and I thought about the basics. The Shy Man was committing crimes and crimes require certain things: motive, means and opportunity. He had to want to kill, he had to have the tools to kill and he had to have the chance to kill.

His psychopathy gave him a motive. He killed because he liked to inflict pain, probably because it aroused him and allowed him to climax. In between killings he probably fantasized and he probably kept trophies and he probably masturbated. He probably didn't have a steady partner although that was not guaranteed; Citizen X of Russia had had a wife and family at home while he was busy killing children.

I was digressing. So the Shy Man had a motive, in fact he was the motive.

Means meant tools. He needed a gun and knives and rope. One victim had been killed with an old European 9mm parabellum full metal jacketed round fired from a pistol, possibly a Luger or Luger copy. Unfortunately there had been about a billion 9mm parabellum full metal jacketed rounds manufactured in the century plus since the calibre had been invented. And there had been about two million Lugers made, not counting Swiss, Belgian, Spanish and Chinese copies. And the knife used was a glass-bladed one, handmade or an antique, pretty hard to trace but easy to identify once found. And the rope was plain, ordinary manila rope, traced back to a job lot brought into the city in the 1970's and probably stored in someone's basement.

So when the cops found someone with a 9mm pistol and ammunition and a glass-bladed knife and rope in their basement they would probably have a good case for arrest and conviction. This didn't help me because the cops were no closer to catching the fuck than ever.

Opportunity was last. Opportunity for the Shy Man meant meeting his ladies and taking them away to play. So what did they have in common?

Paris, the jeweller in 1992, the flower shop owner in 1995, lawyer and husband in 1997, a model in 1998, a waitress in

2001, he stalked but missed an accountant in 2003 but he caught her and her son in 2005, then a bank teller in 2006. I could omit the husband and son, they were incidentals, they were debris to be cleared out of the way, so that gave me seven victims.

I assumed the cops had run checks to see if they knew each other, if they had gone to the same schools and so on.

But what did they have in common? Each woman was between eighteen and forty. Each woman was white. But what else?

And, the million-dollar question, what the hell did they have in common with Claire?

I filed the question away in the hungry part of my brain and started to make breakfast.

Dawn had come.

#34

On the radio (I had it turned to the right wing flake talk channel) there was an early morning interview with Illyanovitch. The guy doing the interview basically agreed with everything he said and Illyanovitch agreed with everything the interviewer said so the whole thing was kind of pathetic and pointless. What was interesting was that Illyanovitch kept coming back to the same idea, that university students would support me because they distrusted Illyanovitch even though he supported their rights to protest on bicycles as long as the parade route was filed in advance. Wasn't that reasonable, he asked the audience.

After awhile the audience phoned in to agree with him and I turned it off.

"Brenda." I said it out loud and I was kind of sad. I liked Brenda. But she was the only one I had told about talking to the students in reference to the bicycle protest. And I knew someone was leaking stuff to Illyanovitch, so it had to be Brenda. I had thought it was probably Dean but when I'd followed him he'd been kissing a girl, not leaking data. It was circumstantial and light but it was enough for me.

I woke Claire and Fred and took an eight-block walk to a random phone booth that probably wasn't tapped and Reese answered on the first ring. "Morning. The lovely Claire or the full Monty?"

"Let me guess, it's not call display because I'm using a clean phone booth. You gave me my own separate number to reach you? Probably a discreet cell phone?"

"Good guess."

"Someone has been leaking stuff to Illyanovitch and I figured out who."

He was quick. "Why do you think someone's leaking?"

"The debate and today. Illyanovitch had complete records on me; those would have taken time to put together. Also he didn't know about the blond guy trying to punch me, Dean set that up, I think on his own. And I fed Dean and Brenda different information about the university trips and Illyanovitch used the stuff I gave Brenda."

Reese was silent. "Have you spoken to Dean or Brenda? They both came highly recommended. I'd hate to think it was either of them."

"No. I want you to double check. I don't want them to think I know about it. I'm enjoying their paternalistic and insulting way of dealing with me."

He was amused. "And how should I check on them?"

"Call Dean up and see if he told Brenda about his plan to get me punched."

"I can do that."

"And, do you have Brenda's home address?"

I heard him rustling papers and then he said, "Yes."

"I can break in and check her place out."

He laughed. "Interesting approach."

"The word you want is 'direct.'"

"And what would you expect to find?"

"Something linking Brenda to Devanter. Or a chunk of cash."

"No." He paused. "No. No one pays people in unmarked bills in public bathrooms anymore, or however it goes."

It was my turn to be amused. "It happens often. Especially with amateurs and professionals. Cash has no conscience and no memory."

Reese firmed up his voice. "No. If it happened she got paid electronically."

"Wanna bet?"

He laughed again. "With you? I think not. Leave this to me."

"Okay. Call me."

"I can do better than that, how about lunch?"

We made a date for a downtown steak house and I went home where I found Elena waiting for me with Claire and Fred. She was talking cheerfully to Claire and scribbling on a notepad. As I came in she greeted me, "And the prodigal jogger returns!"

The note she handed me read, *"Cops have your place bugged, be careful. They asked me to take Claire shopping on a prepared route to see if Shy comes out. We got 40 officers covering the route, snipers on the roofs and etc. and they wirred me too. Joke is the brass is pissed at you and hope S.M. takes you instead of her!"*

She laughed and I said, "Just trying for efficiency since beauty is out."

Then I wrote on her note, *"Wired is spelled with one 'r.' And I know about the bugging."*

Elena read it and so did Claire and then Elena shredded the note and flushed it down the toilet.

While she was in the other room I took Claire in my arms. "How are you?"

Her face was lined and there were bags under her eyes. "Tired." She leaned in close and whispered, "Terrified. Is there anything else we can do?"

I said, "I can't think of anything."

I didn't like the idea of Fred as a decoy as he rode with Claire. I'd have to do something about that. The poet says that death takes the exceedingly young.

But he wouldn't take Fred. I didn't know how but I wouldn't let that happen.

I did like the idea of forty cops watching my wife and son and ready to protect them. And I liked the idea of Elena being there. She would fight tooth and nail to protect Claire and Fred.

And if the Shy Man came for me, I'd take him apart. Quickly if I had a gun. Slowly if I had to use my fingers.

Claire closed her eyes, kissed me and left. When they were gone I shut all the doors and windows, changed the batteries on all the alarm systems and checked them out to make sure they were working. Then I cleaned and was unsurprised when Brenda and Dean phoned to cancel the day's travels.

At one I was downtown in a plush chrome restaurant at a good table with Virgil Reese, who immediately ordered.

"Chopin vodka martini, three ounces of vodka, one big olive, no pimento, five drops of vermouth, clean glass rubbed with lemon peel, splashed with Shooting Sherry."

The waiter didn't even blink but turned to me. "And for you?"

I mocked Reese gently, "Coffee. In a thin-sided china cup. Medium roast. White processed sugar. Cream. And a spoon."

The waiter left and I turned to Reese. "Chopin vodka?"

"Polish potato vodka. It's fantastic."

"So how did it go?"

He grinned but there was no amusement. "It was Brenda. She told me right away. Devanter bought her for $5,000."

"And how did he pay her?"

The drinks came and I sipped the coffee and Reese took a mouthful and relaxed. "Cash. Like you said."

I bowed to him. "No applause, simply throw gold and virgins."

He grunted. "Out of both."

The waiter came and we ordered blue, baked and tossed and he left. I drank some coffee. "So what did you do?"

"Offered her another five to keep us informed of what she was telling Devanter. Without telling Devanter that we knew about her. And I told her I wouldn't sue her ass."

"Good." I knew from past experience that killing a spy or otherwise removing them rarely worked. A new spy would simply be introduced and then you'd have to waste time finding that one. Co-opting them always worked better. "And did she have any new data?"

"Apparently Devanter's freaking out because you're gaining ground on Illyanovitch."

"Am I?"

"Not really. You're just solidifying a block of disenfranchised voters."

I stared into the distance and asked, "Can you still enter another person into the race?"

Reese stared at me. "Sure. Why?"

"We need a dummy. Someone right wing, further right than Illyanovitch. Someone to bleed off votes."

Reese leaned back. "I can do that right away. But who?"

I grinned. "Tell Dean to get the blond guy. Also tell him not to tell Brenda anything about the plan. And wait until the last possible day; I don't want Devanter to steal the dummy idea from us."

Reese looked at me intently. "You are pretty good at this kind of political infighting."

"Yep."

"Ever done it before?"

"Nope."

The food came and we ate. Near the end of the lunch though he got quieter and finally I asked what was wrong.

"I'm wondering why you became a thief. It seems like such a waste. You have a good mind. You're flexible and creative."

I started to laugh and Virgil got offended so I held up my hand. "Sorry. It's just a question I've heard all my life. I've honestly got no answer. I could tell you that it had to do with childhood abuse. Or that it's genetic. Or that everyone steals; Raymond Chandler used to say that no one ever made a million dollars honestly. I could tell you that no one puts up statues to nice people. I could list off famous thieves. But I won't tell you any of that. I'll just tell you that it's what I was at the time and I'm something different now."

Virgil smiled and it was unpleasant, then he paid the tab and was gone.

#35

I knew that Claire and Elena would be out late and I knew Veronica would take good care of Fred so I stayed downtown. I also knew that many cops would be busy watching my house and keeping a cordon around Claire, which made it a good night to commit crime. So the first thing I did was count the money in my wallet and I found I had over $400—more than enough.

Cheerfully I went to work. First a quick stop at a bargain shop for cheap runners, dark sunglasses, oversized track pants and a matching hooded jacket, a baseball hat and a pair of canvas gardening gloves. At a newsstand specializing in pornography I bought a $20 selection of cheap tools; screwdrivers, needle-nose pliers, a wrench, a women's compact mirror and a disposable carpet cutter. At a pharmacy beside the library I bought a small box of surgical gloves, a pair of women's sheer stockings, a little key light, a roll of clear packing tape and a bottle of rubbing alcohol.

Then I went to visit Reynolds and Lake, Alastair Reynolds's

law office, which occupied a high floor on a newish office building right on Portage Avenue. I treated it like a regular burglary and circled the building slowly, checking out the view from other buildings and angles first. Then I checked out the routes into the place and there were three —ground floor, attached garage that connected to the officebuilding at six levels, and an underground walk system. The last was part of the rabbit warren that ran under most of the downtown businesses, survival tactics for the subarctic winters.

I wrote off the ground floor (it went directly through a big lobby with security guards and a jewellery store). And I wrote off the underground because it was patrolled by other security guards who spent a lot of time rousting people who wore hoodies and track pants, the very disguise I had in my bag. I made a note to dress like a lawyer next time.

That left the parking garage, so I checked that out. Lots of expensive cars, an irregular patrol by a fat chick who didn't get out of her pickup truck and many, many cameras. In other words, not a bad way to break in. Not a bad way at all.

I pulled on the baseball cap and dark glasses and walked through the lobby of the office building and took the elevator up to the seventeenth floor. There were two security guards behind the big desk in the lobby and they didn't look twice, at me which made me feel pretty safe. I was wearing the disguise because if things went wrong the cops would run video tape and look for anyone doing what I was doing. Which was casing the joint by walking through it and around it over and over.

On the seventeenth floor there were investment firms, an executive job search agency full of men and women in suits and, in a nice corner office, Reynolds and Lake, Attorneys. I wandered up to their door and found it a solid slab of oak with brass inserts and two Medco Maxum deadbolt locks. Those were serious pains in the ass to pick, break or disable.

There were two bathrooms on the floor as well. So after I scouted the floor I visited the men's and found it had three stalls, two urinals and a locked closet.

I stared at the closet for a minute and then checked the lock. It was a Mastercraft combination lock on a hasp and I smiled to myself and went to the garbage. In five seconds I had an empty can of root beer I washed out in the sink and then took with me into a toilet stall. Six cuts with the carpet cutter got me a piece of aluminum about one inch by two inches with two half-inch cuts in one side. Then I made two more slices so my piece of aluminum looked kind of like an M and folded the two outside legs in. I pocketed the empty can until I could find a recycling bin and went to the closet and wrapped my little lock around the left arm and then pulled it down so the point went into lock mechanism. At the same time I pulled down on the lock itself and it popped open instantly.

The closet was full of shelves of cleaning supplies, a couple of big aluminum pails on wheels, some mops and brooms and miscellaneous equipment. It was certainly big enough to hide in easily, but once in there was no way I could lock it behind me, so its use was limited. And, once inside, there was no way to get out.

Ah well.

I went outside and found a coffee shop called the Fyxx where I could rest and relax until night fell. Then I changed in an alley, leaving my clothes, pocket knife and wallet in a pile of garbage (except for the cash) and went around to the back of the parking garage, which was open, with many thick concrete pillars. With my back to one of the pillars and the surgical gloves on my hands I opened the compact and checked around the corner.

Nothing. No people and no cameras.

I did the same on the other side of the pillar—still nothing and no one.

So I went in, bypassing the man in the pay booth on the basement level.

The only downside of my whole plan was that I looked like a thief. Dark track pants and jacket, hood up, black baseball cap worn down low over my face covered with pantyhose. Dark glasses. At a distance I'd look strange, up close I would look like a thief or a rapist. Period.

Oh well.

I moved slowly, keeping to the shadows, scanning with the mirror for people, cameras and anything moving. Listening for conversation or music or breathing. I even sniffed repeatedly for the smells of cigarettes or perfume that might alert me to someone nearby.

On the third floor I found the entrance to the office building, a glass door that led right into the office building. The lock was a good one, a Schlage five-pin sucker that I could pick in about three minutes if I had my tools.

However, I had gotten rid of most of my tools when I'd gone straight and they weren't easy to find. Claire had insisted I lose all of the tools I'd collected over my life of crime; the lock picks, the clean guns, a few pounds of commercial grade explosives, the lock pick gun, my selection of skeleton keys, my cell phone jammer, my radar detector, the big fishing case of makeup for disguises and so on.

All gone when I'd gone straight.

And the stuff I had acquired over the past year. That stuff I'd used once and then destroyed, trying to leave as few traces behind as possible.

And I didn't have the time to improvise so I stared at the

door and tried to come up with something subtle but nothing jumped into my mind. Then I realized the idiot who had put the door on had left the hinges facing out.

Two minutes with the screwdriver levered the hinge bolts out. Then I pulled the door out entirely, fiddled with the dead-bolt to open it (easy enough when you can reach the face plate) and put the door back in place. I opened it and walked into the office building, leaving the door lock jammed open behind me. I knew anyone who used a key would find the door unlocked; as long as they didn't look too closely it would be good.

And back to my skulking—thirteen floors worth of stairways, checking every few feet with the mirror. The odds of running into a security guard were pretty low, they probably patrolled once an hour or so and as long as I was quiet I should be safe. By the time I reached the seventeenth floor I was bored to tears but I went into the bathroom, jimmied the lock again and climbed into the closet.

When I'd been there earlier I'd noticed that the seventeenth floor had hanging ceilings like most office buildings did and that meant I didn't have to worry about the doors to Reynolds and Lake with their serious locks.

It was a personal motto—over, under, around or through. I kept trying to translate it into Latin with no luck.

However, it gave me the answer to the kickass locks Reynolds and Lake had. I would just go over.

There were strong shelves on the sides of the closet. I moved most of the cleaning supplies and then I used the shelves to climb up to the ceiling and push through the sound-dampening panels into a three-foot-high crawl space full of dust, hanging wires and other junk. The key light served to light it up quite well and I looked around and tried not to sneeze.

I reached down and picked up one of the industrial rolls of cheap garbage bags and started to lay them out in front of me in the general direction of the offices. It took a while but I had to move slowly anyway and laying the bags down encouraged precision and silence. The bags served three purposes: they kept me fairly clean; they allowed me to measure the exact distance, as each bag was thirty inches long; and as a bonus they gave me a route back to the bathroom. As I went I taped them together.

Throughout I was very careful to stay on the iron supports that held up the panels themselves. Those were wired into the ceiling and as long as I spread my weight over three of them I'd be fine so I placed my weight on toe, knee and hands and moved along.

In thirty minutes I covered the 120 feet and reached the corner of the building which meant, in theory, that the offices of Reynolds and Lake had to be beneath me.

I pulled open the last panel and held the mirror down so I could see.

I expected to see a room full of cops with drawn guns.

But there was nothing.

#36

The ceiling was two feet above a bookshelf, which gave me a nice route down to the floor, almost like a ladder. It only took a second to wrap tape around my hands and pick up most of the dust off my clothes and then I climbed slowly and carefully down and went to work.

There was lots of light streaming in through the windows to let me work and the first thing I did was check the whole office out, an inch at a time. It was a nice space, oak furniture and bookshelves, dark leather on the furniture, good quality bindings on the books and a nice thick-weave carpet. The desk was huge, oak as well, with a green felt blotter protecting the top and an expensive-looking laptop on top of that.

"Qosmio X305-Q708?" I said quietly. It looked fast and pricey and I ignored it and opened the drawers, looking to find out whose office I was in. Most of the drawers were locked but one that wasn't was full of boxes of business cards I recognized, ones for Alastair Reynolds.

Past experience told me I should check out the rest of the

office before I started work so I did and found a central waiting room with a desk for a receptionist, a nicely appointed bathroom, a second office almost as nice as Alastair's and a tiny kitchenette with fridge, microwave and a complicated machine that seemed to make coffee. It had an Italian name I couldn't read so I assumed it was for coffee and left it at that.

While I was in the second office the security guard came by—I heard the elevator door open and froze in place and watched through a door open a crack while a large kid in a white shirt and black pants checked all the doors by the light of a big flashlight. Then he left and I went back to Alastair's office.

The desk was ticking me off. I hate locked doors and drawers, unless I lock them. In all other cases they're just a professional challenge.

I found a pair of brass paper clips in one of the open drawers and used my needle-nose pliers to straighten them out. Then I flattened one end of one of them and bent it. That went into the tight grip of a big-jawed spring clip and I had my tension bar. The second paper clip I bent two or three millimetres from the end and I had my very own rake.

First I inserted the tension tool into the base of the keyhole and turned it to the side to put pressure on the pins. Then I slid the rake back and forth across the pins, pointing upwards and shuffling them into position. After about five brisk passes I pulled the rake out and finished twisting the lock with the tension bar and it was open.

I was disappointed in its contents; it was full of random legal papers I had no time to read. The second drawer held marginally more interesting stuff, notebooks and address books. However, I still had no time to read them so I put them back and checked out the third.

In that drawer was a heavy-framed, multi-barrelled pistol. The gun was a four-shot monstrosity from some American company called a COP, which stood for Compact Off Duty Police. It was made of blued steel with black rubber grips and I lifted it out cautiously and cracked it open to find it loaded with four .357 magnum hollow point rounds. Also in the drawer was a box of sixteen extra shells.

It was nasty, inaccurate and fairly useless at any long range.

But up close it would wreck someone's day entirely. The hollow-point bullets wouldn't penetrate too many walls and staring down four third-of-an-inch-wide barrels at the same time would cause most people to reconsider their options.

I left it there but took a few seconds to open the side plate and use the pliers to twist the firing pin a little off centre. With luck that would mean he'd get misfires if he ever tried to shoot the damn thing.

Once everything was locked away again I fired up the laptop and was pleased to find it wasn't password protected. If it had been I would have had to search for the code but I was sure it would have been written down, it always was somewhere handy. Generally on a back page of an address book or on a piece of paper hidden in a book or under a blotter or even taped somewhere handy. But in this case I got a cheerful loading page and I was in.

First things first. I went to the start menu and then connected and disconnected the Internet. Apparently the office ran off a password-coded wireless router somewhere. But that wasn't important right now; first I had some work to do.

There were two forms in a file labelled legal forms, one a generic letter with Reynolds's name, address and so on designed to be cut and pasted into an email to a target. It ended with the typical: "This communication, including its attachments, if any, is confidential and intended only for the person(s) to whom it is addressed, and may contain proprietary and/or privileged material. Any unauthorized review, disclosure, copying, other distribution of this communication or taking of any action in reliance on its contents is strictly prohibited ..."

Then a second letter, this one more formal and designed to be attached. It began with a rude little:

Attention: (insert name)

Dear Mr./Mrs./Ms. (insert name)

Re: (Action—Defamation/Libel/etc.)

Please be advised that we are counsel for Mr./ Mrs./Ms. (client).

We are informed by Mr./Mrs./Ms. (client) that you have been ... etc.

And then lots and lots of space for whatever incomprehensible legal mumbo-jumbo was necessary. It ended with:

I trust that this formal notification shall suffice to prevent any ... etc.

Yours truly,

Reynolds and Lake LLP

Per:

Alastair Reynolds

(in a fake computerized signature and then typed) and CC at the very bottom.

This was going to be easy.

First I copied the letters a few dozen times and then I opened up Alastair's address book and cut and pasted until my fingers were sore. Now each letter was addressed to one of Reynolds's business associates and clients and claimed they were defaming Cornelius Devanter. With that done I fired up the Internet Explorer and cut and pasted email messages and attached letters to them for another hour.

Each time I hit "send" and each time the Explorer did not send as it was not connected to the Internet. But it stored each letter and attachment.

And as soon as the Internet was fixed the letters would all go out.

And the shit would hit the fan.

So much fun.

I shut down the computer and put it back in place. Then I tossed the secretary's desk and found her list of passwords in a file neatly labelled "Pass Codes" in her desk. The code for the wireless connection was "Beelzebub" so I memorized it and put everything back where it belonged. Only then did I climb back into the ceiling and make my way to the closet. There I settled in uncomfortably to wait.

At 7:00 the guard came into the bathroom and peed.

Thirty minutes later two young men came in and I could hear them arguing about who had gotten more drunk the night before. When they left I pulled off my stocking mask and came out of the closet to find the coast was clear. I was at risk for a few seconds while I rearranged the cleaning supplies I'd moved but then I was done. In the farthest toilet stall I pulled off both pairs of gloves and cleaned myself up with wet paper towels and duct tape and stuffed everything into another garbage bag. I put that garbage bag into my shirt to give me a fat belly.

Then I left, heading back through the garage and fixing the door with one hand as I went.

#37

I got minor grief from Claire and Elena who were both sitting in my kitchen, drinking coffee and chatting about nothing in particular.

"Hey-hey, the missing link returns."

"Oh, fuck off."

"You first."

I kissed Claire and hugged Elena and they both wrinkled their noses. Elena said, "You smell foul."

I had changed back into my normal clothes in the alley after retrieving my wallet and so on. She was right; I did smell foul from having my clothes lying in the garbage. "Meetings with business people. Too long without a shower."

"Ah." She pulled a sheet of paper towards her and wrote, "*Anything?*"

I shook my head and said, "That's where I'm heading. What about Fred?"

Claire answered, "Veronica is bringing him to work with her."

Elena got up to leave. "Work calls. Thanks, Claire."

She smiled and it was lopsided. "Anytime."

I went into the shower and scrubbed off the filth. Then Claire joined me and that worked better than coffee at waking me up.

Because I had to work though I also chugged a pot when I was finally dry.

Brenda, Dean and I hit the west end of the city. More walking and talking. More worries about rising crime rates and rising taxes and no one wanted to hear that the crime rates were falling. And no one wanted to know I could do nothing about the taxes.

Every little while Brenda or Dean would go make phone calls and once I did a radio interview via cell phone while sitting at a park bench, eating a smokie dog with relish and mustard. At my feet a narrow creek ran towards a bigger one and a dead fat-headed fish caught in bulrush stems swayed in the current. Clustered around its eyes and anus were a legion of crayfish and water beetles eating their way in to where the good stuff was located.

"My opponent is too close to the police. Over the past five years, since he's retired, he's attended ..." Dean mouthed the number eight to me. "Eight police funerals around the country. He is a member of four fraternal police organizations and still banks at the Police Credit Union. Do you expect him to be dispassionate when it comes to his brothers in blue?"

The interviewer yammered on for a while and then I got my turn. "Actually, 'brother' is his term. And it's good that he still has that loyalty. But a police commission requires a dispassionate, logical and doubting point of view. And that Mr. Illyanovitch does not possess. Hell, he's refused to testify against fellow police officers three times in the past for various reasons."

Dean nodded vigorously. He was good at finding out information, very good indeed.

"My final message is vote for me. Vote for change."

The host thanked me and hung up and I went back to more walking and more talking.

At six a four-door sedan without whitewalls and with way too many antennas showed up and Sergeant Osserman got out. For a second I just stared at his skull face and puppy-dog brown eyes and wanted to kill him or main him but the feeling passed.

"Mr. Haaviko."

"Hello, Sergeant Osserman. And how are you?"

"Good. Can we talk for a bit? Maybe in the car? The mosquitoes are biting something fierce."

They were. I was still getting used to Manitoba mosquitoes. They seemed more persistent than any others I'd run into over the years. But a rule with cops is never to get into a car with them, never to get into any space they controlled, so I suggested we talk right where we were.

"Just wondering about the bracelet. Any more packages from the guy?"

"Not a one. Have you found out anything new?"

His bland little brown eyes focussed on mine and he lied, "Nothing, nothing at all."

Osserman had nothing else to say and he stood there on the sidewalk and looked off into the distance. I wondered how he had found me and decided he could have called either Dean or Brenda or he could have had me followed. I didn't really have a third option.

Finally I turned to him. "Mr. Osserman, I never had a

chance to ask you; what do you think of me running for the commission?"

Osserman shrugged. "Not much. I'm not political."

"No opinions on it at all?"

"Not really. I'm not sure how much the commission actually does. But I wish you luck."

"Really?"

He gave a tight-lipped smile. "Yes, really."

Then he left and I stood there and finally decided I believed him. Brenda and Dean had kept about ten feet away during the conversation and now they wandered back slowly.

"Hey, did Sergeant Osserman call either of you to find out where we were today?"

They both looked at me blankly and shook their heads, which meant that Osserman was having me followed and whoever was doing it was really good. This worried me because I was operating at maximum paranoia, which meant I should have noticed something. Although perhaps that was professional ego.

Dean gave me a lift home and Brenda rotated in her seat and handed me a small black leather case.

"Here. A present from us." Inside was a Nokia cell phone and charger. "It already has our numbers programmed in."

"Thanks." I hated cell phones, they removed privacy, cops could trace them through broadcast towers to find out exactly where the user was and any idiot with forty dollars worth of electronics could overhear your conversations. I also knew a guy whose phone had rung while he was burglarizing an apartment, which sent him to the can for two years plus a day.

Brenda just looked at me and smiled. "You hate it, don't you?"

"Yeah."

"Learn to deal with it." She grinned. "Like my friend says, it's time to put your big girl panties on."

She turned around back to her laptop and left me alone with my cell phone. Which promptly rang so I answered and found Reese on the other end.

"Hello sir, this is your lawyer speaking."

"A lawyer. One of my lawyers."

Reese was smart. By announcing he was my lawyer he was serving notice to anyone listening in that this was a privileged phone call.

"Same thing. Just wanted to tell you that the dummy is in place. It'll be announced tomorrow at noon."

"Why noon?"

"To max out on publicity. And we're doing it on Tuesday because you only announce things on Friday if you want them to be ignored."

"Makes sense. Anything I should do?"

"Just relax. It'll be fun." There was a long pause. "We should talk."

"We should? Why?"

"Certain things happened to a friend of ours." I wondered if he was talking about Reynolds. "And I want to discuss them with you."

"Sure. Soon."

"Now might be a good time."

"Later, like you said. Just relax. It'll be fun."

He growled and hung up on me but he was right, it was fun.

#38

The announcement went out at noon but at 9:00 that morn-ing I was in a used computer place way down in Saint James paying $350 cash for a battered laptop already loaded with basic software. It was two years old and slow as molasses but it had a wireless hook-up and the battery would last for an hour or so before needing a recharge. I had chosen the shop because they didn't have surveillance cameras, despite the fact that I was wearing a basic disguise of non-corrective glasses and a baseball hat.

I had left my work cell phone at home and at 9:15 I phoned Reynolds and Lake and got hold of Reynolds via his secretary. When he answered and told me he was in his office I told him I was a potential client and on my way over. Then I hung up before he could accept or refuse.

At 9:45 I was in the office building and by 9:50 I was back in my favourite bathroom stall and connected to the Internet through "Beelzebub." I had wiped the computer down with toilet paper moistened with rubbing alcohol and was wearing surgical gloves.

At 9:56 I had found the North American Man/Boy Love Association website and from there I just drifted into two questionable sites that linked to it. Then I went to four other sites newspaper research had recommended to me, sites I didn't like to think about.

Without looking and without remembering what I saw I clicked on images and short movies and advertisements.

I looked for youth and innocence and I found horrors.

What I was doing was laying a careful track on the Internet. One that would lead anyone examining it straight back to Reynolds's server.

But it was still unpleasant and disgusting and I wondered if I was, in fact, looking into something similar to the Shy Man's brain.

At 10:42 the computer battery said it was about to give out so I backed out of "Beelzebub" and shut down. Then I slid the computer into its plastic bag and left.

At 10:58 I dropped the laptop into the second-floor garbage disposal crusher in a downtown mall.

And at 11:45 I was back canvassing old Saint Boniface with Dean and Brenda.

#39

Claire and I met for dinner that night at home and stared at each other while Fred stared at us both.

"I can't keep doing this."

"Me either."

We were talking in circles and eating take-out Italian food that reminded me of being a thief and Claire of failure. I missed making our own meals, the peaceful chaos of babysitting and all the rest.

Claire picked at her salad and sneered at the lettuce. "How much longer?"

We both had pads and pens at our elbows. I started to write while I answered, "The election is in two months. Hopefully it'll start to slow down soon."

I wrote: *"No idea where S.M. is. No idea how long it will take. Thinking about taking you away from here. Maybe back to Banff, putting you up with your folks and hiring some folks to provide security."*

She read it and slid it back. "No." She waited. "Well, it might slow down. I hope it does. Maybe we can send Fred to my parents for a visit?"

Fred looked up, pleased someone had used his name.

I ate some spicy sausage and tomato sauce on whole wheat spaghetti and thought about it. I wanted to protect my family but I wasn't sure if I could. Getting Fred out of harm's way would help, if I was sure the Shy Man didn't know where he was. If he got Fred he could make Claire and me do anything.

Absolutely anything.

"That might be an idea."

And I wrote: *"Do your parents still have the mobile home? If they took Fred with them on a tour of the States for a few weeks that would be safe."*

Claire smiled. "I think that's a great idea."

After supper we burned our notes in the kitchen sink and then made love in the back bedroom while Fred watched an episode of a Samurai Jack cartoon thirty feet away. Every few minutes we would check on him through a crack at the edge of the door.

At eight Reese showed up and he and I took a ride.

Downtown we took a walk around the Forks, an upscale shopping mall and market at the confluence of the Red and Assiniboine Rivers. People had been meeting there for 10,000 years and now it hummed with commerce and yuppies and drunks and trains. Reese and I moved down to the riverfront walkways and moved two abreast along the well-lighted path.

"Brenda tells me that Devanter hit the roof after our dummy came onstage today."

"I know. He called me on my cell and set up a meeting for tomorrow morning early, at like seven."

"That is early. He lives in the apartment above his office, did you know that?"

"No. So those early meetings are a way of showing how important and hard-working he is?"

"Pretty much."

We stepped around two young women kissing.

"And how did our dummy sound?"

"Good. Here's a quote: 'Bring back the death penalty for killers and rapists and child molesters. That is the way to achieve justice, not this coddling. Mr. Illyanovitch is a good man but he does not have the will to go to the end. And Mr. Haaviko is a lying, cheating and manipulative son of a bitch who cannot begin to understand the world around him.' And more like that."

"And the crowd?"

"Loved him. Oh, he's also pressing charges on you about that fight you two had at the speech."

"Ah? Interesting. Give me a second."

I took my cell phone, called Lester's office and told an assistant to press charges against the dummy as well and to talk to the cops the next morning when he got a chance.

The young woman took down every word and I asked, "Are you recording this?"

"Of course." She sounded offended.

"Okay. And tell Lester I will of course not speak to the cops without him being present."

"That's it?"

"That's it. Good night."

And she hung up.

Further down the walkway along the Assiniboine River,

Reese and I came upon three young men fishing with spinning rods in the fast current.

Reese stared into the brown water. "So what does the dummy do here? Goodson is not impressed about laying out more cash for this."

"How much is the dummy costing?"

"Five thousand. He's a university student, an actor. A good one."

I absorbed it. "It'll pay off in the long run."

"All right. Now, what does the dummy do?"

"He bleeds off votes from Illyanovitch by hitting him at the root of his constituency; we want the dummy to appeal to the law and order crowd. To protect himself from that Illyanovitch will have to start being more right wing and the distance between him and me will grow. We want to give the voters a clear choice."

"And the point of all this?"

I shrugged. "Simple strategy. Divide and conquer. We are aiming for the ballot question; the last question asked by the voters before they cast their vote."

"You seem to know a lot about this. How is that?"

"Is it important?"

"Yes."

"In prison I had lots of time to read. I read a lot of political biographies—Huey Long, Stephen Harper, Vladimir Putin, Sarkozy, Nixon, Elizabeth the First of England, Kissinger, Reagan, Bush one and two, Philip the Second of Spain, Ivan of Russia and so on."

"Ivan the Terrible?"

"He wasn't that terrible. Anyhow, all the data's there. You just have to see it." Politics and crime, crime and politics, lines blurred. Both were about manipulation, and the borders blurred all the time. In Japan members of the Yakuza sat in the Diet, in Russia the Senate held its fair share of Mafiya, in England a convicted perjurer and a white-collar thief sat in the House of Lords, in the United States a senator had to be pried out of power like a limpet after accepting bribes.

Reese absorbed this information and then took my arm and leaned in close. "Did you hear about what happened to Reynolds?"

"No. What?" I thought about being curious and hoped it showed on my face.

"He snapped and sent out cease and desist orders to about a hundred people to stop talking about Devanter and Illyanovitch. In my business it's followed with an injunction or restraining order."

"So?"

Reese shook my arm. "He sent it to people who had nothing to do with Devanter or Illyanovitch. He sent it to lawyers and judges and cops and millionaires and businessmen. He snapped."

I was curious. "So what's happening?"

"He's in serious damage control mode now and practically paralyzed. He's had to delay two cases I know of from going to court and reschedule at least ten meetings. Devanter is furious with the dumb shit. And, to top it all off, there have been dozens of complaints with the Law Society of Manitoba and even a couple to the police for harassment."

I pulled my arm free and kept walking. Reese followed and went on, "And that's just what I know about."

A duck flew over our heads and Reese paused and then asked, very casually, "You didn't have anything to do with that, did you?"

"Me?" I thought innocent thoughts and hoped they showed.

He held up his hand. "Before you answer, you should know, anything you tell me is privileged."

My criminal mind was very doubtful about the necessity of telling him the truth and I really could think of no reason to risk it. "Sure. But me? Never."

He looked doubtful. "Okay."

"Now, would it be all right if I went and visited Mr. Goodson?"

"Sure. You should call him first. Do you want me to come?"

I stooped for a stone and flipped it out to pop a plastic bag floating in the river. "No."

"Why not?"

"I want to ask him a question you don't want to hear. And you really don't want to hear the answer."

"Ah. I'll call and get you permission. Tomorrow?"

"Or the day after."

When I got home Claire was drinking straight from a bottle of Benedictine liqueur. In front of her was a fancy sheet of thick paper with tiny words written in beautiful script. Holding it flat to the table was the Beretta pistol and the unsheathed Mauser bayonet.

I wanted to reach for the bottle but took the paper instead. It said,

> *Dearest Clarice!*
>
> *I'm so sorry you couldn't make it for coffee but I hope you enjoyed the chocolate and flowers.*
> *Shall we have dinner? We have so much to discuss and so much to plan.*

I hope your husband will have the dignity to step aside in respect of our love.

I long for your embrace and look forward to the continuation of our beautiful relationship.

Signed,
A Wretched Englishman! (You will forgive the pun, my one true love!)

I sheathed the bayonet and carried it with me to check the doors and windows and set the alarms. I wondered how the Shy Man had found out Claire's full name was Clarice, which she never used and which she hated. I wondered where he was.

When I got back Claire had corked the bottle and had pulled the magazine from the gun and the bullets from the magazine and was reloading. She stared into the distance while pressing firmly down on each brass cartridge against the resistance of the spring. I had taught her to do that every night to double check that the magazine was still working.

She saw me and smiled brightly. "I think it's time for a change."

"I couldn't agree more."

#40

I called Devanter the next morning at 6:00 from a pay phone up on Main to cancel our appointment. I got his answering machine but I told the machine that there was a family emergency and it seemed to understand—or at least it didn't argue with me. Then I took a brisk jog to Salter Street where I caught a bus downtown. From there I hit the hamster trails that connected most of the city buildings until I found the parking garage under the Millennium Library. I used the rear entrance to the park and then crossed two more streets to a big hotel.

If anyone was following me they were really good.

In the hotel I used a pay phone to call Sandra Robillard, a gangster who ran her deceased husband's crime organization. She was smart and fairly honest and she owed me. Or I owed her. Something like that. In any case we knew each other.

She answered and swore at me for about three minutes for calling her that early before I could say, "This is a friend."

She kept swearing for four more minutes.

"Are you done?"

"Yes. You can reach me at ..."

She gave me a number and I dialled. In the south end of the city, right near the edge, I knew she would be rummaging for a new cell phone, one still in its packaging. When she'd used it once she'd sell it on eBay or destroy it. These days it was the only way to avoid police surveillance and it was almost foolproof as long as you could also avoid having your rooms tapped.

She answered on the first ring. "Who are you?"

"Monty."

"Thought so. What do you need?"

"A meeting. A job."

"What's in it for me?"

"Five large."

"Where are you?"

I told her and she was there thirty-seven minutes later on a battered old English Triumph motorcycle. She was wearing lavender silk pyjamas and a huge black helmet and she handed me one of my own when I came forward.

"Get on, bitch."

A reference to the seat I took behind her with my hands around her waist. At least I hoped so. I got on and she floored it and soon we were on the Perimeter Highway near the bridge north of the city. That's where she pulled to the side and stripped her helmet off to let the wind run through her shoulder-length black hair. She was slim, in her mid-to-late twenties, with a dark tan, big green eyes and no ability to feel fear.

"Five thousand? For what?"

I leaned against the bike and ran my eyes idly over its smooth, clean lines, so much nicer than any Harley I'd ever stolen.

"For taking my son Fred to Banff and delivering him to his grandparents."

"That's it?"

"Yes. But I don't want the cops to know and there may be a guy who wants to get Fred."

She wrinkled her nose. "A three-year-old?"

"Yep."

"Why?"

I shrugged. "Different reasons. Francis Bacon said that those who had children were hostages to fortune."

"Fuck anyone who steals kids. And fuck Francis Bacon. Anything else?"

"Yep. There's a bonus for you if you agree. The bonus comes up front. Will you help?"

"Of course."

"The cops have got about twenty detectives and uniforms watching my house."

Sandra smiled slowly. "They do? Me oh me oh my. Isn't that interesting."

I knew what she was thinking. It had suddenly become a great time to run loads of cigarettes, booze, dope, guns, stolen cars, counterfeit electronics, displaced hookers, hot building material, just about whatever into or out of the city. Since she was a serious smuggler, knowing where twenty cops were at any time was a very nice thing indeed.

She nodded abruptly. "Deal. When?"

"Tonight?"

"Sure. What kind of stroller does Fred use?"

"Mostly he uses a wagon."

"We need a stroller. Do you still have it?"

"Yes." We still had it and I hated it, a luxury model Claire's parents had given her when Fred was born. It had some collapsing panels and flaps, so that Fred could still fit in it, if uncomfortably. I described it to Sandra.

"Well, dig it out and use it."

I agreed and described the device. She nodded and I handed her five thousand in fifties as we hashed out a plan. Finally she said, "Okay. Let's go. Any more planning and this'll turn to shit. My husband used to say that crime ain't a symphony by Beethoven, it's free-form jazz by a drunk guy with a sax."

"Who said that?"

"My husband. Before he died. Let's go."

"Umm. Can I drive?"

She looked at me suspiciously. "Why?"

"I want to. Also holding you when you're wearing silk pyjamas is worse than holding you naked. And I don't think our relationship is ready for the thoughts such activities engender."

She smothered a smile and I drove myself within ten blocks of home and got off. At a convenience store I bought another cell phone and an hour's worth of minutes and brought it with me to Claire. She took it without question and walked to work, making the call to her parents as she went, about the only time we could be sure the cops didn't have a shotgun microphone on her.

That evening she told me the discussion went something like, Mom and Dad, please take my son on a three-week tour of the States and don't tell anyone about what you're doing. And Dad said, okay, it's Monty, isn't it? What did that dumb sonofafuckingbitch do this time? Nothing Dad, it's not Monty, it's me, just do it. And then Mom got on the phone and shut Dad up and he wandered off to check the Winnebago and sharpen his knives. And Mom said, how bad, and Claire said, bad. No one should know where Fred is, including me, so leave for three weeks and come back and call Monty's lawyer. And Mom said, deal.

I felt considerable relief. Claire's dad didn't like me but he really liked his daughter and he really, really liked his grandson and I felt he would have no compunction gutting anyone who tried to touch him. Claire's mother was even tougher than her dad and I was pretty sure she carried a pistol when I was around. Just in case.

Around noon Devanter called, pissed off at me, and I rescheduled for the next morning.

That night Claire and Fred and I went to the Globe Theatre in Portage Place with his stroller packed with clothes for him. We had explained he would be taking a trip to visit his grandparents and he nodded as though he understood. He didn't, but he was a good kid and he tried.

When we arrived at the theatre Claire went into the bathroom and I stood outside immobile while Sandra came down the hall with a smiling young girl, maybe sixteen, pushing exactly the same kind of stroller as the one Claire and I used for Fred.

The girl went into the bathroom and Sandra stepped beside me and talked out of the corner of her mouth. "No worries—1,447 klicks to Banff and I'll run it in twelve hours. Fred will be in his grandparents' arms by noon at the latest. Susie's the girl making the transfer, she's bringing her baby girl as cover, and she's one and a half, so she'll be company for Fred. The baby's waiting downstairs with Long Tom."

Long Tom was Sandra's lieutenant, reliable and vicious with a strong sense of loyalty. "Great. Is the car clean?" I meant was she running dope or guns. If she was, I would be pissed.

"Yes. It won't be on the way back though."

"That's fine."

A large African woman walked past us, swathed in fabrics

of unbelievable colours. When she was gone Sandra said, "Is it bad?"

"Yes."

"You need back-up?"

"Just what you're doing."

"All right. There's a Browning Hi-Power in the men's bathroom. Fourteen rounds of 9mm military surplus full metal jackets. It's in a plastic bag on top of the toilet paper dispenser of the second stall from the end. It's clean and I've run a few rounds through it myself. It works fine."

I stared at her and exhaled. "Thanks."

"Least I could do. You need anything else just call. I'll hold onto the number you've got for a bit."

When Claire came out of the bathroom I had the gun under my light summer jacket tucked into the back of my belt where no one could see it.

And Fred was on his way to see his grandparents.

Claire and I walked home silently. Because the cops were listening I turned the Muppets on full blast when we were inside and watched Claire cry. When she was empty I walked upstairs and told a bedtime story to Fred's empty bed.

I did Dr. Seuss's *Oh The Places You'll Go.*

And by the end I was crying too.

#41

The next day I went to my meeting with Devanter at 7:00. When I got to the building his secretary was waiting outside the front doors, wrapped in an expensive lamb leather coat against the morning chill.

"Mr. Haaviko."

"Ma'am."

Her mouth twisted unhappily when I said it. Then she led me up and through her office and into Devanter's suite. The place looked the same and I glanced around idly while waiting for Cornelius to arrive. I didn't have long to wait before he came slamming down from his loft wearing an impeccable dove grey suit with a lavender silk shirt and the same tie as before.

"Mr. Haaviko. What the fuck is happening?"

"Just what you paid for. By the way, you owe me $5,000. That would help right now. I've got expenses."

He snorted. "You get sweet fuck all." He stomped to the desk and pressed a button. "Honey? Coffee for two."

I walked over to the wall with its displays of planes and such and stared at a streamlined blimp rendered in exquisite detail. It was on the lowest level, even with my eyes, stuffed onto the same glass shelf as something that looked like a shark with wings. Stencilled on its side was the word PELIGROSO. There was nothing on the blimp though, just clean lines, huge engines and a tiny cockpit hung from the bottom.

I glanced around and saw an empty shelf about five feet up between two other blimps.

"Nice. It looks smaller than the others."

Something hit me in the back and I turned to find an elastic-wrapped bundle of twenties on the floor. I knelt down and picked it up and started to count as Devanter gestured me towards a chair.

"Now what the fuck does that buy me?"

"What you wanted. A loss on the part of Goodson."

Devanter sat down across from me and his eyes flickered over my shoulder and then back to me. I wondered what was over my shoulder as the coffee arrived and I helped myself. As I stirred in my sugar and cream I turned to check the wall and saw that Devanter's eyes had been somewhere near where I'd been standing.

Interesting.

Also, flipping the money at me wasn't something I'd thought Devanter would do.

Devanter cleared his throat. "Here." I turned and he was offering me a little metal vial with a tiny spoon sticking out. "It's good Peruvian flake. One of my pilots brings it up for me from the Panama free zone. Help yourself."

"Thank you, no. I'm straight, remember?"

"Right." He dug in and snorted a tiny mound of crystal and I saw his eyes sparkle. "Ah ... firstest with the mostest."

Interesting quote. It rang bells—I remembered reading up on cowboys and gunslingers and finding that same quote. I watched the cocaine slam into Devanter and then the quote's origins came to me. Nathan Bedford Forrest, a Confederate Civil War general in the States, an illiterate autodidact who went on to found the Klu Klux Klan and the namesake of the Republican wet dream Forrest Gump. Someone had asked him about the secret to his success and that had been his response.

I drank some fantastic coffee and wondered what was going on in Devanter's little mind.

He put away the cocaine and drank some coffee and sneered at the taste. My body remembered what was happening in his mouth and nose—the coke took away your sense of taste. Devanter shrugged and said, "Distinguish the superficial from the substantial."

That sounded familiar as well. "What do you mean?"

"Well, tell me what you know about Daniel McDonald."

"Mr. McDonald is the latest man to throw his hat into the ring for the police commission job. He's right of right wing, a little flaky, pretty, young, and impassioned. My handlers Dean and Brenda have checked him out and claim he's a student and an actor. Brenda goes on to claim he's a much better actor than student."

Devanter nodded and poured more coffee. "And what are you going to do?"

"Stay the course. McDonald and Illyanovitch are in exactly the same place so all I have to do is keep hitting the same point and it's all good. Then I fade out at the last minute."

"What about Illyanovitch?"

"What about him? You telling me he's worried about some wannabe? I've debated the man, he has nothing to fear. Tell you what though, McDonald took a swing at me and it's on camera. I can press charges, which might take him out of the running."

He digested that while I waited and finally asked, "Where's Reynolds?"

Devanter's face tightened and got red. "He no longer works for me. Call me if he tries to reach you."

"Certainly."

"As for McDonald, you do that. Fuck him up."

"Sure." I got up. "Anything else?"

"No. Nothing."

I walked out. Two blocks away I bought a handful of change from a vegetarian restaurant and drank coffee. At nine I used a pay phone to call the biggest Indigo bookstore in the city and got hold of the ordering desk.

"Good morning, this is Cornelius Devanter. Are my books in?"

"Let me check, sir. Address, please?"

I gave it and there was a pause.

"No sir, we have nothing listed for you."

I hung up and called the McNally Robinson bookstore and did the same thing. They admitted they were still waiting for my copy of *The Book of 5 Rings*. I thanked them and hung up gently.

Then I drank some more coffee. *The Book of 5 Rings* was a book on philosophy and war by a Japanese swordsman from about 500 years ago. It was required reading by movers and shakers in the business world. They believed the strategies of war applied to business.

That fit in with the way Devanter talked and acted. I finished my coffee and went to the library and waited for it to open. Then I went in and used the Internet to search out the pattern of his tie—he had worn it twice and once it had gone with the shirt and the second time it hadn't. A blue tie with tiny designs that looked like tridents.

On an English site I found it, an SAS regimental tie. The Special Air Services, British commandos and killers. Out of curiosity I kept looking for the tie clip, the little knives, and found those too, an emblem of Gurkhas, Nepalese mercenaries renowned for their use of the kukri knife.

I leaned back. So. Devanter carried a pistol and he had gotten training. And he quoted military truisms and he wore military mementoes.

All that screamed that he was a fetishist. A new insight into his mind but not one that was of much use to me.

I ran a search for "Peligroso" and found it meant danger in Spanish. Also that it was an unmanned drone built by one of Devanter's companies capable of carrying four guided missiles and circling the world on a single load of hydrogen peroxide fuel. It was his best seller.

In a two-year-old *Jane's Intelligence Review* there was an article about Devanter's company building a micro rigid airship for military/security work. Information was sketchy about statistics and possible sales but the ship was described as being two-man, unarmed and very reliable. A snippet from a sales promotion read, "Perfect for Counter Insurgency!"

Frankly, it sounded very much like what I'd seen in Devanter's office.

I called Claire and found she was at home and working. She answered very coldly and I asked her if anything was wrong. "No honey, I just got an obscene phone call."

"Ouch. Bad?"

"Pretty filthy. I've called the phone company and the cops. The cops are sending someone down, is that normal?"

It wasn't. "Maybe they got a lot of calls recently."

"Maybe."

I read between the lines, must have been the Shy Man. The cops would have the number then but I wondered if it would make any difference.

"Love you."

"Love you too."

At an Alamo rental location I used Claire's credit card to pay for a Ford Mustang convertible and started up to Goodson's place.

It was a nice drive and, despite myself, I enjoyed it.

#42

The old man was on the cedar porch when I arrived. Still in the rocker made of antlers and still with the red blanket on his lap. I walked up from the parked car and saw his right hand under the blanket and realized again how old Goodson was. His face was calm and he wore the dark red wool long-sleeved shirt buttoned to his neck with yellowed bone buttons and faded jeans that ended above his ugly, twisted toes sticking out of a pair of battered leather sandals. The red of the shirt clashed with the blanket.

"Mr. Goodson."

"Mr. Haaviko." He spat loudly off his porch onto the ground and turned his deep-set brown eyes back to me. "And how are you?"

"Good."

"And how is our dummy, Mr. McDonald, working? Oh, sit down."

The other antler rocking chair had been replaced with a canvas and aluminum director's chair. I sat down and stretched out my feet.

"Thank you. Long ride. Mr. McDonald is working just fine." I looked around the clearing and the porch and smiled. "I kind of like this kind of plotting, I don't have to be terribly subtle about meeting with you or Devanter."

"And what is our dummy supposed to do?"

"Bleed off support from Illyanovitch. Nothing else."

"I see. You attack from the front and McDonald attacks from the flank?"

"Pretty much."

"Did you hear about Reynolds?"

"Yes."

The old man closed one eye and stared at me hard with the other deep-set brown orb. "And did you have anything to do with that? The mass email accusations and the child pornography?"

"Nothing whatsoever ... child pornography?"

His eye was unwavering. "Child pornography. Reynolds contested his cease and desist and a judge signed off on a search of his computer records. The cops found he did send the original emails from his own computer, it still held copies of the forms he had used; the cops also found he liked to look at kiddy-diddling stuff as well."

It had worked. I shook my head. "Nope. Not me."

The old man grunted non-committally and went back to watching the trees. I stared at him and didn't say anything. He was old and he was looking it. His face was still thin and sharp with patchy white hair but someone had combed it for him.

"Well? Virgil said you wanted to talk."

"I did. Why does Devanter have such a hard-on for you? And why do you have such a hard-on for him?"

"I told you."

"You told me shit and lies. You're laying out forty grand plus for me and Devanter's doing that and a lot more for Illyanovitch. You're both risking money and imprisonment and for what?"

Goodson leaned his chin against his hand and stared with clear eyes. For a long time there was silence.

"Mr. Goodson, notice that I'm not bringing a threat here. I think you have the same attitude towards blackmail and threats that I do."

He nodded. "Probably."

I went on like he hadn't said anything. "I bite off the hand that threatens me and rub salt in the wound."

He smiled and I saw he had either very good teeth or very good dentures. "Pretty much."

"So tell me why."

Goodson nodded. "All right. Is that why you didn't bring Virgil?"

"Yes."

The old man brought his hand out from under the blanket. It held an old brass handbell that he rang twice. A young woman, plain-faced, freckled and smiling, came out and said, "Yes, master?"

He snorted. "Wiseass."

"Too young for wisdom, maybe a smartass. What do you need?"

"Rye for me." He looked at me and I added, "Lemonade, ice tea, anything cold."

The woman nodded and bent down to kiss Goodson's head. "On its way."

He cursed and watched her go with pride. "Never marry 'em. Take my advice. Never marry pretty women."

I looked at the door she had used and shook my head,

"Never make a handsome woman your wife. But she's not handsome, she's beautiful."

Goodson's eyes flicked to me in surprise. "Beautiful?"

"Yep."

"What the hell do you mean?"

I twisted in my chair. "I dated the prettiest girl in the world once. Slept with her too. She acted like she was giving me the best thing in the world and that I should be grateful. Afterwards I realized that her tits were real but that her smile was fake."

The old man laughed and asked, "What else?"

"She was a dead lay and had bad breath and she never learned to value anything up until the day she died."

"In other words?"

"Be happy with what you've got. Appearances can be deceiving. Don't judge a book by its cover. Pick an aphorism."

The woman brought out a full bottle of whiskey and a small glass for him and a pitcher of lemonade with a glass full of ice for me. "Here you go. Ring if you require service, oh most illustrious master."

She left smiling and the old man grinned back at her like he was about twelve and then turned back to me. "In school I learned that Roman emperors had a slave ride behind them in their chariots. The slave whispered, 'this too shall pass,' during parades. That's the function that girl plays for me—she reminds me I'm full of shit sometimes."

The lemonade was fresh and real and I drank two glasses before the old man poured his first.

He held it up. "Cheers."

"Cheers."

Then he started. "What's the worst thing you ever did?"

#43

None of your business." I remembered flames and screams and shut it all away back where it belonged. The power of the reaction scared me and I filed it away to think about later.

Goodson looked at me intently and then finished his drink and poured more. While I collected myself he lit a cigarette.

"I don't like to think of it much either but sometimes I think of the worst thing I never did. That helps."

He stared off into the distance and tapped ash onto the planks of the porch. "I was born in Germany, in the Black Forest. When I was very young I joined the local glider club. We flew off a little airfield a long walk from home but I went there every chance I could get. I'd leave at 4:00 a.m. every Saturday to watch the launch and later I got to go up. And when I was older I joined the flying corps—the Luftwaffe. I loved to fly and it got me away from my father and mother who lived in a cottage in the middle of a giant copse of oaks and from which I almost never saw the sky or the sun."

He drank and filled his glass again.

"When the war started I was too young, by '41 I was flying a Junkers tri-motor and soon we invaded Russia and there I was. By September I was flying a Messerschmitt Bf 110 out of an airbase outside of Leningrad. We were there to support our troops during the siege of the city and I was there from the beginning to the end—872 days, September 1941 to the end of January 1944. I was a member of a *Zerstörerwaffe*, a destroyer force with thirty-two planes, and I started as a fighter pilot but Bf's were slow and I became a fighter-bomber and later a night fighter, a *Nachtjagdgeschwader*."

"So Goodson is not your name?"

"It is. I changed it legally in Canada in 1952."

I drank some more lemonade and watched the long shadows and listened as Goodson went on.

"*Nachtjagdgeschwader*. It sounds so brave but it wasn't. Up in the clouds with radar and my victims couldn't even see me. So cold I drank vodka the Ukrainian auxiliaries brewed up straight just to keep awake."

"Is that where you got the drilling?"

"No. I had one but it got left behind with the plane. I bought the gun at auction last year. As a reminder."

He reached out to touch the cased weapon behind his chair and smiled. "So we flew and I shot down Russian transports bringing food to the starving city. And I strafed convoys of trucks on the ice bringing in coal and blankets. And I dropped bombs on barges carrying away the wounded. And my comrades died—shot, burned, suicided, cut up by partisans, slaughtered by typhus and the flu. In April of 1942 we were brought up to full strength and involved in Operation Ice Impact, an attempt to sink the Soviet ships in the Lenningrad harbour. It failed completely."

The old man rested his hands on his knees and then lit another cigarette.

"Mostly we just bled. The planes were considered obsolete but they weren't. They were just not as good as the best. Our squad had some models that carried up to two tons of bombs along with machine guns and automatic cannons. And the planes were reliable, like clockwork all the time except when they didn't work."

I laughed and so did he.

"The Spanish Blue division was stationed nearby and we'd trade schnapps for brandy and trade stories for news. But they were cold men, good comrades but cold men. I learned about the difference between a Castilian and a Catalan there on that cold patch of bog. I thought I knew tough soldiers until I saw them and then I understood why the Spanish empire had lasted as long as it did. Small men, tough, tireless and never smiling. As cold as the winter."

Goodson drank from his glass and shivered. "There was a priest or a monk. The others called him Fra, brother, I think, Fra Santiago; he was a handsome young man, a lieutenant. He and I used to talk and once or twice I took him up to show him the widening gyre, what he called it. He spoke English and loved Irish poets and he'd make me recite them while I flew. That's how I started to learn English with him teach me Yeats and Shelley.

"Santiago was the one who told me the greatest mistake the Spanish had ever made was converting and killing all the Jews in the 1500's. They were the ones who understood money; they had learned it to help them survive over the years. So when the money from the Indies started to come in the Spanish didn't know what to do with it and so they pissed it all away in great golden streams feeding wars in

Flanders and burning the English in towns like Mousehole and Penzance."

A deer, a doe, stepped out from between two trees just past my car and snuffled the air. Her head twisted from side to side and she turned back into the darkness. The old man just kept talking.

"The prick dictator Franco had sent the Spanish Blues north to kill communists and that's what they did. They had their own hangers on, Kozzaki and Lithuanians, and they did not take many prisoners. Or so I heard but it was a hard war—Stalin didn't want Leningrad to survive, he was focussed on his namesake city Stalingrad. And for us the high command kept changing their mind, first to take Leningrad at all costs and join up with the Finns and cut the Murmansk supply line that fed Ford trucks into Russian hands. The next month it was to attack Moscow in the centre and kill Stalin. Then it was to station battleships in Norway to cut the supply line to Archangel where Allied aid was fattening the Soviets. Then it was to concentrate all the forces on Stalingrad far to the south and capture the Baku oil fields. No one took too many prisoners, not then. It was a different time. So we flew and bombed and shot. And in the city they were eating their dead."

He said it quietly.

"Eventually Franco bowed to political pressure and called his soldiers back but they surely did not want to go—they had gone through the Spanish Civil War and saw their beloved enemies in every Russian face. When the Blues left the last thing the Fra said was that God writes straight in crooked lines. I thought about that for a long time. And I had time waiting for more fuel to come up so I could fly again, learning to fix the engines and clean the guns, anything to keep out of the lines where it was a real meat grinder."

It was a beautiful afternoon, hot but bearable under the trees and the old man's voice went on, "One day in the early winter of '43 I got special orders and a full load of gas—rare things indeed. And a team of specialists took my baby apart and stripped out the machine guns and the cannons until she was naked, and then they put on these two fat dachshund bellies, one under each wing. Long aluminum containers specially built and shipped out when the front was screaming for ammunition and the soldiers were praying for food. Those got loaded under tarps while I sat in my dugout and crushed lice crawling through my beard."

The woman brought more lemonade and pills for Goodson and never looked me in the eye. She went inside and Aerosmith started to waft out under the door, "Dude (Looks Like a Lady)," I think, and that made me think of lost opportunities from childhood.

The old man kept talking.

"My orders were given to me by a tightarse, a civilian member of the Reich Ministry for Public Enlightenment and Propaganda direct from the Ordenpalais in Berlin. He was escorted by an SS Major from the Reich Security Main Office—they were badasses amongst badasses and, if I hadn't been completely drunk at the time, they probably would have scared the piss right out of me. My orders were to fly over Leningrad on headings this and that at a height of 1,000 metres and open my dachshund bellies while travelling at a stalling speed."

A fly landed on the old man's face, just under his left eye, and he brushed it away.

"The orders were suicidal considering the flak over the city and the Yakovlev fighters and the Sturmovick ground attack planes but I listened anyway. Before supper I checked the plane out for one last time with a mechanic. While he was distracting two RSHA guards I undid the housing of one of the dachshunds and found it full of little booklets of cheap paper. I took one, tidied up and went and ate my potato soup. While I ate I read the booklet under the table. It was just a bunch of slips of paper glued into place. I could read Russian a little, we all could by then, and it said, 'A week's worth of Rations Book for Leningrad.' And I knew that my cargo was counterfeit ration books."

The music inside changed to "Everybody Loves Me Baby" by Don Maclean.

"After soup there was vodka and I wrote on a corner of a scrap of newspaper while I drank. The major had told me I was carrying 2,600 kilos of extra weight—maybe 1,000 would be the containers, the rest the ration books themselves. By my calculations I had perhaps 80,000 of the damn things. I would drop them; the citizens would pick them up and think such a blessing. And they would go to the kitchens and there would not be enough food and they would riot and the army guns would come out and they'd massacre their own."

The old man rubbed his chin. "We knew that the citizens still in the city were living on 500 calories a day. Enough to let you die slowly. Enough to make you hurt. We knew the army had set up special teams to fight cannibalism. And the major and the bureaucrat wanted me to drop hope on them— I was amazed. I would have dropped white phosphorous or high explosive or delayed charges loaded to go off at nearby movement or anything else without blinking. I could have fired explosive incendiaries into a school or strafed a line of old women lining up to trade for fuel oil, but I could not drop hope. My mind rebelled."

I was afraid to move and shake Goodson from his reverie. His voice went on, "There were six or eight million Soviets in the city when we started and we killed more than a million and a half through guns and bombs but mostly through starvation and disease. When the rivers were free of ice you could walk from one side to the other on bloated corpses and there were a lot of rivers. So off I flew, the weight had been calculated precisely and so I went solo, no radio man, no radar operator, and no rear gunner. Just me."

His voice trailed off and then got stronger. "Alone. And I climbed slowly and turned northwest and headed out over the Baltic, that cold, amber-laden sea. And I turned north and then east and then I was over the city with my hand on the jury switch, just cables slung through a hole in my cockpit that ended in toggles. Drunk on vodka, scared, hating the Soviets below me and the shitters behind me with their fucking games and rules and cruelties. Hope, they were using me to drop hope. Who could defend against that? And my hand was on the toggles."

There was no music in the house now and even the wind had died as the old man took a deep breath and said, wondering, "I couldn't. Standing orders were to follow a different route back but I didn't, I went back over the Baltic, that cold sea and I dumped my ration books into that hungry sea and went and reported that my mission had been accomplished. And they gave me a medal. And, a few weeks later, the siege was broken and we fled south. And I couldn't find any fuel for my plane somewhere in Poland and I shot it in the nosecone while my engineer laughed—to put it out of its misery, I said. I made it to Austria, barely, and kept going. It was chaos but I was determined and lucky. And when I heard English being spoken I surrendered, then I was tried and sent to a prison camp here in Canada for two years. There I read about the Nuremberg trials. Some of the other prisoners were furious over what was happening but I wasn't. I read a special report the Russians had delivered, a diary from an eleven-year-old girl, a baker's daughter from Leningrad, named Tatyana Nikolayevna Savicheva. The diary talked about starvation and the death of her sister, then her grandmother, and then her brother, then one uncle and the other, then mother, all starved to death. It ended with 'Everyone died. Only Tanya is left.'"

The old man's voice trailed off.

#44

It was getting towards evening and I needed to pee after drinking two pitchers of lemonade. I told Goodson and he pointed towards the trees, so I went out and pissed on a birch tree while thinking about what he had told me. When I came back he had assembled the drilling and was weighing it on his lap.

Without pausing I started, "None of that explains why Devanter wants you so bad."

"His dad found out about my past. He threatened to tell the public. I couldn't risk that."

"So the son still has the proof?"

"Yes. Cornelius has copies of my military records, photos of me receiving medals, newspaper reports from my village, confirmation records, birth records, even copies of letters from Goering—he sent them out to anyone who got any kind of decoration. Transcripts of my trial and sentence in Canada and so on."

"Are you wanted anywhere?"

Goodson looked at me uncomprehendingly and then said, "No. I've done my time. I'm a free man."

"So why doesn't he use what he's got? If he hates you so much?"

"I'm not entirely sure."

It didn't make sense and I said so. "So Devanter senior had the information way back when. I take it he blackmailed you? To do what?"

Goodson pinched the bridge of his nose. "He had me bow out of a huge contract in '68 to build a freeway system right through Winnipeg. The joke was on him though, the whole deal fell through and they went for a Perimeter Highway with Peter Leitch's company in '69."

"Did you help with that?"

"Me? Well, maybe I knew it was a possibility. It was a long time ago that it happened but maybe I knew it was something that might happen and maybe I mentioned it as a good idea to some movers and shakers. I never could figure out why the old man didn't use the information afterwards, he sure had lots of opportunities."

"So he never used it, or even threatened to use it?"

"Nope. He just held onto it after that. We still fought but never over so much money. That much never came up again. After '69 I spent some time and money and tracked down the agencies Devanter had used—private agents in London and Germany, historians in Berlin and Moscow and the Pinkerton's here in Canada and the U.S. I tracked them all down and bought them off where I could."

The old man didn't make sense. "Why would you do that?"

"To find out if senior was bluffing with me. Me and him we fought for how many years, sometimes it was the only thing that seemed worth doing and sometimes he bluffed. But he wasn't bluffing. He had all the data in his hands."

I stood and turned away from Goodson and started to pace. It was a conscious effort to leave him with a loaded shotgun and rifle behind me but I put my hands behind my back and started to walk back and forth.

"You've still got the records you collected?"

"I do. In a safe place. Under an assumed name in a town I've never visited because accidents happen."

"Let me ask you something, why the fuck do you care what Devanter senior might have said or what Cornelius might say now?"

"It would ruin me." He said it simply.

"No it wouldn't. You're what, eighty-five? eighty-seven? You have no children, no family, no nothing. You've got money and power and that's about it. So why the fuck do you care what happens now?"

"I hate to lose."

I stood in front of him. "Old man, everyone loses. Get the fuck over it. Life is hard and then you die."

His eyes flashed and his knuckles whitened on the wood of the gun. "You don't have to tell me that *dummes Scheiss!*"

"I guess not. I shouldn't have to but here I am telling you anyway. Are you worried about public opinion?"

He thought about it. "Yes ... I think so."

"You live in a house three hours from the only decent-sized city within two days' drive. You deal with everything through lawyers and corporate structures. What do you care about the public? You don't have any contact with anyone that you don't control." Goodson stared at me and I went on, "And you didn't do anything that you haven't paid for. The law can't touch you and you don't care about society. So what else is there for you to worry about?"

"Ah."

"However, you're not good at giving up. I think that's your problem. You just can't stand losing."

Goodson stared at me with open mouth and the young woman came out with a wooden tray with folding legs. She put it down between me and Goodson and then brought out a covered bowl full of thick-limbed pretzels, a bowl of dark brown mustard with a spoon and a third big bowl of Spanish peanuts. She checked my lemonade and Goodson's whiskey and left.

As she went back into the house she gave me an indecipherable look.

I spread mustard on the warm, soft pretzel and ate it slowly, and when I was done I started to talk again. "You're at the end of the game and it's the hardest part to play. It's only a loss if you consider it a loss."

"It's not that easy."

"How so?"

"Think of the power of words. Think of the press who change the word 'rock' for 'stone' when describing the actions of Muslim youths throwing pebbles at Israeli tanks. Shooting a teenager who throws a rock at you is a lot more acceptable than shooting a boy who throws stones."

"Interesting."

"Sticks and stones may break my bones ..."

"I get it already."

"And in Afghanistan and Iraq our soldiers get blown up with Improvised Explosive Devices. Because our enemies could never build or use a bomb—they're too stupid. I don't want to lose and that's what all this is about, I'm willing to pay for it. And I don't want to be called a Nazi."

He had a point. "Okay. It's your money and you get to call the tune." I ate some peanuts. "So why doesn't Cornelius use what he's got to fuck you up?"

"No idea."

I had two ideas, sort of, anyway. "Number one, he doesn't use the information because he knows it's useless. Number two, he doesn't use the information because ..."

"Because what?"

"Let me think here. He's got a weapon but he doesn't use it. Why? Because it doesn't work, that's one possibility. Or because it's dangerous to him."

"Dangerous to him?"

"Yes. Dangerous." I ate peanuts and paced back and forth while the old man finished his rye. "Can you prove that Devanter senior blackmailed you?"

"No. I can prove he collected the information though. I bought out the inquiry agents in London lock, stock and barrel. Including their correspondence with Devanter senior. Like I said, I wanted to find out exactly what he knew."

I finally understood. It was like a big burst of light behind my eyes and everything fell into place. I sat down. "Mr. Goodson. You can do anything you want and Cornelius won't do jack shit."

"How can you be sure?"

"Because you have proof that his father discovered you were a Nazi and didn't tell anyone. If you come forward and tell the press that, they'll freak out. Then they'll realize you're not wanted and then they'll start wondering why Devanter senior gathered up all the information in the first place."

The woman came out and put her hand on Goodson's shoulder and I kept talking.

"And, Mr. Goodson, that's why Cornelius doesn't want to

use what he's got. It embarrasses his father and his father is dead and can't defend himself."

Goodson stared at me and the woman said, "Aubrey? It's time for you to go to bed."

He got up slowly, staring at me. "Maybe. Maybe you're right. So all I have to do is release the information myself."

"Yes."

"And I win."

"Yes."

He smiled and the woman led him inside. I waited until she came back.

"Is he going to be okay?"

"He's an old man. But this has helped."

"Really?"

"Yes. You see, he hates to lose and that's what he thought was happening. He thought he was losing."

"And now he doesn't?"

"I think so. He never understood that to the living we owe respect, but to the dead we owe only the truth."

"That's very deep."

She smiled and showed dimples. "It's not mine. It's a quote from a smart man called Voltaire. For Aubrey no one ever dies and so he saves the truth very carefully indeed just in case he needs it. And really, after all, how can you lose to the dead? They're dead and gone, right? They don't keep count."

I left, feeling disquieted. I treasured the truth myself and held it close to my chest. It was my weapon and my armour. And I certainly wasn't going to waste it on the dead, or the living either, for that matter.

#45

I got back to town late and left the Mustang parked in front of the house. When I walked through the door I found myself facing Claire with the Browning partially disassembled on piles of newspaper. Beside her elbow was the Beretta.

"Hi honey! Miss me?"

"You have no idea. Fred's been a doll though."

She sneered and gestured with her chin at the life-like toy doll in the corner of the dining room.

When the gun was cleaned and oiled and reloaded we went upstairs and slept on opposite sides of the bed.

There was an interview scheduled in a local television station and that's where I went first after dropping off the Mustang.

I had left Claire staring grimly into her cup of coffee with dry toast and a congealing fried egg on a plate at her elbow.

We'd spoken perhaps three words to each other.

I walked. On the way to the station I made good time and I dawdled along Portage Avenue, trying to spot the cops and

255

wondering if they were still tailing me. At a doughnut shop downtown I grabbed an extra large double cream and single sugar and a sour cream old-fashioned and watched for cops while I stood at a high bar up against the window.

"Excuse me." A young woman came up beside me with her own coffee. I moved to the side and she pulled out a thick paperback and started to read. Her place was marked by a large, homemade bookmark and she put it beside her coffee.

Was she a cop? I looked her over carefully. Late twenties and fairly short but nicely built with hazel eyes and light brown hair. I could see through her white t-shirt and saw lace around the cups of her bra.

She caught me looking at her chest and seemed amused. "Are you done?"

"Ummm. Yes."

I turned away and decided she wasn't a cop for three reasons. One, I had never met a cop with lace around the cups of their bra. Two, she had challenged me and cops on tails didn't do that, they were trained not to react. And three, she was reading *Il Milione, The Complete Travels of Marco Polo: The Yule-Cordier Translation* and I doubted a cop had ever read that.

There was careful printing on the bookmark and I caught part of it.

"Excuse me?"

Without looking up the woman said, "No you can't buy me a drink and no I don't come here often and no, you don't know me. Any other questions?"

"Actually, can I read your bookmark?"

She slid it across to me silently and read it for me, "Seduction isn't making someone do what they don't want to do. It is enticing someone into doing what they secretly want to anyway."

"Thank you."

She didn't say anything else and I left. Sometimes all it takes is a single idea to form to jell everything into a cohesive whole. And the bookmark was that idea.

I still had a little time before I had to be at the station and I walked erratically through the downtown streets and thought. Maybe the Shy Man was having relationships with his victims, just inside his mind. Maybe he was loving them in his own, destructive way.

Maybe he was seducing them.

Incidents break down into patterns; that was a basic rule of being a bad guy. It was almost a superstition.

If you're addicted to cocaine you run out of it eventually. Then you have to rob someone to go buy more cocaine but you run out of it eventually and then you have to rob someone to go buy more cocaine but you ... A pattern of behaviour leading to the incident of the robbery. This happens and then this other thing happens.

And sometimes incidents become patterns.

So. Maybe the Shy Man was having a relationship in his sick little mind. He met his victims somewhere or he saw them, somehow he connected with them. Then he sent them gifts, made phone calls, asked them out for coffee and maybe lunch and dinner and so on. All like a normal seduction/relationship.

Which would normally end with the couple falling into bed unless either partner decided against it.

But in the case of the Shy Man in the end the victim was taken apart.

Because that was the incident that ended the pattern and allowed him to start again.

He wasn't stalking his victims, he was seducing them.

And in his mind they were helping. Because seduction required that the other person wanted to be seduced.

I got to the station with ten minutes to spare and both Brenda and Dean met me with concerned looks on their faces. Brenda spoke through tight lips as she started to brush at invisible fluff on my shirt and jacket.

"We thought you weren't going to make it."

"I did."

Dean looked worried. "This Candy is trying very hard to be noticed at a national level in her industry. She will ask some provocative questions and will expect some provocative responses."

I looked at them both intently. "Advice?"

They looked at each other and then Brenda spoke. "Go for broke. The station is getting good ratings; this might be your only chance. I say go for it."

Dean nodded. "It could be your best chance."

A young dark-haired man in a cheap business suit came and got me, introducing himself as Fred the production assistant. He led me onto the stage where two cameras were locked in place, one pointing at one chair and one at another. Between the chairs was a small table with glasses of water and from everywhere hot, bright light shone down and I regretted my grey suit for temperature reasons alone.

I sat down in the indicated chair and after about ten seconds Candy came out and sat down opposite me. A technician hooked us both up with little microphones attached to lapels and belt-mounted power packs. Candy was wearing a navy blue pantsuit and had her hair done up tightly around her face but the effect was still ruined by her overly wide mouth that seemed to want to smile no matter how cold she made her expression.

"Mr. Haaviko? May I call you Monty?"

"Monty is good. Candy, right?"

"That's right. Shall we start?"

She was talking to me in a condescending way that I quite enjoyed. I think she thought she had me cold but that was okay. I love it when people underestimate me.

Dean and Brenda stood off to the side with two technicians and someone I didn't recognize. Lights on the camera turned green.

"Let's go."

Candy started, "Good evening everyone, my name is Candy Sawchuck and I am here with Montgomery Haaviko, who is running to be the commissioner of the new police commission."

She gestured to me and I nodded. "Happy to be here, Candy. Thanks."

She turned back to the cameras and her smile vanished. "He is also a convicted felon."

I think she expected me to be shocked. "I am that too."

"So why should the people trust you?"

I laughed and it wasn't even forced. "They shouldn't. But then the citizens should never trust the people in power."

"What do you mean?"

"I mean that right now the people have an opportunity to make a change. Up until now the police have policed themselves and now that's going to change. But my opponent is an ex-cop and if he wins then what will really change?"

This was not what Candy was expecting. "What do you mean?"

"I mean that there is a definition of insanity I quite like. It says that insanity is doing the same thing over and over again and expecting a different result. That's what we're doing if we put cops back in charge of policing themselves. It hasn't worked before so why should it work now?"

In the sound room Dean covered his eyes and Brenda grinned widely while one of the technicians looked a little stunned.

I was on a roll so I kept talking. "Let's talk about effective policing. Effective policing is sometimes counter-intuitive to the people involved and that causes a lot of stress, especially for the police themselves. Sometimes what they want to do is not in the best interests of society."

Candy cut in. "Can you give me an example?"

"Certainly. Imprisonment. Many police officers believe that stiffer penalties result in a reduction in crime."

"Are you implying it doesn't?"

"Yes." I drank some water. "Stiffer penalties do not reduce crime. Check out the countries with the highest imprisonment records: the United States has 715 people per 100,000 behind bars, Russia has 584 people per 100,000 behind bars, South Africa has 402 people per 100,000 behind bars and Canada has 116 people per 100,000 behind bars. So, the United States should be the safest, right?"

"Well, not necessarily ..."

"Right. The United States had about 4 murders per 100,000 people, Russia had about 20 murders per 100,000 people, South Africa has 50 murders per 100,000 people and Canada had about 2 murders per 100,000 people. Harsher penalties, more arrests, more people in prison does not mean a safer community. Yet many people are invariably in favour of longer sentences."

"Why do you suppose that is?"

"Because it seems like it should work but it doesn't. It's predicated on prevention through fear, and criminals are optimists."

"They are?"

"They are. They never think they will get caught. But on a regular basis the idea of more prisons and more prison time gets passed around all the time. It's normal, along with ideas that protecting the police means the same as protecting the community—and that is not necessarily so. Listen to the language being used by those who support more police and longer sentences, they talk about police taking out the trash, protecting society, damage to justice and enforcing the law. There are some very strong and negative words being used here. But let's be honest, the truth is that the system is doing what it is supposed to be doing—reviewing each case one at a time and making impartial decisions."

Candy looked intrigued. "And why does the system do that?"

"Our society spreads the blame around when we deal with justice. Which is what our society is designed to do."

"Excuse me?"

"We say judge, jury and executioner. We divide the roles in criminal cases. We blindfold justice to make sure she is impartial. That is central to our idea of justice. We do not allow judges to rule in cases where they know the accused. We do not allow police officers to investigate their brothers and sisters. We do not allow prosecutors to prosecute people who have murdered their children."

I drank more water and turned to the cameras.

"So why should we give more power to the police? We should spread the power and the responsibility around even more. Justice is not easy; if it were there would be no recidivism. Experts tell us things that are counter indicative, and following the ideas always generates resistance. And most of the resistance comes from the police themselves, which is normal."

"I'm sorry Monty, I don't understand."

"Okay, here's another example. In England the police are travelling to areas with high vehicle crime and finding vehicles that are in danger of being stolen. Then they put stickers on car windows to inform the owner that their vehicle is at risk. They even have boxes to mark to inform the owner on how the vehicle is in danger. To many this is counter-intuitive—it tells the thieves what and how to steal."

"That sounds reasonable."

"But it also forces the owner to take action. It puts a police presence on the street. And it attracts the press so stories like this get out and people start to think about the world they're in."

Candy thought about it. "That's interesting. Is that what really happens?"

"It is. But police resistance to the idea is widespread despite the fact that it is working. Theft is dropping in the areas where the stickers are being delivered."

"I guess that makes sense."

"Okay, now let me give you an example of what I'm talking about right here in River City." Candy didn't laugh; I guess she wasn't a big fan of musicals and had never seen *The Music Man*. "Right now the police union is up in arms over a proposed plan for the service to start cutting the amount of time plainclothes officers spend in investigative units."

"What do you mean exactly?"

"Units like vice, organized crime and so on. In the new rules detective sergeants could get rotated out after four years, compared to the current five. And constables could get rotated out after one year instead of three."

"Why is the union complaining?"

"Because they feel that inexperience of officers in the premium units could hamper conviction rates. This is possible. But by changing the rotation rates the service is going to put more police officers with more experience back on the streets—which is where they do the most good."

"That seems to make sense. But you say the police union doesn't feel that way?"

"Nope. But they're offering a possible result by describing the cases falling through, one that may or may not happen. Yet the plan will offer a concrete result—one we know will happen. The more police on the street the less crime you have. Period. I don't mean police in cars or storefront offices or helicopters or submarines. I mean police on the street, walking around, talking to people, introducing themselves ..."

"Hold on. You believe police on the street solves crimes?"

"No. It prevents them." I took a drink of water and then took Candy's glass and started in on that. She waited until I put the glass down. "So there are two viewpoints here. One that this will lower the crime rate and the other that it will increase the crime rate."

"Yes. And the citizens need to hear both sides of the story. But they only hear one voice."

"And you'll provide a new voice?"

"Yes. I'll provide a different voice. I will be a change. And it's time for a change, isn't it?"

#46

When the cameras were off Candy shook my hand and said, "That was the dumbest fucking thing I've ever seen. You have just alienated half of the city."

"You think so?"

Brenda and Dean came up, both looking stunned, and Dean cut in, "Half at least. Maybe more. Jesus, Monty, what the hell were you thinking?"

I shrugged. "I was thinking of sending a message."

"What message? That you're nuts?"

Brenda said, slowly, "No. Not that. Actually I think Monty told the truth. Not that that's a good idea."

I nodded. "And fuck 'em if they can't take a joke."

Candy hid a smile and Dean and Brenda wandered away. The last I heard they were both muttering something about tequila shooters.

I thanked Candy and the technicians and washed my face in the bathroom.

Outside I took my jacket off and hung it over my shoulder.

My stomach growled and I realized I was starving so I looked around the parking lot for a hot dog vendor or something but there was nothing. While I was trying to decide what to do I heard a low cough behind me and a voice say, "Mr. Haaviko?"

I turned and saw a small, slight man in his late forties or early fifties about six feet away. He was wearing black wool pants and a long trench coat with a black felt bowler hat on his head. His right hand was in the pocket of his coat, an umbrella was hooked over his wrist and his left hand was open at his side. His face was closely shaved and his eyes were pale brown behind thick-lensed granny glasses. He looked vaguely familiar.

"Yes?"

The right side of his coat swung open and I saw his right hand and for a minute I saw double and felt confused and then I realized he had stuffed his empty sleeve with something to give it a shape and then tucked the empty sleeve into his pocket.

In his real right hand was a huge pistol held at waist level.

My hands became fists and I feinted left and started to move towards him. But he had already pulled the trigger and the gun went boom and something very hard hit me in the chest and knocked me backwards onto my ass

For a second I couldn't breathe and I was sure I was dying.

It wasn't so bad actually. The dying I mean.

Although I very much missed Claire and Fred.

Then the man was kneeling on my stomach and slamming his gun into the side of my face. Not hard but over and over again.

I tried to get my hands up to protect myself but I couldn't, my arms just refused to move. As he hit me I could swear he was singing low, as though to himself, something about a girl's knickers and how you could see them if you wanted to pay.

I woke up puking into a canvas bag over my head in a moving vehicle. I couldn't remember getting knocked out. Which is normal, you never remember getting knocked out.

My head ached and my nose and mouth were full of the stench of vomit. Not to mention the fact that I was dizzy, nauseous and my legs and crotch were damp. Which meant I had pissed myself.

A cultured voice pierced my pain. "Mr. Haaviko? I assume you're awake?"

I tried to say yes but wasn't sure what actually came out. However, the man seemed to understand. "That's good."

The car or whatever turned a corner and the voice went on, "That's very good. Now. If you behave everything will be fine."

The car turned another corner and accelerated and a radio came on, a police band radio full of panic and confusion. "If you do not behave I will cut the tendons behind your ankles and knees. Then things will get really bad. Do you understand?"

The police radio made sense; sometimes bad guys used them to keep track of cops.

"Yeshh." I could not feel my hands or my arms and I seemed to be unable to move my feet as well, oh well.

"Excellent. Your understanding and acceptance of this whole situation is very edifying."

He shut up and I got to listen to the radio and it wasn't good. My concentration was bad and I knew I was concussed but I could still make out some key words and numbers.

"Status 1—status 3." That meant cops were available and

had arrived. There were lots of those. Something big must be going on.

The language codes came back to me very slowly indeed but they came back. I had memorized hundreds of them over the years and they were hard-wired in. By reflex I had memorized the codes before I came to the city.

A very calm, professional voice said ,"Listen please. We have code 2705. We have code 9902. We have code 9906." That meant offensive weapon and violence and a mental condition.

The words didn't make sense to me and then they fitted in.

A different voice came on. "We've got D4G and she's definitely DOA." That meant multiple gunshot wounds and one dead lady.

"10-33." Officer needs help. My brain was starting to work, which was nice.

"10-75. 10-75. 10-75. Looking for the latest 10-75. Folks, keep your eyes open." 10-75 was a police hater, a classic. Oh God, I started to throw up again when the car hit something and bounced.

"Code 3." A hot response, an emergency response. I must have passed out again because there was a blank space, then a voice speaking in plain English.

"We have one officer down and one missing. We are looking for Officer Morgan. We believe he has been kidnapped. He is a white male, twenty-eight, six foot four inches high, 240 pounds. The situation is extremely serious. His partner is dead—shot and stabbed multiple times. We believe there are multiple assailants. Extreme caution is required."

My head started to clear again and the police radio was turned off and a regular station came on. "And this just in, a police officer was ambushed and murdered this morning. Her partner was kidnapped at the same time. Police are looking for the officer who is described as a young Caucasian male. Anyone with any information is requested to contact the police immediately. However, the perpetrators are armed and extremely dangerous and are not to be approached under any circumstances."

The radio turned off and the cultured voice spoke again. "We will be home soon. If you behave good things will happen. There may even be cake. We should have no troubles with the police; they're very busy and should be for a long time. They get so stirred up when one of their own goes missing, don't they?"

The car went down a decline, quite far down in fact and then it levelled out and the car stopped.

"And here we are! Home again, home again, happy is the sailor home from the sea!"

#47

The engine turned off and a door opened. Then it closed and then another door opened and something caught my legs and then I was moving.

And whoever was doing it was grunting and panting like it was hard work.

Then I was falling and slamming into concrete and I was out again. When I became conscious again I was on something that rattled and rolled.

"... and you, sir, are quite ridiculously fat. I don't know what Clarice saw in you! However, it is nothing we cannot deal with."

I heard rattling and then an electric engine started and we were going up. Strange smells managed to cut through the vomit in the bag on my head. Smells of chemicals and something musty I'd never smelled before.

"And here we are. Your home away from home so to speak. For as long as you choose to spend here."

Something touched my hands and then they were in front of

me and then above me but I could still barely feel them. There was the sound of a smaller engine and I was moving upright, pulled by something implacable, and the pain from my chest was incredible and for a second I couldn't feel my head hurt.

Then the bag was off my head and I could sort of see except for the blood and vomit caked onto my face. The man in front of me looked curious and unremarkable and slightly, vaguely familiar.

If I had seen him I had immediately forgotten him.

His nose wrinkled in a strangely delicate motion. "Phew. You stink, sir."

He fumbled at his feet and came up with a plastic squeeze bottle and a rag. In his other hand he held a short knife, about three inches long and very broad, made out of what looked to be black glass, all carefully chipped to sharpness along the edges. He held the knife to my throat and started to clean my face with the rag.

"In case you're wondering, you were shot with a teakwood round from the shotgun barrel of my pistol. A .63 inch diameter eight-inch length of good quality teak. Quite expensive and imported from Annan, or whatever they call it now. It's kind of like getting hit with a small car, I imagine."

The black glass knife, the casual kidnapping, the level of violence dealt to the police as a distraction, the insanity in the actions of the man in front of me.

The Shy Man.

It had to be.

The man reached up and mopped my face with cold water. "It's based on a lovely idea the British Army used against rioting anarchist yellow communist niggers in Hong Kong in the late 60's. 1960's, that is. In the 1860's they would have used real lead, which would have stopped a lot of problems dead."

He twisted my face to the side to check his handiwork. "Of course, in Hong Kong they fired the teak rounds into the street and bounced them up into their targets."

He patted my cheek once and twice softly and then a third time hard. "But you're a big tough guy and I didn't have time for that."

After he had cleaned me for awhile he took his jacket off and put it somewhere behind him. I still wasn't focussing very well but I could see a holster on a belt around his waist. And in the holster was a huge walnut-handled pistol.

"Are you looking at my gun?"

He said it almost coquettishly.

"Yes. It's a nice gun."

"You like it? It's a LeMat revolver, circa 1856. Black powder and brass cap design."

The Shy Man grinned sweetly like he was talking about his new car. My brain was working a little. The black powder meant it was an antique and therefore fell between any kind of gun control rules and regulations. It also meant that the Shy Man could make his own ammunition; hell, he could even make his own black powder if he wanted. It wasn't hard to do—just charcoal, sulphur and saltpetre.

He held the gun up where I could see it, a big, heavy, forward-pointing design with an octagonal barrel about a foot long and a short, fat barrel under that. The hammer was huge and the butt was slightly rounded and came with a place to attach a lanyard to make it hard to lose the damn thing.

"It holds nine shots plus the shotgun and I can cast my own lead balls from child's soldiers that I buy at antique swaps. The bigger barrel underneath is a shotgun. It was designed by a French-descended doctor in New Orleans during the American Civil War; despite that it's quite a good gun. This particular one was built in Birmingham, England and was supposed to be shipped to the Dixies but it never happened. A very elegant device, not at all like those crude Remingtons and Colts or those ridiculously déclassé modern guns."

"It's very nice."

"If you're good I'll blow your brains out with it. It will be quite an honour. Okay?"

I could only nod weakly. Then the knife came up again and he started to cut off my clothes. With smooth, slick motions he cut my clothes into ribbons and let the ribbons fall to the ground. He wasn't that careful and lots of blood flowed as well.

Then the Shy Man left and I closed my eyes and tried to focus through the pain.

After awhile my eyes went into focus and I could see a wooden wall across the way from me. There were words written in flowing script a foot high, words in gold-coloured paint in a language I didn't understand. It looked like Arabic but I wasn't sure. Under the artistry were words in old-style English calligraphy about the same size:

"In the narrow passage there will be no brother, no friend."

Then the rest of the room slid into my perception. It was over thirty feet long and narrow, about ten feet, with a fifteen-foot-high ceiling. Holding the ceiling in place were multiple six by six inch square wooden posts running from the floor to the ceiling. Everything I could see was wooden, walls made up of planks and panels, and there was dust everywhere. And there were strong smells, all sorts of them, chemicals and moist dirt and a kind of musk and animal smell. Acid smells and oil smells and electrical smells. Up against the far wall were low piles of something dark and hairy. My eyes focussed more and I saw that the floor was made of splintered old wooden planks and that the light was dim and seemed natural.

The best time to escape from any situation is right after you're captured. That's when you're the most alert and the least damaged. That's what the rules say, but I looked above me to check the situation and sighed. It's hard to escape when your hands are tied together with chains and ropes and are hung from an electric winch so your toes just barely touch the floor. It's also hard to escape when your ribs are bruised and probably broken. I looked down to check my chest out and found a dinner-plate-sized bruise, purple and angry, in the middle.

I figured I was probably concussed and in shock and I thought about that and listened to sounds of echoes and the hum of electrics and then I closed my eyes and went to sleep.

That's another rule of bad guys: if you can't do anything else, sleep and recover energy. And with practice you can sleep standing up, although I do not recommend it.

#48

The Shy Man woke me up by throwing a bucket of cold water on me and singing out, "Here I come with a sharp knife and a clear conscience!"

I didn't react and he took another rag and dried my face. "I have to move you. If I leave you like this for too long your shoulders will separate and that's bad. But I don't want to have any shit from you either. For that reason I will be putting these ear muffs on."

He held them in front of me and they were big state-of-the-art muffs used by shooters. "And I will be covering your eyes with duct tape as well. You will move in the direction I indicate and stop when I tap you. If you fail I will cut you up a very great deal. Do you understand?"

"Yesh." I tried to act groggier than I felt and he put the muffs on, sealed my eyes and stuffed a gag into my mouth before lowering me to the ground with the engine. When I was unhooked he let me get to my feet at my own speed and then pushed me to the side until I hit one of the posts.

I had been in some pretty bad situations before but I had never felt more alone and helpless.

With more force he made me turn around until the post was at my back and raise my hands. Something cold went around my chest and was tightened. Then something around my waist and knees and ankles. Finally my hands were brought down and separated.

I couldn't feel either of them and he massaged them until I screamed and then forced them around the back of the post where something else cold went onto my wrists and secured them.

Then the Shy Man went away and I was alone in the absolute dark of my very own skull.

And I guess time passed.

Most of my eyebrows left when the Shy Man tore the tape off my eyes and I screamed into my gag. In front of me the man took a clunky-looking tape recorder from his jacket pocket, examined it and put it carefully in a corner out of my view. Then he cut my gag free and pulled the muffs from my ears and I took a deep breath and coughed.

The noise awoke a young man bound with broad strips of blue fibre tape over a railing in front of me. His arms and legs looked lumpy and I realized they had been broken. I could only imagine the amount of pain he was in.

I stared at the young man. He wore a blue uniform and his hat was on the floor. He still had his gun in his holster and he began to yell into another piece of tape across his mouth.

From where I was I could see lettering on the wall, industrial script that read "Lots A-G, mink and fox—commercial farm." Then I started to recognize some of the smells as the musky, dusty smells of furs, but old ones.

Between me and the cop a ladder led down onto a dim warehouse floor and we seemed to be in a loft overlooking everything. From where I was I could see that the dim light was coming through dusty narrow windows in the walls and ceilings. Down on the warehouse floor was a long, battered station wagon with a sign on the side that read "Antiques and Marvels."

The name resonated in my head. I remembered Alex and Claire at the Red River midway walking over to a booth with that sign above it. And in the booth had been the man who had shot me, wearing a smile and gesturing towards a tabletop loaded with expensive crap and antique china.

I looked down and saw that I had a chain with a big padlock around my chest and the same around my waist, knees and ankles.

The ladder shook and the Shy Man came up. He was wearing a transparent plastic raincoat and nothing else and carrying a roll of plastic sheet and the black glass knife tied in a bundle on his shoulder.

Silently he began to unroll the plastic under the cop and then he pulled the knife out and checked the blade by cutting an idle gouge in the cop's side.

Then he looked at me and repeated the line, "And here I come with a sharp knife and a clear conscience."

I said, "Wait …"

But he ignored me and took the cop apart.

When he was finished the cop was still breathing intermittently, and the Shy Man had lost his raincoat and the knife had broken somewhere. He got to his feet breathing hard and pulled the cop's pistol and examined it with a child's wonder. The Shy Man was covered in dried and fresh blood, and other substances and flecks of meat hung in his hair.

His eyes were expressionless as he took his glasses off and licked the lenses clean.

Then he shot the cop in the back of his head.

The noise echoed as he re-holstered the weapon on the corpse and climbed back down the ladder.

He left me with the body until it got dark outside. Then he came back from behind me and held a new black glass knife in front of my eyes. "Obsidian is a fascinating material. Volcanic glass and capable of holding an incredible edge. Some surgeon even performed an appendectomy with one. A little brittle perhaps but still …"

He held a plastic bottle in front of me. "Thirsty."

"Yesh."

"Well. I want you to read out a message for your wife into a tape recorder. Then you can drink."

"Fuck you."

His face became still. "What?"

"Fuck you."

He lost it and started to hit me. But he wasn't that strong and he never used the knife. He also hit me most of the time in the stomach, almost never in the face.

But I never said a word. I did not cooperate. I didn't give him any words he could string together on a tape to make a message to Claire.

I gave him nothing and I took the beating and in a way I kind of enjoyed it.

He was punishing me for getting caught.

So I took the beating and I laughed and that made him hit me harder.

Finally I gasped, "My wife. Why my wife?"

He screamed, "SHE'S MINE NOW!" Like a switch he calmed

down. "At the fair, she picked my mother's favourite china pattern. It shows great taste and talent. It was a sign from God."

He nodded solemnly and I laughed at him for real. Which made him lose his patience and start to hit me again. Eventually I became unconscious.

My mind drifted in shock. I went back to the first time I had ever been arrested, the cop looking at me from a great distance. His face melted until he became the young guy the Shy Man had taken apart.

And he said, very slowly, "Everything not compulsory is banned. Everything not banned is compulsory."

He squeezed my testicles and twisted and the pain spiked right past where I should have passed out but there are limits to pain.

The endorphins produced by the brain define those limits. Those wonderful drugs that are oh so close to opium, to heroin, to codeine, to all my old and true friends.

And I enjoyed those too.

I travelled to a steak dinner with Smiley outside Kansas City. A dinner neither of us planned on paying for because we were going to rob the place. A dinner served in the velvet room by a naked forty-year-old woman wearing high heels and stockings that tied into dents beneath the line of her pubis.

I had come back to the restaurant years after the diamond job and I had come because I remembered the rich men in the place and the way they paid in cash and wore good jewellery. I had told Smiley and he had agreed.

. He always agreed.

In my memories Smiley was saying words I had never heard.

"And then of course there is my friend who shot himself in the head to avoid a tequila hangover."

"You made that up!"

"Probably."

And the woman brought us hundred-year-old brandy in snifters a foot across. And you could cut the steak with the edge of your spoon. And the smell of the woman was not perfume. And the weight in my pocket was the most expensive pistol I'd ever stolen, a $5,000 Korth-Waffen revolver.

And I knew someone was going to die that night. And I was right.

I drifted in and out of consciousness and I laughed when I could and the Shy Man grunted and screamed and started to use the tip of his knife to cut me but that was nothing.

I remembered a beating by cousins with bicycle chains and the pain of a meth explosion. I remembered a cop shooting me in the face and the powder blinding me. And I remembered a girl saying, "Let's not ruin our special friendship ..."

The first dinner with Claire after months of chasing her.

"I have severe mental problems dealing with garnish. You know, this little sprig of parsley that looks so lonely sitting on the plate next to the hamburger. What's the point? It's too damn small to have any nutritional value. And it looks so forlorn sitting there next to the grease so it can't be there for visual reasons. Just one of those things God didn't mean for us to understand."

Claire waited until I was finished, then she reached over, took the parsley and chewed it up. "It freshens your breath, you asshole."

"Ah. That was my second guess."

The Shy Man had worked himself until his mouth foamed and he spat as he grunted and kicked and swung. The pain was a fucking joke.

It was a friend.

And inside the pain I remembered being alive and I loved that and smiled and that made the Shy Man even angrier.

I used to have a girlfriend who believed, really believed in magic. She used to make love and then crouch over me and whisper, "To bind Fenris the gods spoke to the dwarves and told them to make the chain Gleipnir from six things: the noise of the footfall of a cat, the beards of women, the spittle of birds, the breath of fishes, the nerves of bears and the roots of stones."

Now I understand she was trying to hold me. At the time I thought she was nuts, a great lay but nuts.

She believed in magic though and whether I did or didn't was unimportant.

The Shy Man finally stopped like his batteries had run down.

#49

I woke up still chained to the post. The Shy Man was painting my cuts with iodine and the pain had brought me round.

"I had a dream last night. I have it every night. I was looking at a pencil drawing on a museum wall. It reads for me from right to left."

He had recovered his voice and had cleaned up. He was methodical in his motions but I kept my mouth shut and he went on.

"First it is a recumbent women, her face blocked by her left elbow, hand behind her neck. Her right hand is on her belly, her left knee blocks her sex and her right leg is straight. Her breasts are full with erect nipples."

The smell of the iodine mixed with the reek of my waste, as my bowels and bladder had cut loose at some point. He ignored that and kept talking as though we were having a conversation.

"Her legs end in a mess. From the mess is a falling female dropping back. She uses her left hand to unbutton her shirt and her right to throw away her tie. She has pants on and a belt. Her hair is straight and falling forward and it shades her face. Her legs end in a mess."

There was a rhythm to the way the little fuck was talking. It was poetry.

"From the mess stands a third woman. She faces me with braced legs and a policeman's uniform and hat. No jacket. In her hands is a revolver in a two-handed grip pointing at me. Her hair hangs free in wisps and frames a perfectly blank face. She has just killed me."

He looked up at me. "What do you think it means?"

My voice was rusty. "That you're a fucking loon."

The accusation didn't bother him. "I prefer to think of it as a warning. An anti-entropic pulse message sent winging down the wires from the future me to this me. It's telling me what to look out for."

When he was done he just stared at me, confused. "Actually I don't know why I told you that."

Then he left and I was alone again.

The math in my head was relentless. Without food I would die in roughly a month, and it would probably take longer. I would suffer from weakness, confusion, irritability and so on and finally hallucinations, convulsions and so on. Without water I would die in a couple of days, probably less, and I would suffer from exhaustion and rage and finally slide into shock.

Or I could bite through my tongue and bleed to death in about five minutes. That was my last card though. My version of "You can't fire me, I quit!" And I didn't want to do it unless I had too.

In truth death takes care of itself.

What I wanted was one clean shot at my friend with the knife.

If I died getting that shot that was just fine. Indeed it struck me as being a pretty fair trade.

He came back with a very old Polaroid camera and some flat packs of film still sealed in plastic.

"Mr. Montgomery Haaviko. Are you wondering how I found you?" I shook my head but he kept talking. "I simply called your assistant Dean and claimed to be a photographer and he told me when and where you would be. It was that easy."

I tried to wiggle but the chains were too tight, stainless steel does not give.

"I hate to lie so I am going to take your photograph."

His smile was bright.

"And are you wondering about Officer Morgan?" I shook my head again but he still ignored me. "I knew the police were watching you and your wife and I needed you so I gave them something to worry about. It was easy. I found a cop car and took my LeMat with one teak round and used it on the driver through the window. Then I switched to the revolver barrel and shot the other one and then cut her up some. So very simple."

The Shy Man stared thoughtfully into the distance. "So very easy to distract the great unwashed. If you know how. So easy to get them to react emotionally."

He loaded the Polaroid and pointed it at me. "So now I'm going to send these to your wife and see if she'd like to come have our date."

I shook my head and the Shy Man was amused. "You don't think she'll come?"

The camera flashed over and over again.

"I think she'll come. She loves you very much and would do anything to save you. And if she doesn't come then she's a bad woman and deserves to be punished."

#50

Claire came.

The Shy Man explained how he had sent the pictures to Claire's work along with a new cell phone so he could give her instructions.

He had thought it all through. He knew the cops could track a cell by triangulating the receiving towers. And he explained how he would make Claire disrobe at one point and change in a hotel room into clothes he had provided while he watched her through the phone's camera. That way she could bring no weapons.

He knew about the cops watching our place. And he knew that everyone in the city was on edge looking for the cop killer and the kidnapped cop, and he relied on that fear and tension to eventually make everyone tired. Because then they'd start to make mistakes.

No one can be alert all the time.

I stared at him when he said he knew about the cops, and he shook his head violently. "Do you think I am some ass?

Some impatient child? I always watch very, very carefully. And I never act until I am sure. It wouldn't be honourable. But now I know she loves me! And I love her because I am a gentleman."

Fucking loon.

Sometime on the second day I could hear the elevator start up on the floor of the warehouse and then Claire came into my view. Her hands were held in front of her, linked with heavy iron manacles that looked like more antiques.

She was wearing a white silk dress with brocade across her breasts and on her neck.

Behind her was the Shy Man in his black wool suit with the LeMat in one hand and the obsidian knife in the other.

His eyes were dilated as Claire stepped forward and kissed me.

"Hey!" The Shy Man was outraged.

In the kiss Claire pushed a square of metal into my mouth. It took a second before my numb and swollen tongue recognized it. A double-sided razor blade, a throwing star for the poor.

Good girl.

She was crying as the Shy Man pulled her back and hit her in the back of the head with the heavy barrel of the revolver. My wife wobbled and the Shy Man wrenched her arms up and attached them to a rusty iron hook hanging from an engine on the ceiling beam near the wall ten feet away from me.

Then he turned the engine on until Claire was on her tiptoes.

He turned to me and took my manacles off and re-fixed my hands in front of me. Since the chains were still on I could do nothing. The manacle looked like hers, heavy, iron and square.

He had fixed a second engine above me and he looped the manacle through that and undid my chains, one-two-three-four.

I was weak as the blood surged back into me. I played up on the weakness but he had the gun pointed at Claire's lower legs.

So I had my shot but I passed on it and then I was in the air, dangling too.

Claire finally got some words out. "No tears to see me?"

"De-hy-d-rat-ed."

"We can't have that!" The Shy Man brought his water bottle and squired it into my mouth and I barely managed to avoid swallowing the razor. When the water was in me I smiled at Claire. "You look great."

The razor made my voice sound strange but the Shy Man didn't notice.

Claire answered, "And you look like shit." She turned to the Shy Man. "I'm here for our date. You can let him go."

"No." Neither Claire nor I acted surprised as the Shy Man turned to me. Neither of us had expected him to keep his promise. "I'm going to beat you to death and make your wife watch. Then we can be together without distractions."

He ended in a scream and his eyes were alight with some strong emotion. He holstered his pistol and removed a lumpy pair of black leather gloves from a jacket pocket.

"I bought these from a police supply house. Sap gloves with powdered lead sewn into the knuckles and palm. I want you to feel this." Then he was screaming again. "I want you to FEEL everything!"

I didn't feel it but I faked calm. "Ah, you've got it wrong."

He paused in pulling on his gloves and looked confused. "I do?"

"Yeah. You keep acting like I'm the dangerous one. I'm not, she is."

I pointed, hard to do with your hands cuffed above your head but not impossible, and he turned to look at Claire.

I grabbed my right hand with my left and squeezed as hard as I could. The pain was staggering, but compared to the beating and the cutting and the fear it was nothing.

Nothing at all.

Sometimes an animal in a trap will gnaw its own leg off and ambush the trapper when they return.

Or so I've heard.

And Vikings in the good old days would sometimes cut off their own hands to make the Fountain of Tyr, a gush of blood to blind their enemies in a fight.

Or so I've been told.

Compared to that breaking some second-rate bones in a hand is a fucking joke.

I squeezed some more and for a second nothing happened, then the metacarpal bones in the lower thumb and pinkie broke loudly and my hand compressed and slid. I pulled it through the manacles and I was free.

The Shy Man heard the bones break and was turning back quickly, pulling the pistol from the holster on his hip. He moved just in time to catch the razor I spat at him. I missed though and it only gouged a little chunk out of his cheek, under his eye.

I had wanted to hit him square in his left eye and pop that little sack of aqueous humour.

Oh well, the distraction helped, as he flinched.

Then I was in close and my right elbow caught him in the hollow of his throat as my left hand covered his gun.

Nothing on me worked right. My body felt far away from me and I was as weak as a kitten. But sometimes that doesn't matter.

The elbow might have killed him. I felt his thyroid crush in his throat and I knew he'd start to suffocate right away.

But it would take time. Three minutes, probably longer, and one can do a lot of damage in three minutes.

I drew the gun towards me and twisted, getting my palm around the round wooden butt. It was heavier than I imagined, almost three pounds, and I let the weight bring the barrel down until it touched the Shy Man's thigh. By then I had control of the trigger and squeezed it briskly.

BOOM!

The lead .35 calibre round burned down the eight-inch barrel and went right through the Shy Man's calf and then burrowed through his leg and exited through the base of his foot.

He was silent and struggling fiercely but the shot made him lurch away from me and spin towards Claire. As he came around she rested her weight on the manacles above her head and raised her legs, showing a flash of skin and an absence of underwear. The Shy Man paused, transfixed despite himself.

"Get OVER yourself!" Claire yelled, driving her high-heeled feet into his face, and he went down, pulling her right shoe off entirely.

I took the gun from his hand before the Shy Man even touched the floor and got ready to fire a second shot but I didn't have to. The right shoe was stuck to his face, the three-inch heel driven right through his eye and lodged somewhere in his brain. He twitched for a long time and finally he stopped doing even that, which gave me a chance to find the keys in his pocket with numb fingers and unlock Claire and then myself.

We held each other for a long time in silence, her in her silk dress and me naked.

#51

"What are you doing?"

I had pulled on a pair of cloth gloves and had dragged the Shy Man into the centre of the warehouse and put him on top of a bale of very dry elk and bison hides. Claire watched me curiously, then climbed down the ladder.

"Dealing with the evidence." I dragged the cop over beside the Shy Man and then rolled the cop on top of his body. It didn't look right, so I drew the cop's pistol, put it in his right hand and fastened his fingers around it.

"Why?"

I nodded at the corpse. "I don't want to think about him ever again. If the cops come they'll search the place, gather evidence, and try to pin crimes on him. There will be newspaper stories. There will be movies and books and graphic novels and essays. He will become a martyr. A hero to freaks and a person of importance to the unhealthily curious."

Claire sat down at the bottom of the ladder. "I see."

"Yeah. People believe Hannibal Lecter is real—a princely

ghoul. They root for Norman Bates and admire his mother love. They think Jack the Ripper was misunderstood and try to scry truth in the entrails of his slaughter."

My wife was getting into the idea. "That's normal though, they're trying to make sense out of insanity. They're trying to integrate monsters and the things they don't understand."

"I love the way you talk! People blur the lines between fiction and fact. They buy John Wayne Gacy's paintings, Ted Bundy got married in prison, and you can buy serial killer autographs, collect trading cards and buy bestselling books about their exploits. People don't try to understand the monsters, they attempt to martyr them. I don't think the Shy Man here deserves our understanding and I know he doesn't deserve to be a martyr." My mouth turned into a rictus. "I think the Shy Man should vanish."

Claire thought about it. "So ... he just stops?"

It sounded like she was going to go along with it. "Yes. It's not very romantic or satisfying but this is real life. And that is not very romantic or satisfying but at least it's real."

"But I want revenge."

I stared at the corpse. "Vanishing his ass is the best revenge."

Claire kissed me and pulled on another pair of gloves and we spent five-and-a-half hours cleaning the place. First she bandaged me from top to bottom with the contents of a big first-aid kit we found in the Shy Man's station wagon. Then we wiped every place we might have touched with our bare skin and we gathered every note and scrap of paper we could find and filled a double-lined garbage bag with notebooks and albums. We found a little room off his bedroom where he kept trophies by tracing the sound of a hidden fridge inside a false wall. He kept mementoes—for lack of a better word—in plastic ziplock bags and glass canning jars filled with alcohol.

I sent Claire away while I flushed all that.

In reality the whole place was disturbing.

A fairly small warehouse in the middle of the city. Innocuous. With underground parking and lots of storage space.

We were stunned by the greenhouse we found, built from factory-ordered kits and sitting in the middle of the main floor storage area. The space was full of trestle tables growing roses and twenty different varieties of flowers.

I ushered Claire out when I saw the white of bone poking through the loam.

In the Shy Man's bedroom I found a folding stocked Ruger Mini-14 semi-automatic assault rifle with a 75-round snail drum magazine by his bed right beside a four-litre container of non-petroleum lubricant from Costco. Under his pillow were a folding saw and a dried human ear.

In a giant cedar trunk at the foot of the bed I found clothes all neatly dry cleaned, pressed and put away. All for a man and a woman much larger than the Shy Man. I threw them onto the floor and found a black and white wedding picture of an ugly man with a huge moustache wearing a uniform coat and a kilt and, beside him, in a flowing dress, an equally ugly woman.

I looked at them and saw, somewhere between them, the genesis of the Shy Man.

None of his clothes fit me so I rummaged until I found the kilt, a huge, heavy wool monstrosity and a white dress shirt that fit me like a tent but at least covered the bruises and cuts and some of the bandages.

In his main fridge we found jars of a yellow liquid I didn't think about.

By a La-Z-Boy recliner in his living room we found a swear

jar made from an old kerosene tin. It was full of old, tarnished quarters, the kind that still had silver in them.

In the kitchen I found a drawer full of loose cash and change, which I pocketed. I left behind a Luger 9mm pistol with no bullets in the magazine and a First World War trench knife with triangular blade and knuckle-duster hilt.

In a small dressing room I found a velvet-lined bedside drawer with sixty-two pieces of Ms. Paris's jewellery neatly arrayed. I filled another garbage bag with that and added it to the pile.

By the time it was way past dark I still wasn't sure we had gotten everything but I couldn't stand the place anymore, neither could Claire.

I put a chair in the middle of the room and went back to the bodies. There I pulled on five torn garbage bags (the best I could do for a Hazmat suit) and I picked up the Shy Man, who was stiff as a board. I pressed the LeMat into his right hand and got behind his body while pressing the barrel into a hole in the back of the head of the dead cop, who had started to go soft again in his chair. Then I squeezed the trigger.

The low velocity round took his head apart all the way.

I carried another chair from the kitchen into the room and put it beside the dead cop. Then I propped the Shy Man's body into it. I'd found a strange-looking reading lamp with parrot designs in his bedroom and I put that between the chairs and used the Shy Man's fingers to handle it. Then I snaked an extension cord from a kitchen outlet to the light and ran it through his dead fingers again.

When I was sure it would work I plugged the outlet into a digital timer set for 4:00 a.m. and plugged in the whole contraption. I chipped a small hole in the light bulb itself and made sure it hung down into a crystal goblet I filled with gasoline. The gasoline filled the bulb almost to the top where the filament was.

The idea was that the timer would count down and turn on the light bulb. Then the heat and spark of the light itself would ignite the gasoline—at about 495 degrees Fahrenheit. Surrounding the light I piled balled-up newspapers, torn books, broken furniture, cans of paint and formaldehyde, all liberally splashed with gasoline and kerosene I'd found stored near the station wagon.

The lamp would ignite the newspaper and other things and the fire would spread through the wooden building full of dried and splintered wood covered in one hundred years' worth of paint. And the tinder dry furs and hides would catch as well and the fire would burn hot and fast.

Or that was the hope.

I settled the Shy Man's corpse against the chair. With his fingers wrapped around the butt of the gun I pushed the barrel into his left eye, following the hole left by Claire's high heel as much as possible, and pulled the trigger.

His head exploded as well and the body flopped out of the chair and onto the floor like a billet of wet wood. The gun flipped away with the recoil and ended up far away.

I stripped the garbage bags off and bundled them for dumping outside.

On our way out of the building I locked the door from the outside and flicked the key under the crack at the bottom in the general direction of the corpse.

Six blocks away I stuffed the garbage bag into an industrial skiff outside a roller rink that was being demolished. Two blocks past that I got rid of the bundle of garbage bags that had made up my hazardous material suit. A block later I dumped the jewellery into a grease trap behind a dim sum restaurant.

It sank into the foulness and vanished.

After that we just kept walking, putting distance between us and the dead man and the filth of his dreams and desires.

#52

Claire and I didn't say a word to each other until we reached a Salisbury House restaurant perched improbably in the middle of the bridge over the Red River.

Before we went in I asked her, "How do I look?"

She looked me over critically. "Like an idiot." I was barefoot in a hundred-year-old white linen shirt and heavy wool kilt with a sporran full of loose change and cash from a dead psychopath.

Claire went on, "But your injuries are covered. Except on your face."

So we went into the restaurant and there we smiled like idiots and acted like young lovers. We cleaned up in the bathrooms and I ordered three breakfasts—fried, poached and scrambled eggs, sausage, ham and back bacon, rye, white and more rye toast. And coffee. And orange juice.

Claire was aghast. "How can you eat?"

"Easily. We're alive and he's dead."

She stared at me hard and opened and closed her mouth several times as I continued.

"Smile, honey. We're young lovers. Young lovers need to keep up their strength. This is the only reason we're out and about in the city at this unholy hour. Everyone will see us and place us in the proper, slightly naughty category and forget us. If you smile."

We were in a booth in the back and it was 2 a.m., but there were still thirteen people in the place, most nursing coffee and avoiding hangovers. A pretty girl with buck teeth two booths away was eating a nip, a Salisbury hamburger, with grim determination.

Claire finally smiled and I went on, low voiced, "I'm starving. You should eat too."

"I may never eat again."

"He got what he deserved."

She sipped some coffee and made a face. "Did those women? Did the husband? Did the son?"

"No." I thought about the dead and shook my head. "No. I cannot bring them back. I can just try to make sure they're not remembered in conjunction with him. We, you and I, can do that."

She shook her head and, behind her, the girl with the nip lost the battle and booked it for the bathroom with her jaw set as rigid as iron.

"I can go back," I offered, "I can stop everything before it starts and I can clean up the scene I staged. The cops will give me a pass, if they find out. Because they used you as a Judas goat. I can rearrange things so that the cops have a fucking road map. I can place all the blame on him. I can even make you and me heroes."

"Can you?"

"Sure. And I would do it right now if it was a question of public fear ... if everyone still thought there was a monster out there killing for fun. But the cops never told anyone about the Shy Man so there is no fear. No one is worried. And if I don't say anything then the only ones who will continue to be worried will be the cops. And I'm okay with that."

I smiled widely like I imagined a wolf would, if a wolf could.

"And maybe the cops being worried is even a good thing."

"How so?"

"Maybe it'll keep them on their toes, I don't know. In any case my sympathy for them is limited."

She shivered and ordered poached and bacon and rye toast.

Eventually the girl who'd lost the battle with the nip came back and finished it.

I had to admire her determination.

At twenty to four we left the restaurant and walked to a parking garage beside the Richardson building and climbed the stairs to the top. There we watched and, at a little after four, the sky to the north turned crimson and the sound of sirens filled the air.

"Will there be anything left?"

More sirens joined the chorus and lights approached the fire from all directions, dozens of trucks seemingly.

I squeezed Claire's hand. "It is a 130-year-old building, according to a plaque in the kitchen. Splintery wood dried out by 130 prairie winters, coats of paint upon coats of paint, stored furs and hides all dried out and preserved with buckets of chemicals. And closets of methyl alcohol and dry cleaning chemicals." I shook my head and put my arm around her. "It'll burn like the fires of hell."

"Good."

The Shy Man's money bought us a room in the Fairmont Hotel after Claire's credit card was shown to prove we didn't need to spend the cash we spent. For $269 plus tax we got a king-sized bed in a 300-square-foot room. It had air conditioning, a window that opened onto the burning building a few blocks away, an alarm clock, bathrobes, cable television, a coffee maker, desk, hair dryer, high-speed Internet, mini-bar and telephone. A fifty-dollar tip to the Filipino bellboy got me a bottle of Southern Comfort liqueur that I put in front of Claire once we'd dragged the desk over so we could see the fire outside.

We had a great view.

She drank most of the bottle and, when she passed out, I put her in bed and waited.

When she woke up she watched me sleep the clock around.

The next day we went home.

#53

The election was scheduled to take place two months after Claire and I got loose.

At first the press wanted nothing but a piece of me, but watching McDonald and Illyanovitch dance kept them busy as shit. McDonald especially loved being a popular figure and played up his actor-school oratory until he almost made sense. Meanwhile Illyanovitch tried to convince everyone he was as honest as the day was long—he may even have been for all I know.

And for a while no one noticed that I wasn't saying anything.

Brenda and Dean had stayed with me, despite their better judgement. To their shock my standings in the polls rose even faster when my mouth was shut.

Six weeks before the election Claire and I flew to Halifax and picked up Fred from her parents. Well, Claire did; I hid in a hotel room to avoid meeting her mom and dad. Then we flew back to town and I kept my mouth shut some more.

Don't get me wrong. I still met individuals in their houses

but I ignored the press. They just kept running my name and asking, "Where is Montgomery Haaviko?"

When Devanter or Aubrey or Virgil asked me I told them it was part of my master plan.

Five weeks before the election Reynolds told the Crown attorney that Cornelius Devanter was trying to exert political influence in the city to buy one-man helium airships to use by the police. Several city councillors admitted Devanter had spoken to them but no one could figure out if a crime had been committed.

Reynolds gave the information up in exchange for dropping the child porn charges.

When the news hit the public, industry experts said the idea was actually a good one and discussed the importance of legitimizing the rigid airship after the Hindenburg incident.

Someone else pointed out all the advantages a rigid airship had over a helicopter—silence, time in the air, and safety.

Frankly, as a bad guy, a silent danger was a much greater threat than a loud one.

However, the public and the police turned against Devanter and I felt sorry for the guy.

A month before the election Goodson announced that he was an ex-Nazi flyer who wanted to make a substantial donation to the new Canadian Human Rights Museum, the first national museum outside of Ottawa. His admission caused a bit of a splash but everyone stopped talking when they found out he wasn't wanted for anything by anyone.

He also donated $10 million to build a park in St. Petersburg—what Leningrad had been renamed again after the war. Virgil told me privately over ribs in another steakhouse that the donation for the park was $10 million but that it cost $20 million to the local Mafiya and political machine in graft to make sure it happened quickly. They asked Goodson what he wanted it named and he said he leaned towards "Hope" but wasn't holding his breath.

The Russian press asked him if he wanted to be there for the ground breaking and he told them, "Fuck no! I never want to see that place again!"

And everyone laughed.

Three weeks before the election I looked around my quiet house at midnight, slipped out the basement window and snuck through the Kilpatricks' yard and then through two more and was away. In an industrial park near the airport I found the building I was looking for, a long, low structure covered with huge windows.

I dawdled near the front gate for ten minutes until the security guard came forward. He was about six foot eight, white, young, and his hand clasped and unclasped on the big flashlight holstered on his belt.

"The factory is closed."

I had a new hoody up and a baseball hat under it and my hands were in my pockets, making them bulge.

"I'm the one who called, Clarence McFee."

He froze and stared.

It had taken two phone calls to find the factory. One call to find who the factory hired to run security and two calls to them to find out who had the night shift. Then it had taken eleven phone calls to find out where Mr. Clarence McFee lived. After that, two calls had finally reached the man himself.

He stared some more and I brought my hand out of my pocket and tossed an envelope to his feet. "Count it."

I watched his lips as he counted, "Five thousand."

Without another word he let me in and showed me where the printing presses were and how to run them. He had warmed them up and loaded them with the right card stock and I stood in front of the control panel and tried not to scratch my itchy and healing broken thumb and pinkie.

"And I just press this button?"

"Yes." His voice was gravelly. "You understand these ballots are all numbered, right? I mean, you're just doing a reprint."

"I understand. You were very clear. A reprint is fine."

"You don't care that the serial numbers are going to be the same?"

"Not at all."

I printed ten thousand, slipped Clarence a $500 bonus and went home again.

#54

When election day came I went with Claire and Fred and we voted, Claire first and then me, with me wheeling Fred in his stupid baby carriage that barely fit into the little privacy screen.

While the cameras flashed at the top of my head Fred handed me the bundles of already marked ballots and I stuffed them into the box until it was full.

On my way out Candy stopped me for a final interview. "You took a long time in there, Mr. Haaviko."

"I wanted to think about what I was doing. Democracy is a very serious thing, isn't it?"

She nodded and turned back to her camera and I interrupted her, "And did YOU vote?"

She had the dignity to blush and I went on my way.

Dean and Brenda had rented a hotel suite and stocked it with pop and potato chips and each had brought their own bottle of rye whiskey. They constantly skipped into the bathroom and snuck drinks as we watched the results pour in.

Everyone was there, my lawyer Lester and his wife (Lester just back from drying out somewhere tough), Elena the cop and her husband and son, Claire and Fred and I, the Kilpatricks, Veronica Rose and two slightly stunned eighteen-year-olds, the Greek bakers and Frank from the archery shop. And others I barely remembered, people whose hands I'd shaken and babies I'd kissed.

The results kept pouring in and I started to lose.

The Greeks threw the potato chips out the window and produced trays of baklava and Turkish delight while Frank handed out jerked deer meat.

I kept losing and Claire held my hand.

Fred got into a wrestling match with one of Veronica's high school boyfriends while one of the Greeks decided she looked pretty yummy. His words. Not mine. Delivered in a serious and sonorous voice.

Candy showed up with an anchorwoman from another station and I let them in and fed them and refused to answer questions.

The Greek father went to his car and came back with a case of homemade retsina, sweet Greek wine laced with fermented pine sap.

The hotel manager brought up a case of cold champagne that Virgil had sent over and Claire took a glass and whispered into my ear, "Domestic."

By midnight I was the serious loser and the polls were officially closed and the party went on.

By two Veronica had left with two of the Greeks and returned alone an hour later. All the babies were unconscious and tucked safely under a bed. The anchorwoman had shown Claire her breasts and asked her politely to check to see if they were real and she had done so.

They were.

By four an announcement had come on that there were serious discrepancies that had to be resolved.

By five it was announced that someone had stuffed at least one ballot box with 10,000 votes for Illyanovitch and that an investigation was being called.

By eight Claire and I were home with Fred and in our own beds.

#55

Hey, I lost, didn't I?"

Devanter and I were in a steakhouse eating and talking at noon on a beautifully clear September day. Devanter glared at me and spoke through clenched teeth. "Yes."

"And your guy won, right? He did win. At least for awhile. Then there was that whole cheating thing but he did win. Not my fault McDonald was declared the winner. Your guy still won and I lost."

"Yes."

"Then what's the problem? You made the deal, pay up."

Devanter drank from his oversized wineglass and growled. "My guy, as you know, is not in charge."

I touched the tip of my nose and shook my head. "That wasn't part of the deal. You paid me to have me lose. That's what happened."

He growled again, started to say something and stopped. A waiter in black and white hustled by with a tray of steaks and fried fungus in covered dishes. Sitting back, I realized I was enjoying this way too much. I also realized my hand was mostly healed and that the cuts had faded down to a general itching.

"So, the deal is done. You owe me ten grand."

Devanter's face clouded over. He was in a rough place. Goodson had called his bluff and admitted his past, which left Devanter with no cards to play, but he had done nothing afterwards. He wasn't fighting anymore. And his idea to sell the airships to the city was on hold and no one seemed to be taking him seriously. Even his lawyer had turned on him.

Really, nothing was going right for him and he finally growled, "Fuck you. Sue me."

After Devanter had gotten up and left I borrowed the house phone and called Virgil Reese. When he answered I said, "I have a case for you."

"Really?" In the background I heard the scratching of a pen or pencil.

"Yes, sir. Suing Devanter."

"For what?"

"You choose. I've got a contract here and he owes me $10,000."

He started to laugh.

#56

I visited the cop Atismak in the RCMP building down on Portage Avenue. He had a corner office on the third floor just off a bullpen full of men in business suits who looked at me sideways as I was escorted through their desks by a stocky woman who had assigned herself as my guide. She left me at Atismak's door, which was open.

He raised his head from his desk full of papers with a slightly pained look on his face, but when he saw me it vanished and was replaced by blankness.

"Mr. Haaviko."

I was formal. "Mr. Atismak."

He waited and then told me I was welcome to come in. When I was sitting he put his hands together on his desk and rested his chin there. "How can I help you?"

I felt not inconsiderable rage bubbling up but I ignored it. To my surprise it left and in its place was a cold, clinical fury I had never experienced before. I wanted to smash Atismak, to hurt him, to make him into a living warning to anyone who would try to fuck me over in the future.

Instead I opened my mouth. "You can't help me. I just wanted to say that I forgive you."

"Forgive me?"

It wasn't what he expected and he opened his mouth twice and closed it again. Then he asked, wonderingly, "For what?"

"For not telling me about the Shy Man."

"The Shy Man?"

He wasn't very believable so I shrugged it off. "Yes, the Shy Man. You know, when you set me and my son and my wife up."

Atismak licked his lips and opened his mouth again but nothing came out. Then he said, "I don't know what you're talking about."

"Of course."

Silence. I wondered if he was trying to come up with something to say. Probably not, I guessed, he was probably stuck in his role of cop. Either way didn't matter.

I got up to leave. "Anyhow, I forgive you."

"Wait." Atismak found his voice. "How's your wife?"

"She's perfect. I'll tell her you asked."

My smile was real and Atismak stared at it with his head cocked to the side. "Uh. Are you here to confess to something?"

That made me laugh. And then I couldn't stop and finally had to sit down to catch my breath.

"No." My eyes were streaming and I wiped them. "That's good though. I haven't laughed in a long time. I'm just here to tell you I forgive you. I've never forgiven anyone before and it's an interesting feeling. I'm used to vengeance and justice and an eye for an eye and all that other Biblical shit I learned in my misspent youth. I'm forgiving you. Let's leave it at that."

Atismak's hand touched the black telephone on his desk and paused. He could call in many cops and drag me down to the detention cells for a little six-on-one interrogation. He could call the Crown attorney and start the process of having me charged. He could call a judge and ask for search warrants. Instead he drew his hand back and bit his upper lip.

"Okay, we'll leave it at that."

I got up and left. Outside the sun was shining and, off to my right, a wall of thunderclouds filled the horizon from side to side. As I watched a single bolt of brilliant light jumped from one greyly pregnant cloud to another and I heard a distant rumble of thunder.

ACKNOWLEDGEMENTS

I'd like to acknowledge the support and aid of the Manitoba Arts Council and the Canada Council for the Arts. I'd like to praise Turnstone Press for their skill and patience with a very recalcitrant book. Apologies go out to William, Lois, Alison, Sēanin, Morgan and Erik for having to put up with me. Thanks goes to Robert and T., Kathryn L., Wayne T. (for illumination), Sue, Catherine, Talia, Charlene, Perry, and Tavia for support, moral and otherwise. Also thanks to Aqua Books for inviting me to be Writer in Residence and College Beliveau for keeping me honest. A special thanks to C.R. for another perspective. An awkward thanks to someone who wants to remain anonymous.

And, again, my thanks to those in the shadows ... quae nocent.

JAN 30
DIED 2014 TORONTO

Michael Van Rooy was born in Kamloops, BC, in 1968 and grew up in Winnipeg. His first book, *An Ordinary Decent Criminal*, won the 2006 Eileen McTavish Sykes Award for Best First Book by a Manitoba Writer. In 2009 he won the John Hirsch Award for Most Promising Manitoba Writer. In his diverse life Van Rooy has worked as a teacher, a newspaper editor, a bartender, a cheesemaker, and a casino dealer. He is currently a freelance writer and administrator who lives with his family in Winnipeg.

AN ORDINARY
DECENT CRIMINAL
by Michael Van Rooy

... funny, fast-paced and so hugely compelling it's hard to put down. Van Rooy has all the elements—a terrific protagonist, a twisting plot and a writing style that snaps along.

—Winnipeg Free Press

Montgomery "Monty" Haaviko has done the crimes—robbery, assault, embezzlement, arson, smuggling, attempted murder—and has lived the criminal lifestyle, where nothing is permanent. Crime may look easy, but a career criminal can't even follow a TV series. For Monty the endless danger and fear, along with a hard-to-kick drug habit, became too much. Now, all he wants to do is settle down in a quiet Winnipeg neighbourhood with his wife, his baby son, his dog, and his pet mouse, and try something new: an honest job and life as an ordinary decent citizen.

But going straight is hard, even for a guy who was an ordinary decent criminal. And it gets harder. When Monty ends up with three dead break-and-enter artists in his living room, he discovers there are those who won't let him forget his past. Detective Sergeant Enzio Walsh knows all about Monty's criminal history and thinks he'll be the one to put Monty away for good. And then there's Jean Robillard, a minor crime boss and uncle of one of the dead men on Monty's floor. He'll settle for nothing less than Monty's body on a slab.

Fortunately for Monty, he doesn't have to face his nemeses alone. His wife, Claire, at one time a hairbreadth from leaving him for good, is standing by him. And he has plenty of tricks, scams, and schemes he can use to clear his name and save his life.

ISBN 978-0-88801-348-4
$16.00

YOUR FRIENDLY
NEIGHBOURHOOD CRIMINAL
by Michael Van Rooy

...a well-written, convincing, and compelling novel.
Reminiscent of Elmore Leonard and Andrew Vacchs,
this is hard-boiled fiction laced with humour and an odd
wisdom—a book you won't mind losing sleep over.
—Quill & Quire

Ex-criminal Montgomery "Monty" Haaviko would rather be known as the friendly neighbourhood daycare provider, but it's his criminal past that brings him to the attention of Marie Blue Duck. Marie is a human rights activist, and she wants Monty to set up a route to smuggle refugees into the United States. Monty is doubtful and a little insulted, but the money on offer is too good to refuse. Even his wife, Claire, who ensures Monty stays on the straight and narrow, thinks he should take the job.

Monty's carefully laid plans go off the rails when a local criminal, Samantha Ritchot, tries to seize the route for her drug-smuggling operation. Monty finds himself squaring off with Samantha in a power struggle that quickly escalates into kidnapping, torture, and a daring and highly explosive stand-off.

Just when Monty thinks he might have it all under control, his old jailhouse crony, Hershel "Smiley" Wiebe, shows up on his doorstep. Smiley is armed to the teeth, but begs Monty to help him go straight. Monty is more than suspicious of Smiley's motives, but figures if you should keep old friends close, you really should keep old cons closer.

A gripping and aggressive crime novel, *Your Friendly Neighbourhood Criminal* explores how far a man will go to protect his family, home, and neighbourhood, and asks the question, "Can a man do good by doing bad?"

ISBN 978-0-88801-339-2
$16.00